This book belongs to

....

Five-minute Stories

Miles Kelly

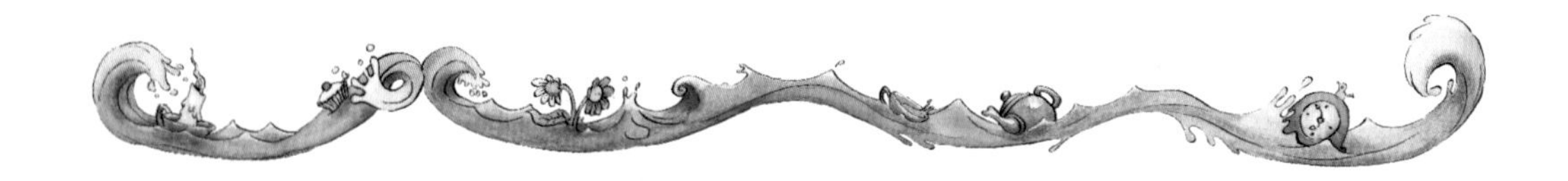

First published in 2011 by Miles Kelly Publishing Ltd
Harding's Barn, Bardfield End Green, Thaxted, Essex, CM6 3PX, UK

This edition printed 2013

6 8 10 9 7

Publishing Director Belinda Gallagher
Creative Director Jo Cowan
Editor Amanda Askew
Senior Designer Joe Jones
Designer Kayleigh Allen
Production Manager Elizabeth Collins
Reprographics Anthony Cambray, Stephan Davis, Jennifer Hunt
Assets Lorraine King

ISBN 978-1-84810-545-4

Printed in China

British Library Cataloguing-in-Publication Data
A catalogue record for this book is available from the British Library

ACKNOWLEDGEMENTS
Artworks are from the Miles Kelly Artwork Bank

Made with paper from a sustainable forest

www.mileskelly.net
info@mileskelly.net

Contents

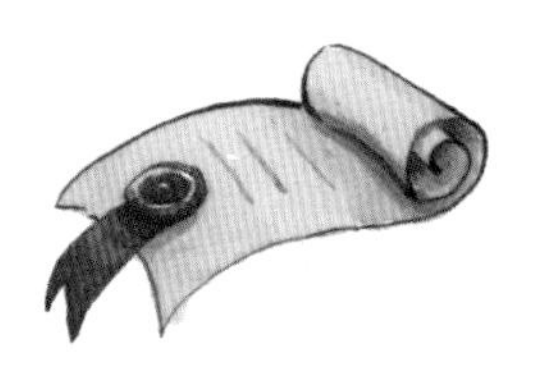

Wise Folk

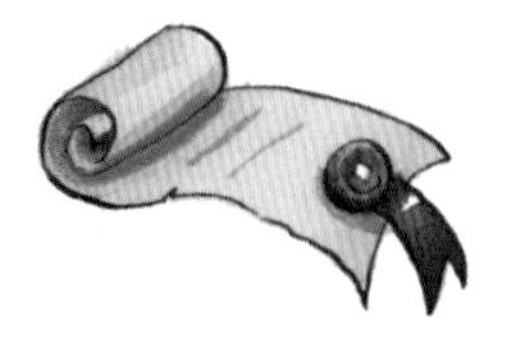

The Thunder God Gets Married 12
The Wonderful Tar Baby 19
The Clever Apprentice 24
The Fairies and the Envious Neighbour 27
Iktomi and the Muskrat 30
Amal and the Genie 35
The Girl who Owned a Bear 41
Singh Rajah and the Cunning Little Jackals 49
The Hillman and the Housewife 54
Jack and the Beanstalk 58

Trickery and Mischief

The Giant Who Counted Carrots 66
How the Rhinoceros got his Skin 73
Under the Sun 79
The Fairy Fluffikins 85

The Pot of Gold 90
The Ogre's Bride 96
Iktomi and the Ducks 103
A French Puck 109

Animal Antics

The Cat and the Mouse 114
The Ugly Duckling 121
The Three Billy Goats Gruff 127
The Seven Little Kids 133
The Sagacious Monkey and the Boar 139
How the Camel got his Hump 145
The Husband of the Rat's Daughter 151
Why the Swallow's Tail is Forked 158
The Old Woman and her Pig 163
Why the Manx Cat has no Tail 168

Girls and Boys

Peter and the Wolf 174
The Selfish Giant 178
The Red Shoes 185
Cap o' Rushes 192
The Sorcerer's Apprentice 198
Hansel and Gretel 203
My Own Self 211
The Little Matchgirl 216

Royal Adventures

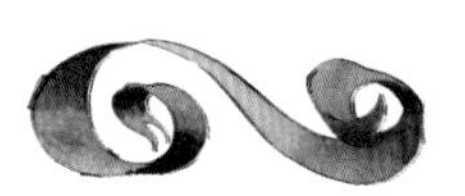

The Seven Ravens 222
The Golden Touch 228
The Sword in the Stone 234
The Princess and the Pea 241
The Twelve Dancing Princesses .247
The Frog Prince 253
The Haughty Princess 259
The Twelve Windows 266

Tattercoats .274
The Three Aunts .282

Fantastic Journeys

The Precious Stove .290
The Three Sillies .296
The Two Frogs .303
Honourable Minu .307
Straw, Coal and Bean .310
Dick Whittington and his Cat .313
Rosy's Journey .319

Good Deeds

Hop-Toads and Pearls .328
Liam and the Fairy Cattle .335
Androcles and the Lion .342
The Lion and the Mouse .345
Whippety Stourie .348

The Elves and the Shoemaker .353
The Fairy Cure .359
Farmer Mybrow and the Fairies .364
In the Castle of Giant Cruelty .370

Favourite Tales

Chicken Licken .378
The Three Little Pigs .382
The Hare and the Tortoise .388
Little Red Riding Hood .394
Goldilocks and the Three Bears .402
The Gingerbread Man .409

Fun and Nonsense

The Pied Piper of Hamelin .416
The Greedy Dog .423
A Tall Story .427
Nasreddin Hodja and the Pot .430

Nasreddin Hodja and the Smell of Soup 432
Lazy Jack 435
Tikki Tikki Tembo 440
The Husband who was to Mind the House 444
Teeny-tiny 449

Magic and Mystery

The Fairy Cow 454
Paddy Corcoran's Wife 460
The Three Wishes 463
The Mermaid of Zennor 468
Pandora's Box 473
Rapunzel 479
The Fairy Blackstick 486
The Smith and the Fairies 491
Billy Beg, Tom Beg and the Fairies 496
The Magic Porridge Pot 503

Index of Stories 511

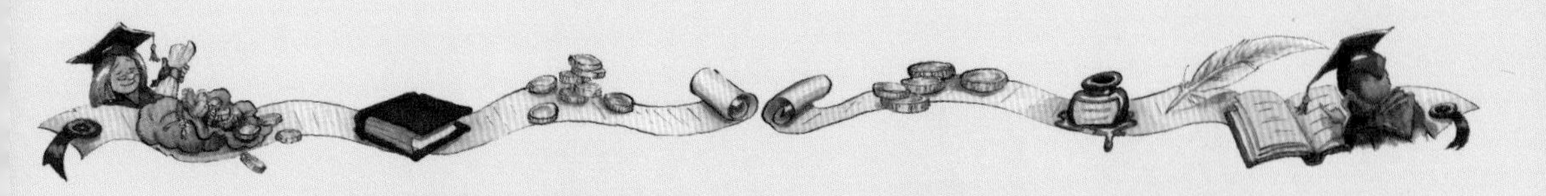

Wise Folk

The Thunder God gets Married

A Norse legend

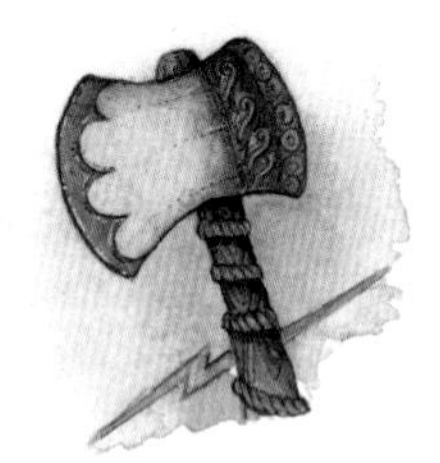

Up in heaven, Thor the thunder god was furious. Someone had stolen his magic hammer. Thor's magic hammer was the terror of the gods. Whenever he threw it, it killed anything that it touched and it always returned to his hand. It was perhaps the most deadly weapon that the gods possessed to protect them against their enemies, the giants.

Now the raging Thor's roaring sounded like the

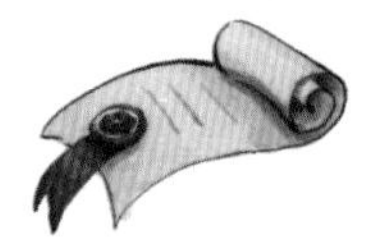

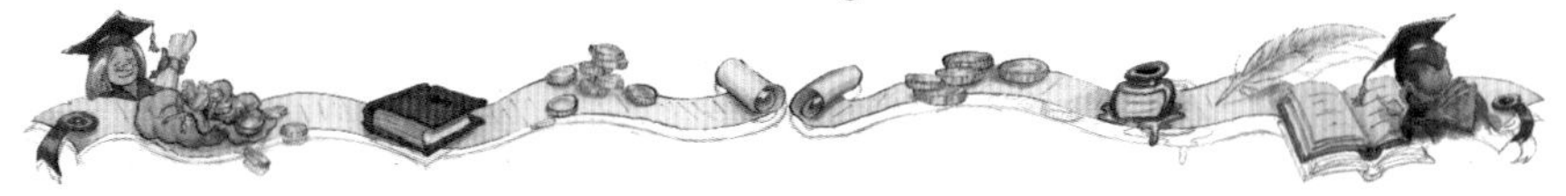

clouds were clashing together. His face was so black with anger that it sent a dark shadow over the whole sky. As Thor grabbed blazing lightning bolts and hurled them, the mischief-maker god, Loki, came nervously to see him.

"I have good news, my angry friend," Loki explained. "I have used my cunning to find out that it is the giant Thrym who has stolen your hammer. He has agreed to give it back on one condition – that he has the most beautiful of all the goddesses, Freya, as his bride."

The thunder god's sulky face brightened a little and he charged off to find Freya straight away.

"Put on your best dress, Freya!" Thor boomed, throwing open her wardrobe doors. "You have to marry the giant Thrym so I can get my magic hammer back."

Freya's eyes flickered with cold fire. "Excuse me,

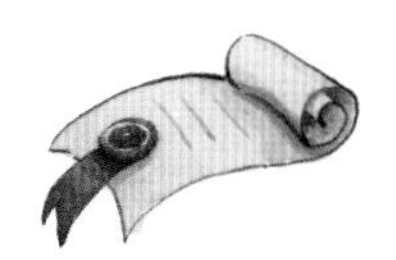

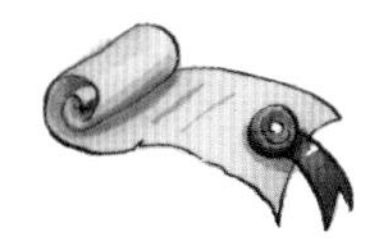

Thor," she said, calmly. "Would you care to repeat that?"

"You-have-to-marry-the-giant-Thrym-so-I-can-get-my-magic-hammer-back!" the impatient thunder god cried at top speed.

Freya stood glaring, her hands on her hips. "Firstly Thor, as the goddess of beauty I don't have to do anything." Thor's face reddened.

"Secondly," Freya continued, "I wouldn't marry that ugly monster Thrym if he were the only creature left in the world." The ashamed thunder god hung his head.

"Thirdly," Freya finished, "it's your problem, you sort it out."

"Sorry, Freya," Thor mumbled, shuffling about

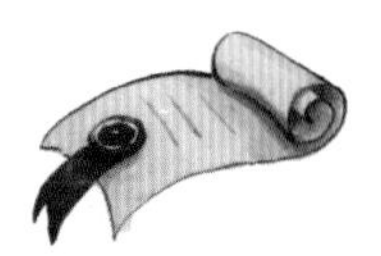

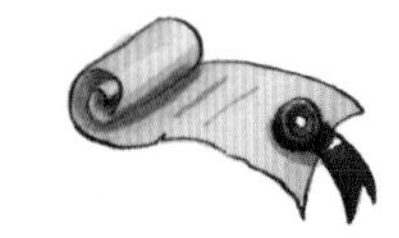

a bit. Then he turned and stormed back to Loki. The two gods sat down glumly and wracked their brains to come up with another way to get back the hammer.

"How about..." Thor started to suggest. Then he shook his head. "No, no good."

"What if..." Loki began. Then his face fell. "No, it would never work."

It looked as if Thor's magic hammer would have to stay in the land of the giants forever – until the god Heimdall had an idea.

"That's absolutely out of the question!" Thor thundered.

"Outrageous!" Loki squealed. "I'll never do it!"

"Well, you come up with another plan then," Heimdall laughed, knowing that there wasn't one.

That night, the giant Thrym was delighted to see a chariot with a bride and bridesmaid in it

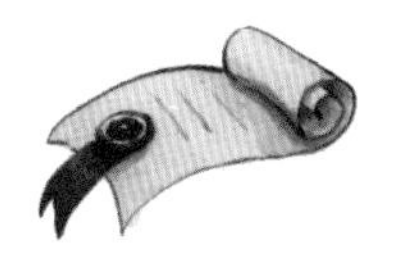

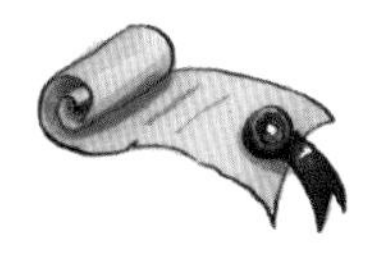

rumbling up to his castle.

"It's Freya!" the gormless giant gasped with delight. "I shall gladly give back Thor's magic hammer in return for the most beautiful wife in the world!" The overjoyed giant commanded a magnificent banquet to be prepared and his guests to be sent for at once.

But Thrym wouldn't have been so overjoyed if he could have seen what was underneath the veils of his bride and bridesmaid – the angry, highly embarrassed faces of Thor and Loki! As it was, the giant was far too excited to notice how big and clumsy the bride and bridesmaid looked in their frilly dresses. Thrym didn't take in that the women had low, gruff voices and huge, hairy hands. And he hardly thought twice about the way that Freya swigged down two whole barrels of beer and ate an entire roast ox.

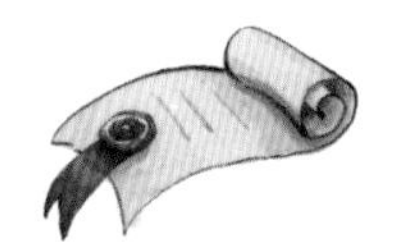

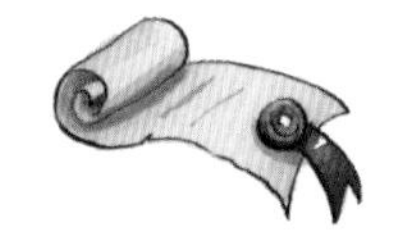

When the guests had eaten and drunk their fill, the beaming Thrym stood up to make a speech.

"My wife and I," he began, blushing bright red, "would like to thank you for celebrating this happy occasion with us. Freya has made me the luckiest being in the whole universe. And now, I will keep my word and give back the magic hammer I stole from that ugly thug of a thunder god."

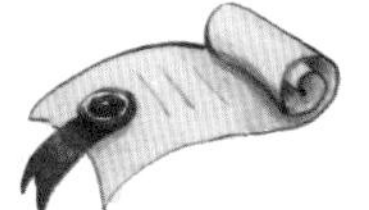

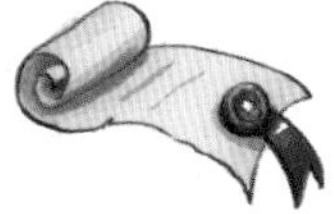

There was a roll of drums as one of Thrym's servants brought in the magic hammer on a cushion. Thrym held it high in the air for his marvelling guests to admire. Then with a grand flourish, he presented it to his bride.

"The ugly thug of a thunder god thanks you!" roared Thor, ripping off his veil and springing to his feet. And before Thrym and his guests could really take in the trick, they were lying dead on the floor and the wedding feast was unexpectedly over.

All the gods were truly relieved to have the magic hammer back in Thor's hands in heaven, where it belonged. But it was a long time before Thor and Loki could laugh with the other gods about how charming they both looked in a dress!

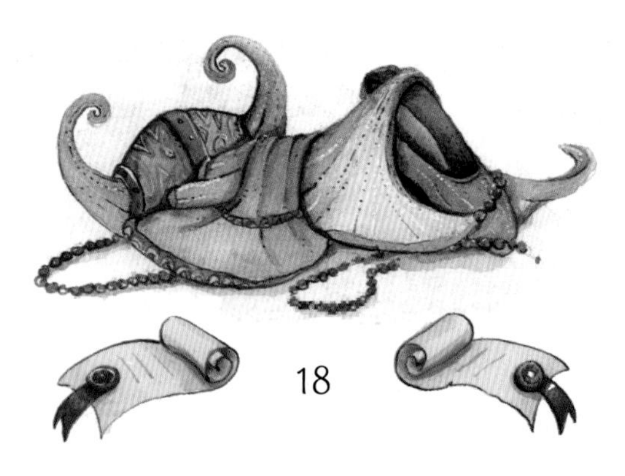

The Wonderful Tar Baby

By Uncle Remus

Brer Fox was doing what he usually did – trying to catch Brer Rabbit. But he'd be danged if this time he didn't catch that pesky varmint once and for all! Brer Fox mixed up a big pot of sticky tar and pulled and patted it into the shape of a baby. Then he lolloped up the road, set the tar baby sitting in the dust, and went to lay low in the ditch.

By and by, Brer Rabbit came bouncing down

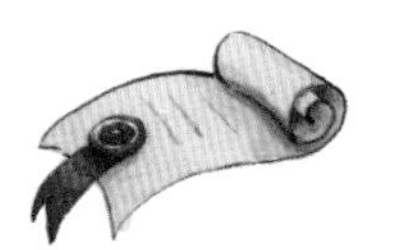

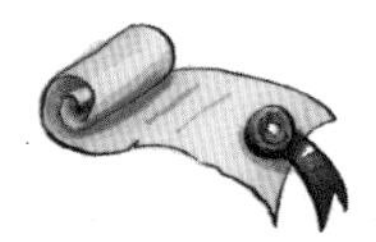

the road. "Good morning," he greeted the tar baby, "nice day, ain't it?"

But the tar baby didn't utter a word.

"I SAYS," shouted Brer Rabbit, just in case the tar baby hadn't cleaned his ears recently, "GOOD MORNING! NICE DAY, AIN'T IT?"

The tar baby just stared straight ahead.

"Ain't you got no manners?" Brer Rabbit asked, crossly.

Still the tar baby stayed silent.

By this time, Brer Rabbit was hopping from foot to foot, madder than a snake in a wasps' nest. "You'd better speak to me civil-like or else!" he hollered.

But the tar baby simply ignored Brer Rabbit.

"Well I guess you've done gone and asked for this!" Brer Rabbit shrieked.

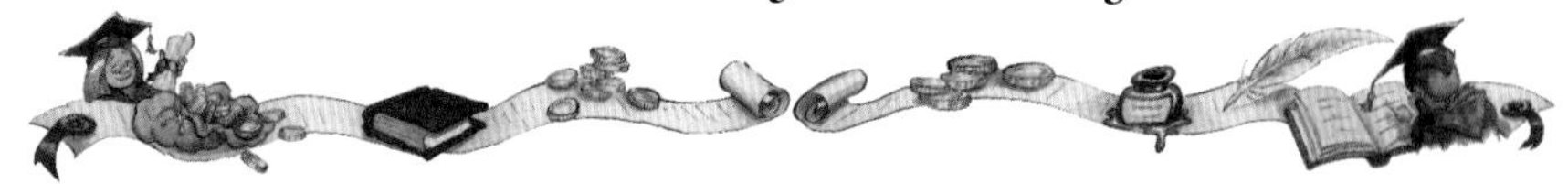

BLIP! He thumped the tar baby straight in the mouth – and his fist was stuck fast to the tar baby's face. "You let me go!" Brer Rabbit yelled. "Let me go – or I'll let you have another!"

BLAM! Brer Rabbit socked the tar baby again and his other fist became glued to its head.

SMACK! He kicked the tar baby and was left hopping around on one leg.

WALLOP! another kick and the tar baby was holding him off the ground. "Right, you've really had it now!" Brer Rabbit screamed.

THUNK! he headbutted the tar baby and found himself stuck eye-to-eye.

All this time, Brer Fox had been holding on to so much laughter he thought he was going to burst. He leapt out of his hiding place and howled, "My, oh my, Brer Rabbit! What type of mess have you got yourself into this time?"

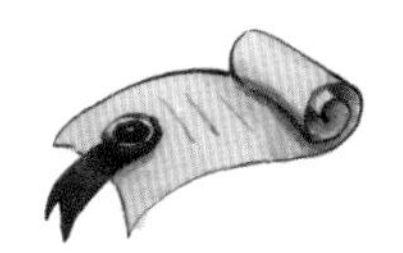

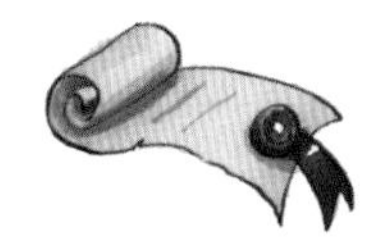

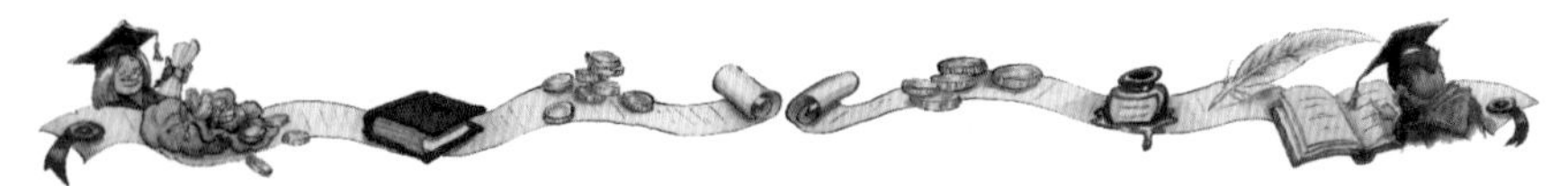

"I suppose you're gonna have a tasty barbecued bunny for supper," Brer Rabbit admitted.

"Yep!" grinned Brer Fox, licking his lips.

"Well I'm glad you're going to dress me up with some sauce and warm me over your fire," Brer Rabbit smiled. "I'd much rather you did that than throw me in that briar patch over there."

Hang on a minute, thought Brer Fox, and his face fell. That no-good rabbit seems quite pleased about being roasted! "I've changed my mind," Brer Fox said. "I'm gonna hang you instead."

"Ain't I glad it's good ol' hangin' and not being thrown in the briar patch!" sighed Brer Rabbit.

Brer Fox frowned. "I mean, I'm going to drown you!" he snarled.

"Fine, fine," smiled Brer Rabbit gaily. "Dip me in the water and at least I'll die clean. Just don't throw me in that there briar patch, that's all!"

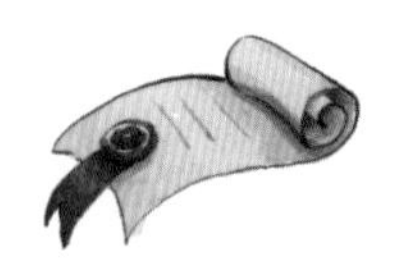

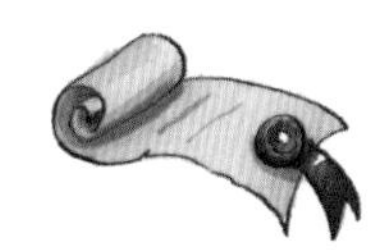

At that, Brer Fox was sure that the very worst thing he could do to Brer Rabbit was to hurl him into the briar patch. He grabbed him round the waist and pulled him hard and – SHLUP! – Brer Rabbit came unstuck from the tar baby. Brer Fox spun round and round and – WHEEEEEEEE! – Brer Rabbit went sailing high into the air and came down – DONK! – into the briar patch.

Brer Fox began to smile contentedly. "I've bested that bunny once and for all!" he chuckled.

A high-pitched giggle came from the far side of the briar patch, and when Brer Fox squinted into the sunshine, he could just see Brer Rabbit hopping away into the distance. "I was born and bred in a briar patch, Brer Fox!" he was singing.

Brer Fox boiled with rage and thumped the very first thing that came to hand. And you know what that was, don't you?

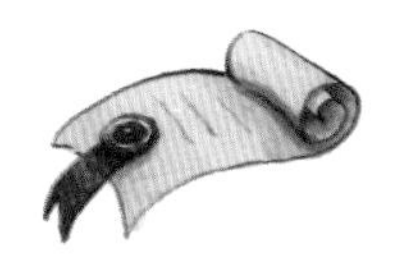

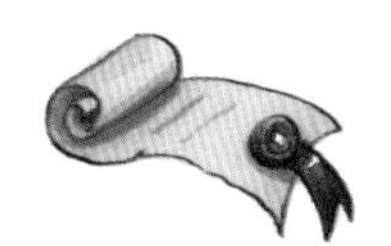

The Clever Apprentice

By Walter Gregor

A shoemaker once engaged an apprentice. A short time after the apprenticeship began the shoemaker asked the boy what he would call him when addressing him.

"I would call you master," answered the apprentice. "No," said the master, "you must call me master above all masters."

"What would you call my trousers?" "I would call them trousers," said the apprentice. "No, you

must call them struntifers."

"And what would you call my wife?" "I would call her mistress," replied the apprentice. "No, you must call her the Fair Lady Permoumadam."

"What would you call my son?" "I would call him Johnny," answered the apprentice. "No, you must call him John the Great."

"And what would you call the cat?" "I would call him pussy." "No, you must call him Great Carle Gropus."

"And what would you call the fire?" "Oh, I would call it fire." "No, you must call it Fire Evangelist."

"And what would you call the peat stack?" "Oh, I would just call it peat stack." "No, you must call it Mount Potago."

"And what would you call the well?" "Oh, I would call it well." "No, you must call it the Fair Fountain."

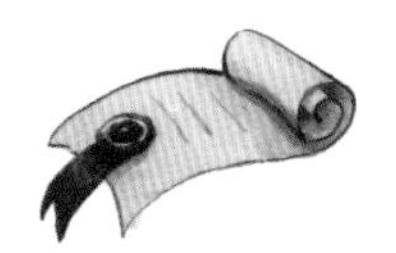

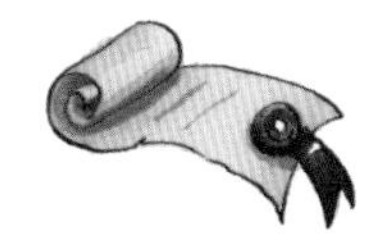

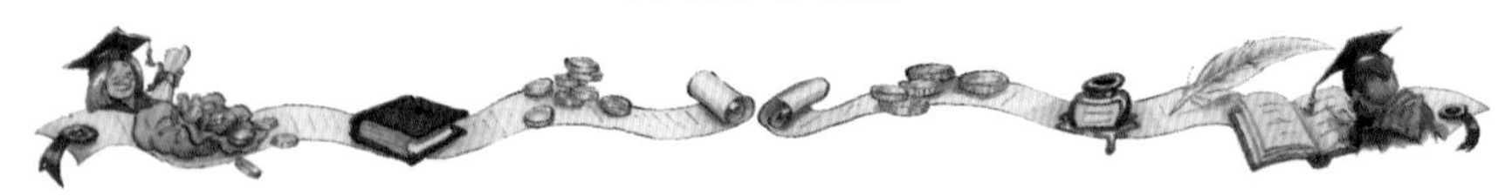

"And, last of all, what would you call the house?" "Oh, I would call it house." "No, you must call it the Castle of Mungo."

The shoemaker, after giving this lesson to his apprentice, told him that the first day he managed to use all these words at once, without making a mistake, the apprenticeship would end.

Then one morning, the apprentice got out of bed before his master and lit the fire. He tied some bits of paper to the tail of the cat and threw the animal into the fire. The cat ran out with the papers all in a blaze, landed in the peat stack, which caught fire.

The apprentice hurried to his master and cried... Master above all masters, start up and jump into your struntifers, and call upon Sir John the Great and the Fair Lady Permoundaddam, for Carle Gropus has caught hold of Fire Evangelist, and he is out to Mount Potago, and if you don't get help from the Fair Fountain, the whole of Castle Mungo will be burned to the ground!

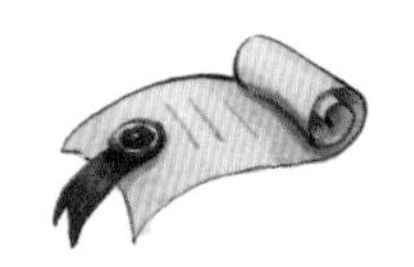

The Fairies and the Envious Neighbour

By Algernon Freeman-Mitford

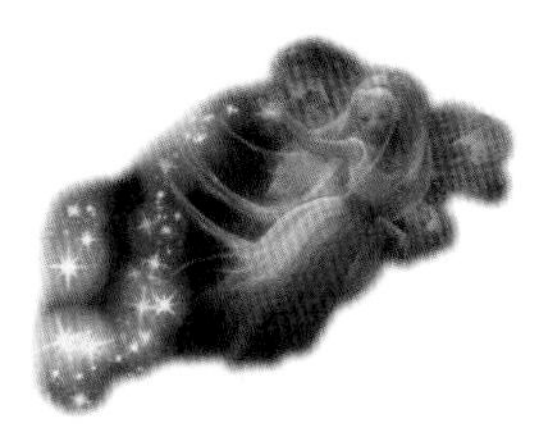

Once upon a time there was a man, who after getting lost in the dark, sheltered in the trunk of a hollow tree. In the middle of the night, a large group of fairies appeared, and the man, peeping out from his hiding place, was frightened out of his wits. After a while, the fairies began to eat and drink, sing and dance. The man, wanting to join in the fun, forgot all about his fright, and crept out of his hollow tree to join in.

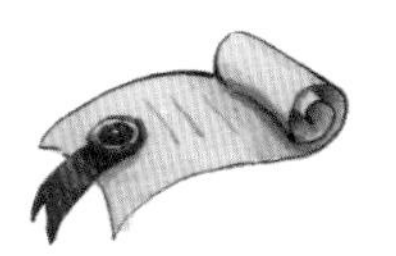

As the sun began to rise, the fairies said to the man, "You're very jolly and must come out and dance with us again. Promise us." So, to make sure the man would return, the elves took a large wart that grew on his forehead and kept it.

The man left for his house in glee, both at having passed a great night, and getting rid of his wart. He told the story to all his friends, who were pleased that he was cured of his wart.

His neighbour, who was also troubled with a wart, was jealous, and went to find the hollow tree.

Towards midnight the fairies came, as he had expected, and began feasting and drinking, with songs and dances as before. As soon as he saw this, he came out of his hollow tree, and began dancing and singing as his neighbour had done. The fairies, thinking he was the first man, were delighted to see him, and said, "You're a good

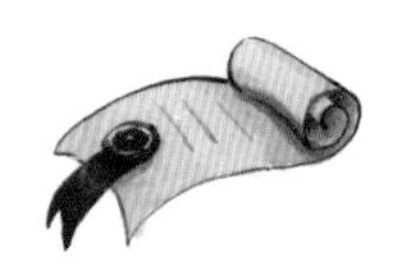

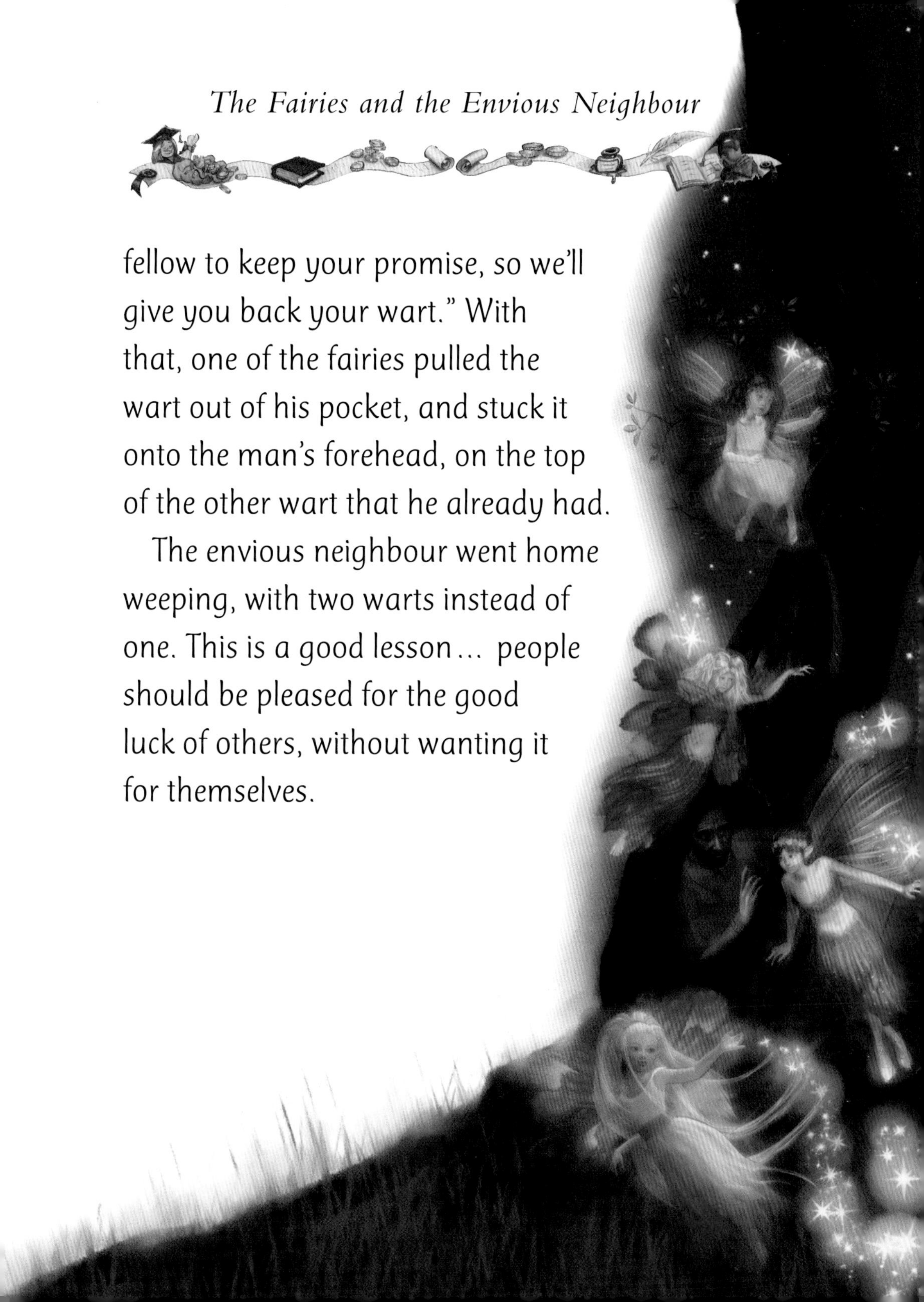

fellow to keep your promise, so we'll give you back your wart." With that, one of the fairies pulled the wart out of his pocket, and stuck it onto the man's forehead, on the top of the other wart that he already had.

The envious neighbour went home weeping, with two warts instead of one. This is a good lesson... people should be pleased for the good luck of others, without wanting it for themselves.

Iktomi and the Muskrat

By Zitkala-sa

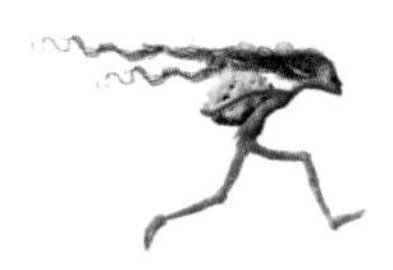

Beside a white lake, beneath a large willow tree, sat Iktomi the fairy with a pot of boiled fish. He quickly tucked in, for he was hungry.

"How, how, my friend!" said a voice.

Iktomi jumped and almost choked on his soup. He peered through the long reeds from where he sat with his spoon in mid-air.

"How, my friend!" said the voice again, this time at his side. Iktomi turned and there stood a

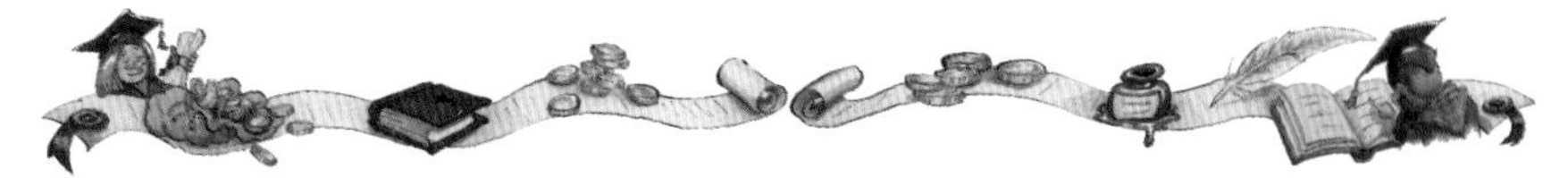

dripping-wet muskrat.

"Oh, it is my friend who scared me. I wondered if a spirit voice was talking. How, how, my friend!" said Iktomi. The muskrat stood smiling, waiting for Iktomi to ask, 'My friend, will you sit down beside me and share my food?'

Yet Iktomi sat, silent. He hummed an old song and beat gently on the pot with his spoon. The muskrat began to feel awkward and wished himself underwater.

After many minutes, Iktomi stopped drumming with his spoon, and looking upward into the muskrat's face, he said, "My friend, let us run a race to see who shall win this pot of fish. If I win, I shall not need to share it with you. If you win, you shall have half of it." Springing to his feet, Iktomi began at once to tighten the belt about his waist.

"My friend Iktomi, I cannot run a race with you!

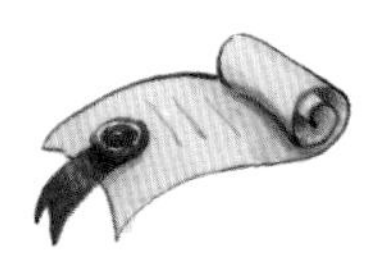

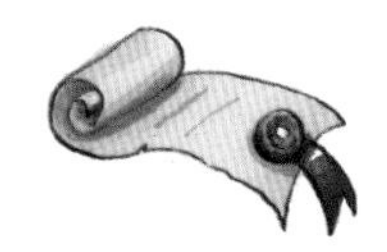

I am not a swift runner, and you are nimble as a deer," answered the hungry muskrat.

"Then I shall carry a large stone on my back. That will slow down my usual speed, and the race will be a fair one." Saying this he laid a firm hand upon the muskrat's shoulder and walked to the edge of the lake. When they reached the opposite side, Iktomi searched for a heavy stone. He found one half buried in the shallow water. Pulling it onto dry land, he wrapped it in his blanket.

"Now, my friend, you shall run on the left side of the lake, I on the other. The race is for the boiled fish in yonder kettle!" said Iktomi.

The muskrat helped to lift the heavy stone upon Iktomi's back. Then they parted. Each took a narrow path through the tall reeds on the shore. Iktomi found his load a heavy one. He puffed and panted, and sweat dripped from his forehead.

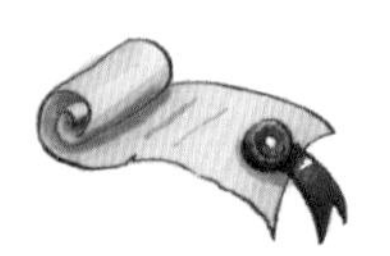

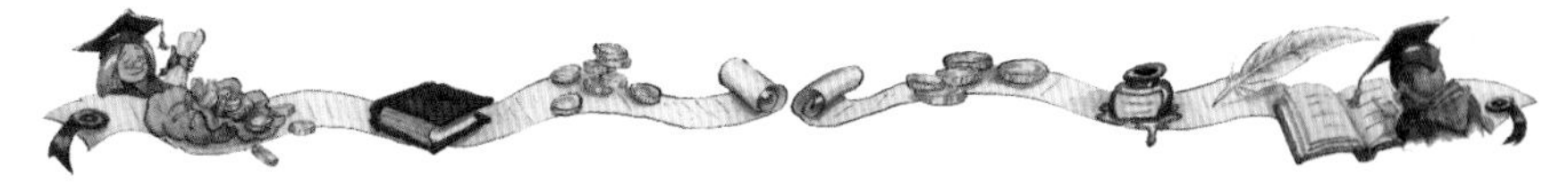

He looked across the lake to see how far the muskrat had got, but there was no sign of him.

"Well, he is running low under the wild rice!" said he. Yet as he searched the tall grasses on the lake shore, he saw nothing moving.

"Ah, has he gone so fast ahead that the disturbed grasses in his trail have already become quiet again?" exclaimed Iktomi. With that thought he quickly dropped the heavy stone.

"No more of this!" said he, patting his chest with both hands. Off with a springing bound, he ran

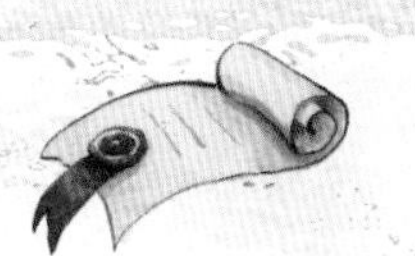

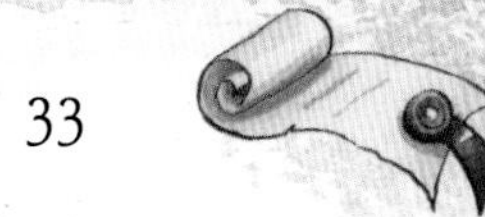

swiftly towards the goal. Tufts of reeds and grass fell flat under his feet.

Soon he reached the heap of cold ashes. Iktomi halted stiff as if he had struck an invisible cliff. His black eyes showed a ring of white about them as he stared at the empty ground. There was no pot of boiled fish! There was no muskrat in sight!

"Oh, if only I had shared my food, I would not have lost it all! Why did I not remember the muskrat would run through the water? He swims faster than I could ever run! That is what he has done. He has laughed at me for carrying a weight on my back while he shot here like an arrow!"

"Ha! Ha! Ha!" laughed the muskrat. "Next time, say to a visiting friend, 'Be seated beside me, my friend. Let me share my food with you.'"

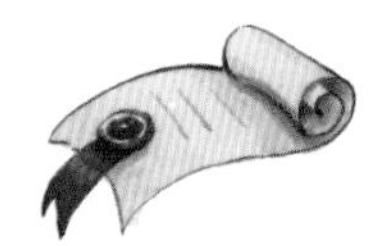

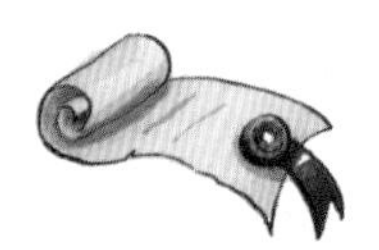

Amal and the Genie

A Persian fairytale

Many moons ago in ancient Persia there lived a bright young man called Amal. He was out one day when he had the misfortune to meet a genie. Now sometimes genies can be good news, but this one was in a very bad temper and he was looking for trouble. Amal had to think quickly. He had no weapons with him, only an egg and a lump of salt in his pocket.

The genie came whirling up to Amal, but before

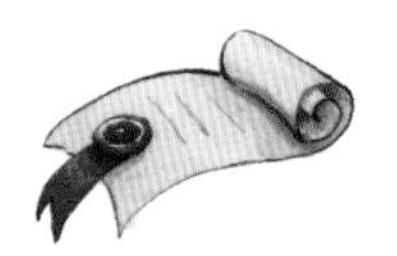

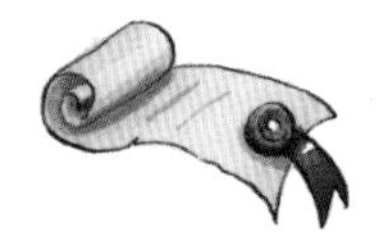

he could say anything, Amal yelled at him.

"Genie! You and I should have a competition to see who is the strongest!"

You might think this was very foolish of Amal, but he knew two things about genies. One was that it is always better to take control first, and the second was that genies are not terribly bright. They are fine at conjuring up gorgeous palaces and flying carpets, but they are a bit slow when it comes to basic common sense.

Well, the genie looked at Amal, and then he laughed. It was not a nice sound, but Amal was not daunted.

"Hah! You don't look very strong," sniggered the genie. "I shall win this contest easily," and he laughed again.

Amal picked up a stone.

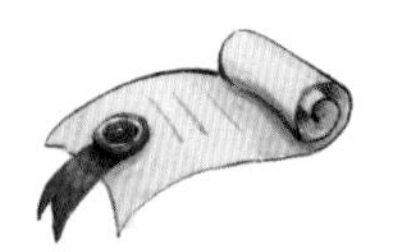

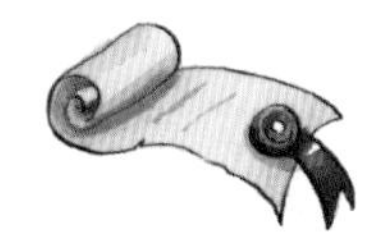

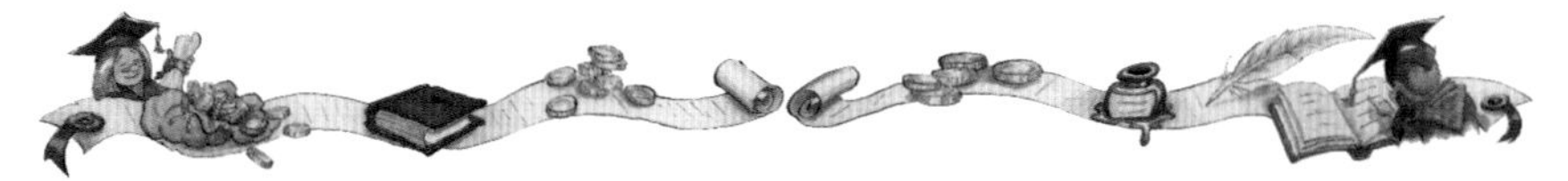

"You must squeeze this stone until water comes out of it," he said, handing the genie the stone.

Well, the genie squeezed and squeezed, and huffed and puffed, but, of course, no water came out of the stone. He threw it down in a temper.

"Not possible!" he snapped.

Amal bent down and picked up the stone, and squeezed. And with a scrunching sound, liquid ran down Amal's fingers. The genie was astonished. And so would you have been if you had been there. What clever Amal had done was to put the egg in the same hand as the stone, and it was the egg that was broken. Genies are not terribly bright and this one was no exception.

Then Amal said, "Well, I win that one. But now perhaps you could crumble this stone into powder," and he handed the genie another stone. Well, the genie squeezed and squeezed, and huffed

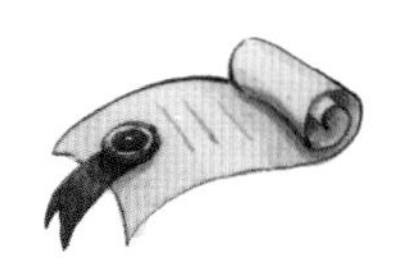

and puffed, but, of course, the stone did not crumble at all, not even the tiniest bit. The genie threw it down in a temper.

Amal picked it up and squeezed. And as he squeezed, powder fell from his fingers with a grinding sound. The genie was astonished. And so would you have been if you had been there, but you can guess what clever Amal had done. He put the salt in his hand as well as the stone.

The genie was feeling that his reputation was somewhat dented by Amal's performance so he needed to get his own back.

"You are clearly a great and mighty fighter," the genie said to Amal. "I should like to give you a meal to celebrate your achievements. Come and stay the night with me," and he smiled.

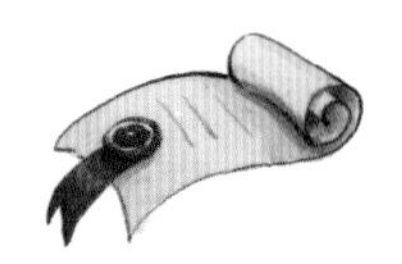

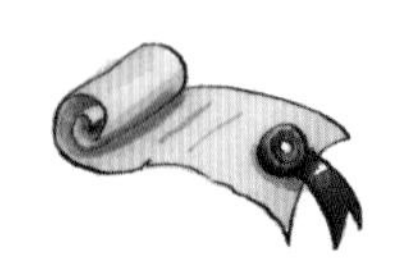

But Amal saw the smile, and kept his wits about him. After a dreadful meal, they both lay down to sleep in the genie's cave. Once Amal was sure the genie was asleep, he moved to the other side of the cave, leaving his pillow in the bed to look as if he were still there asleep. Then he watched. As the first light of dawn filtered into the cave, the genie woke

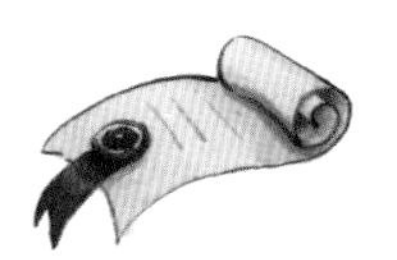

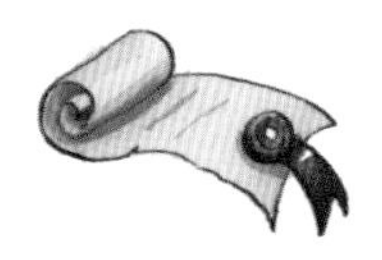

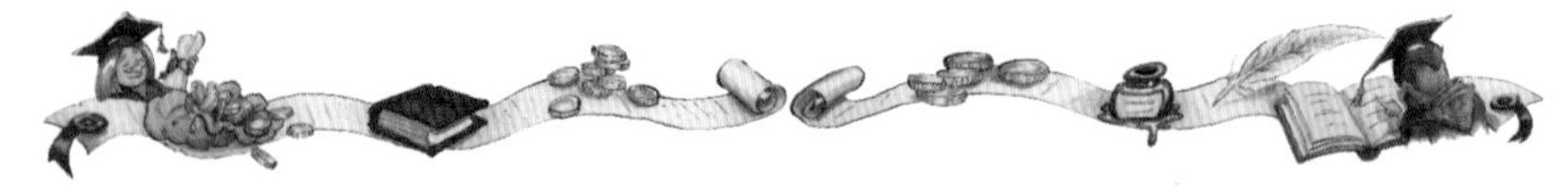

up. He picked up a club, crept over to where he thought Amal was lying and pounded the club down onto the bed. Then he stomped out of the cave to fetch some water for his morning tea.

You can imagine his dismay when, on returning, he found Amal singing to himself as he lit the fire.

"Morning, genie! I thought I would get breakfast ready," said Amal cheerfully. "I hope you slept better than I did," he continued. "Some wretched insect batted me in the face during the night."

Well, at this the genie gave a great shriek and whistled himself as fast as possible into an old oil lamp that lay on the floor of the cave. He wasn't seen again for hundreds of years until a young lad called Aladdin happened to find the lamp.

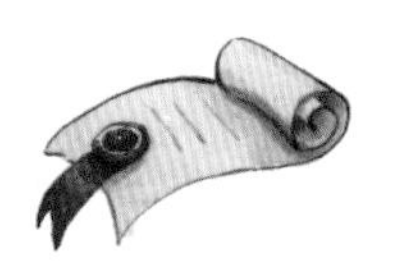

The Girl who Owned a Bear

By L Frank Baum

Jane Gladys was amusing herself alone in the big sitting room upstairs. She was working on her first piece of embroidery – a sofa pillow for papa's birthday. The door opened and closed quietly. She raised her eyes and was astonished to find a strange man in the middle of the room.

He was short and fat, and was breathing heavily from climbing the stairs. He held a hat in one hand and underneath his other elbow was a

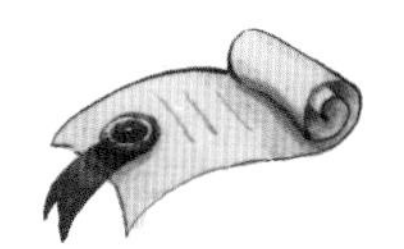

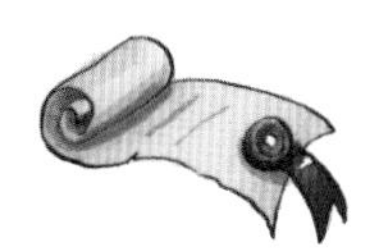

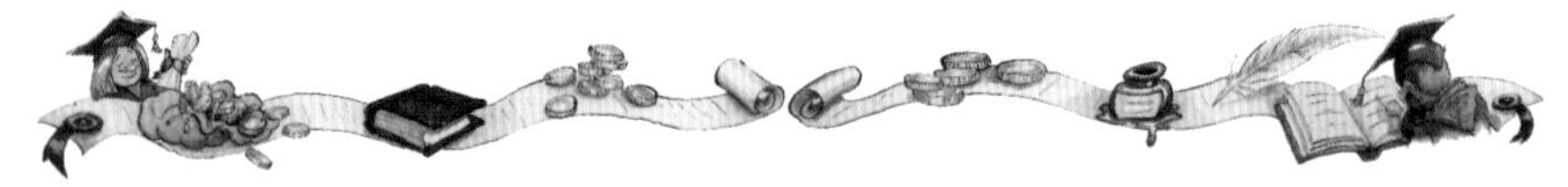

good-sized book. He was dressed in a black suit that looked old and rather shabby.

"Excuse me," he said, while the child gazed at him in surprise. "Are you Jane Gladys Brown?"

"Yes, sir," she answered.

"Very good, very good, indeed!" he remarked.

"What do you want?" she asked.

"I'm going to be frank with you. Your father has treated me in a terrible manner."

Jane Gladys got off the windowsill and pointed her small finger at the door.

"Leave this room 'meejitly!" she cried, her voice trembling. "My papa is the best man in the world."

"Allow me to explain. I called on him the other day and asked him to buy the 'Complete Works of Peter Smith,' and

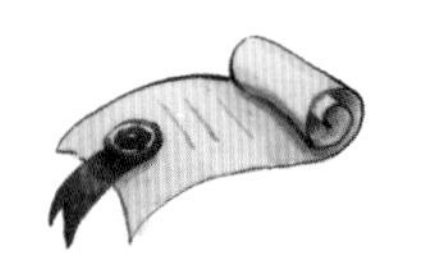

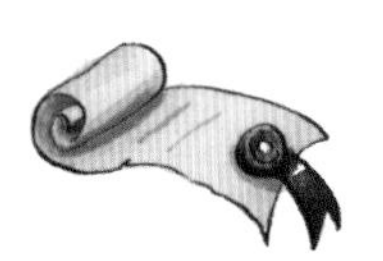

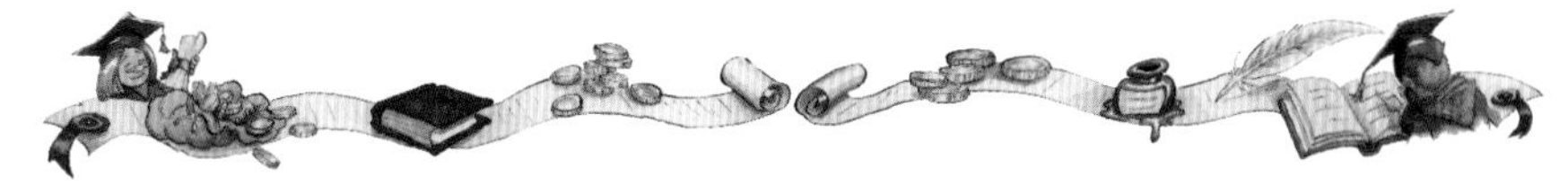

what do you suppose he did?"

She said nothing.

"He ordered me from his office, and had me put out of the building by the janitor! I decided to be revenged. So, I'm going to present you with this book," he said, taking it from under his arm. Then he sat down, drew a fountain pen from his pocket and wrote her name in it.

After handing the book to her, he walked to the door, gave her a bow and left the room.

The child sat down in the window and glanced at the book. It had a red and yellow cover and the word 'Thingamajigs' was written across the front cover in big letters.

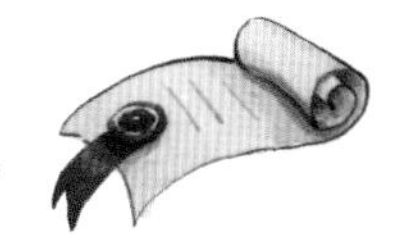

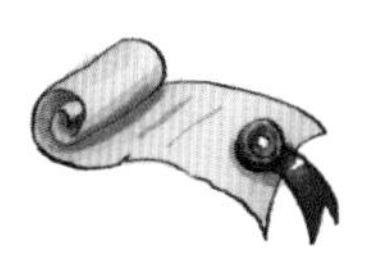

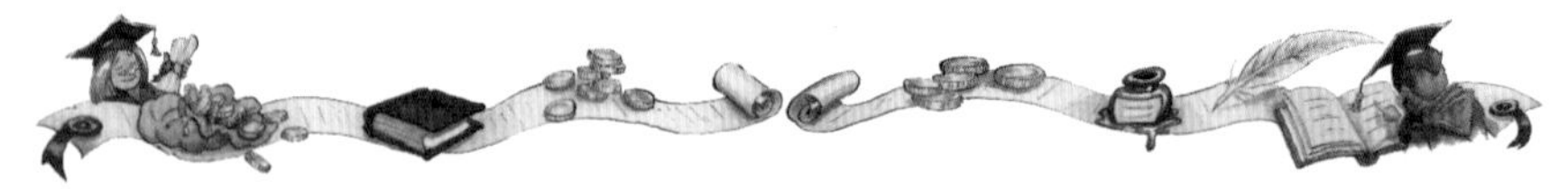

Then she opened it, curiously, and saw her name written in black letters upon the first white page.

She turned a page, and she had scarcely noted that it contained the picture of a monkey when the animal sprang from the book with a great crumpling of paper and landed upon the window seat beside her.

"He he he he he!" chattered the creature, springing to the girl's shoulder and then to the centre table. "This is great fun! Now I can be a real monkey instead of a picture of one."

"Real monkeys can't talk," said Jane Gladys.

"How do you know? Have you ever been one yourself?" inquired the animal, laughing loudly.

The girl was quite bewildered by this time. She thoughtlessly turned another page, and before she had time to look twice, there sprang over her shoulder a spotted leopard, which landed upon the

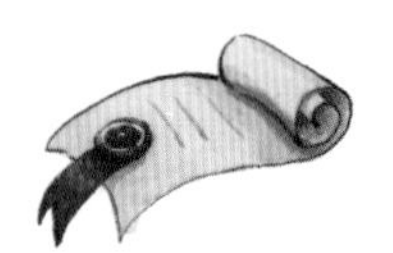

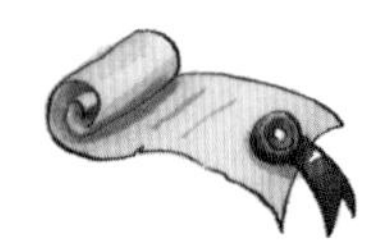

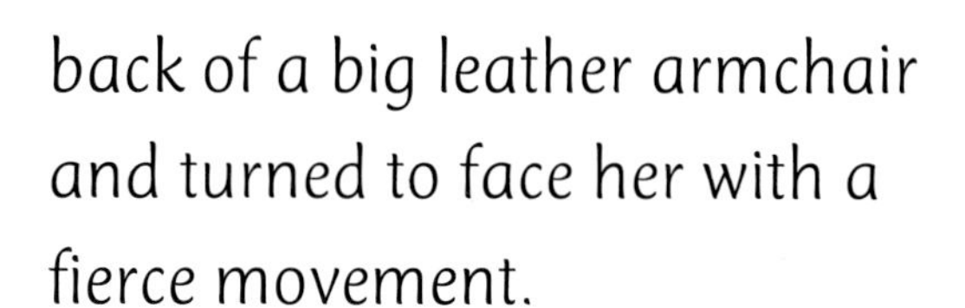

back of a big leather armchair and turned to face her with a fierce movement.

The monkey climbed to the top of the chandelier and chattered with fright. The leopard crouched upon the back of the chair, lashed his tail from side to side and glared at them.

"Which of us are you going to attack first?" asked the monkey.

"I can't attack any of you," snarled the leopard. "The artist made my mouth shut, so I haven't any teeth, and he forgot to make my claws. But I'm a frightful-looking creature, nevertheless, am I not?"

"I suppose you're frightful-looking enough. But if you have no teeth nor claws we don't mind your looks at all," said the monkey.

This annoyed the leopard so much that he

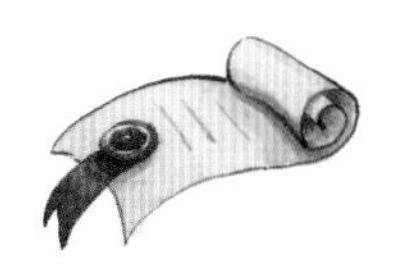

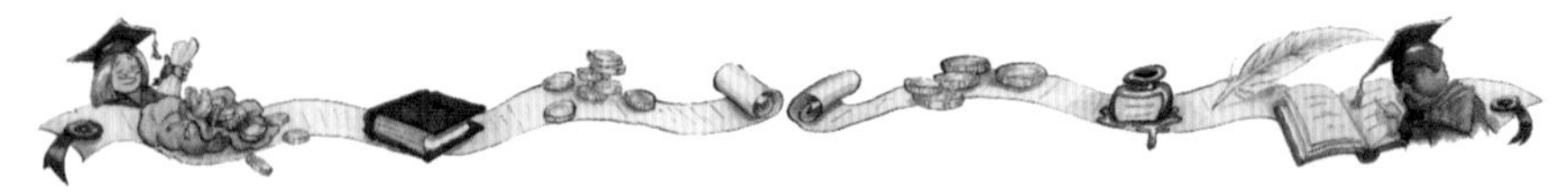

growled horribly, but the monkey just laughed.

Just then the book slipped from the girl's lap, and as she made a movement to catch it one of the pages near the back opened wide. She caught a glimpse of a fierce grizzly bear looking at her from the page, and quickly threw the book to the ground. It fell with a crash in the middle of the room, but beside it stood the great grizzly, who had wrenched

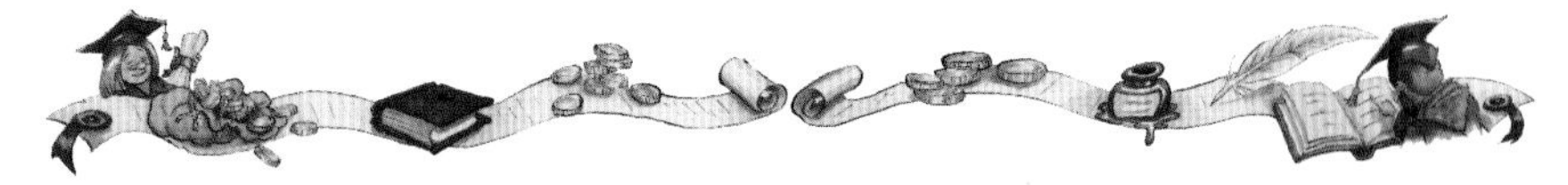

himself from the page before the book had closed.

"Now," cried the leopard from his perch, "you'd better look out for yourselves! You can't laugh at him as you did at me. The bear has both claws and teeth."

"Indeed I have," said the bear, in a low, deep, growling voice. "And I know how to use them, too. If you read in that book you'll find that I eat little girls – shoes, dresses, ribbons and all!"

Jane Gladys was much frightened on hearing this, and she began to realize what the man meant when he said he gave her the book to be revenged.

"You mustn't eat me. It would be wrong."

"Why?" asked the bear, in surprise.

"Because I own you. The book was given to me, my name's on the front page. So you mustn't dare to eat your owner!"

The grizzly hesitated. "Then, of course, I can't

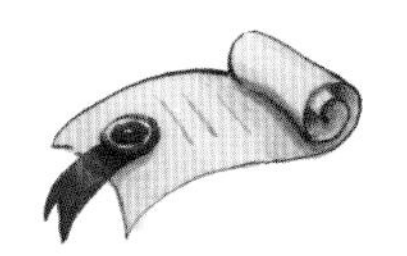

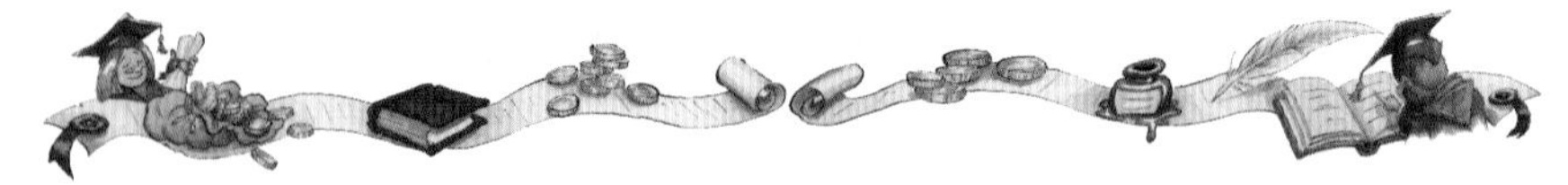

eat you," he decided. "That author is disappointing – as most authors are."

"The fault lies with all of you," said Jane Gladys, severely. "Why didn't you stay in the book, where you were put?"

The animals looked at each other.

"Now, you stupid creatures—"

But she was interrupted by them all making a rush for the book. There was a swish and a whirr and a rustling of leaves, and an instant later the book lay upon the floor looking just like any other book, while Jane Gladys' strange companions had all disappeared.

This story should teach us to think quickly and clearly upon all occasions, for had Jane Gladys not remembered that she owned the bear he probably would have eaten her before the bell rang.

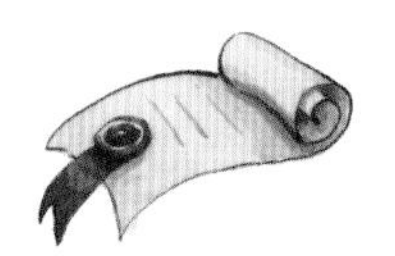

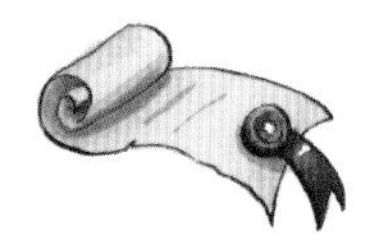

Singh Rajah and the Cunning Little Jackals

By Mary Frere

Once upon a time, in a great jungle, there lived a great lion. He was rajah (king) of all the country, and everyday he used to leave his den and roar with a loud, angry voice. When he roared, the other animals in the jungle were frightened, and ran here and there. Singh Rajah would pounce upon them, kill them, and gobble them up for his dinner.

This went on for a long time, until at last there

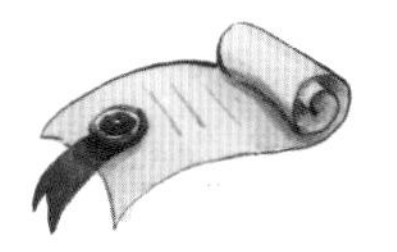

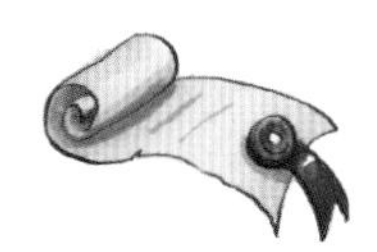

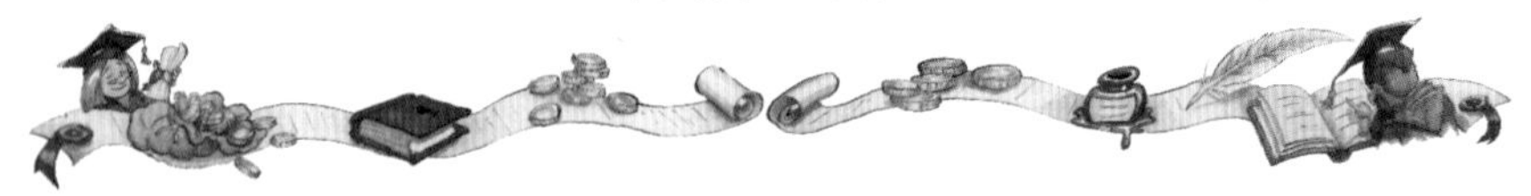

were no creatures left in the jungle but the king and queen of the jackals – Rajah Jackal and Ranee Jackal.

A very hard time of it the poor little jackals had, running this way and that to escape the terrible Singh Rajah, and every day the little Ranee Jackal would say to her husband, "I am afraid he will catch us today – do you hear how he is roaring?" And he would answer her, "Never fear, I will take care of you. Let us run on a mile or two. Come, come – quick, quick, quick!" And they would both run away as fast as they could.

After some time spent in this way, they found, however, one fine day, that the lion was so close upon them that they could not escape. Then the little Ranee Jackal said, "Husband, husband! I feel very frightened. The Singh Rajah is so angry he will certainly kill us at once. What can we do?" But

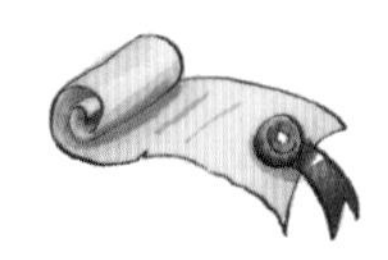

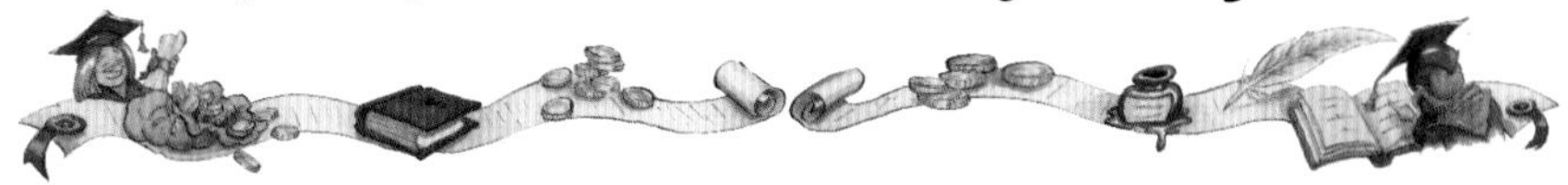

he answered, "Cheer up, we can save ourselves yet. Come, and I'll show you how we may manage it."

So what did these cunning little jackals do, but they went to the great lion's den, and when he saw them coming, he began to roar and shake his mane, and he said, "You little wretches, come and be eaten at once. I have had no dinner for three whole days, and all that time I have been running over hill and dale to find you. ROAR! ROAR! Come and be eaten, I say!" and he lashed his tail and gnashed his teeth, and looked very terrible indeed.

Then the Jackal Rajah, creeping close up to him, said, "Great Singh Rajah, we all know you are our master, and we would have come at your bidding long ago, but indeed, sir, there is a much bigger Rajah even than you in this jungle, and he tried to catch us and eat us up, and frightened us so much that we were obliged to run away."

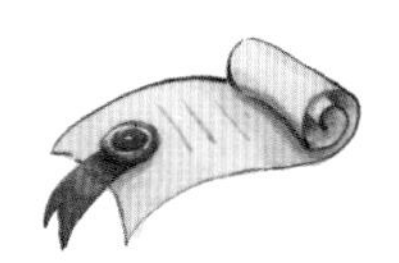

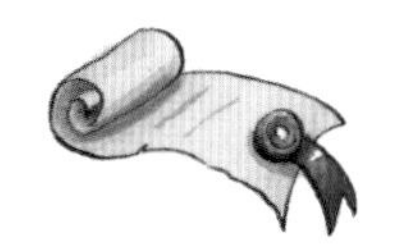

"What do you mean?" growled Singh Rajah. "There is no king in this jungle but me!"

"Ah, sire," answered the jackal, "in truth one would think so, for you are very dreadful. Your voice is death. But with our own eyes, we have seen one with whom you could not compete, whose equal you can no more be than we are yours, whose face is as flaming fire, his step as thunder, and his power supreme."

"It is impossible!" interrupted the old Lion, "but show me this rajah of whom you speak so much, so I may destroy him instantly!"

Then the little jackals ran on before him until they reached a great well,

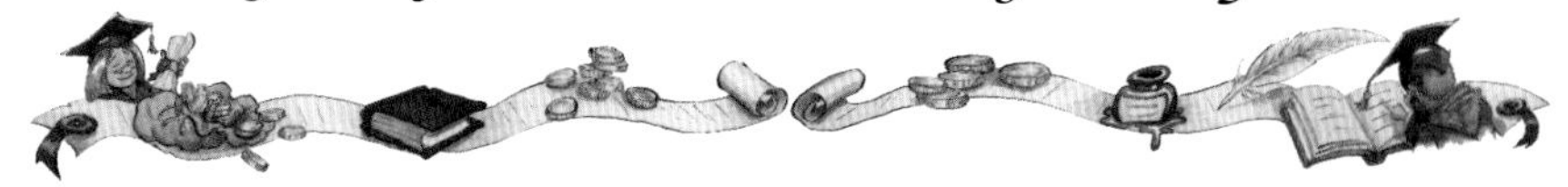

and, pointing down to his own reflection in the water, they said, "See, sire, there lives the terrible king of whom we spoke."

When Singh Rajah looked down the well he became very angry, for he thought he saw another lion there. He roared and shook his great mane, and the shadow lion shook his, and looked terribly defiant. At last, filled with rage, Singh Rajah sprang down to kill him at once, but no other lion was there – only the treacherous reflection. The sides of the well were so steep that he could not get out again to punish the two jackals, who peeped over the top. Singh Rajah was never seen again.

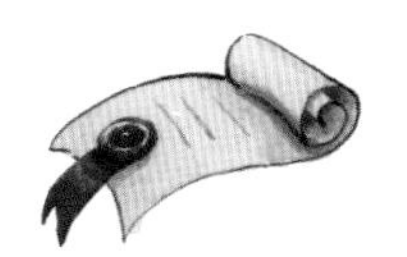

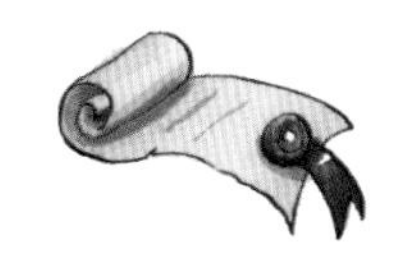

The Hillman and the Housewife

By Juliana Horatia Gatty Ewing

It is well known that the good people cannot stand mean ways. Now, there once lived a housewife who was a good woman, but gave only to others what she had no use for.

One day a hillman knocked at her door.

"Can you lend us a saucepan, good mother?" said he. "There's a wedding in the hill, and all the pots are in use."

"Is he to have one?" asked the servant girl.

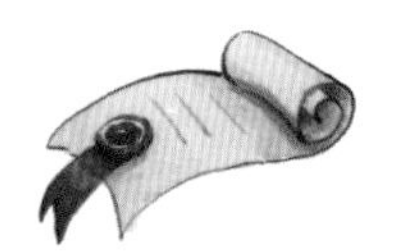

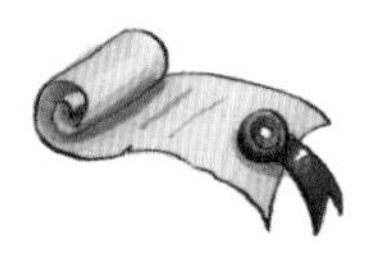

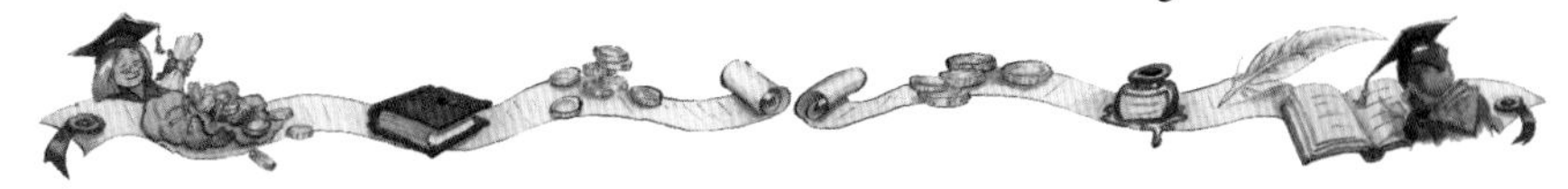

"Ay, to be sure," said the housewife.

But when the maid was taking a saucepan from the shelf, she pinched her arm and whispered sharply, "Not that, stupid, get the old one out of the cupboard. It leaks, and the hillmen are so neat and such nimble workers that they are sure to mend it before they send it home. So one does a good turn and saves sixpence for fixing."

The maid fetched the saucepan and gave it to the hillman, who thanked her and went away.

The saucepan was soon returned neatly mended and ready for use. At supper time the maid filled the pan with milk and set it on the fire for the children's supper, but in a few minutes the milk was so burnt and smoked that no one could touch it, and even the pigs would not drink the wash into which it was thrown.

"You good-for-nothing!" cried the housewife to

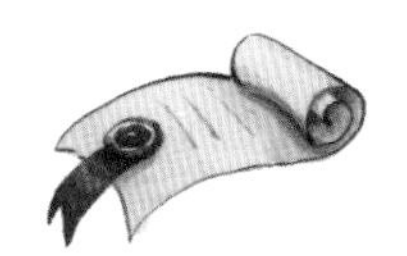

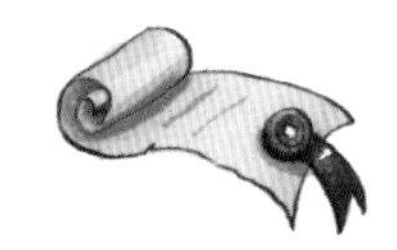

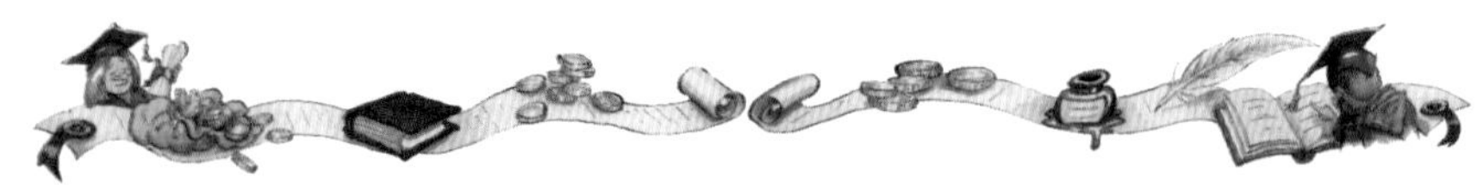

the maid, and this time she filled the pan herself. "You would ruin the richest, with your careless ways. There's a whole quart of milk spoilt at once."

"And that's two pence," cried a voice from the chimney, a queer whining voice like some old body who was always grumbling over something. The housewife had not left the saucepan for two minutes when the milk boiled

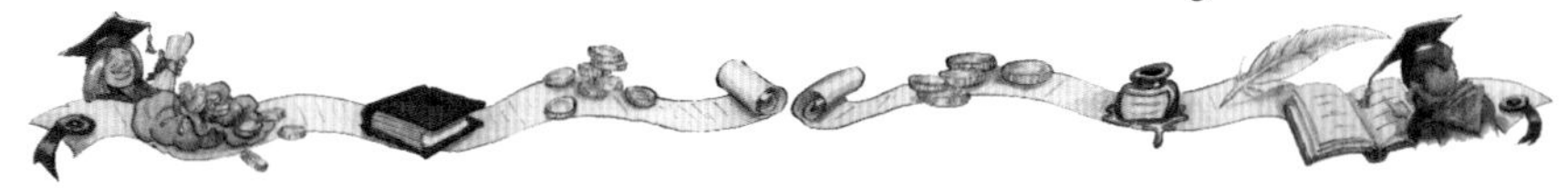

over, and it was all burnt and smoked as before.

"The pan must be dirty," cried the housewife in a rage, "and there are two full quarts of milk as good as thrown to the dogs."

"That's four pence," said the voice in the chimney.

After a long scrubbing, the saucepan was once more filled and set on the fire, but the milk was burnt and smoked again, and the housewife burst into tears at the waste, crying out, "Three quarts of milk burnt for one meal!"

"And that's six pence," cried the voice from the chimney. "You didn't save sixpence after all." With that, the hillman himself came tumbling down the chimney, and went off laughing through the door. And from that time on, the saucepan was as good as any other.

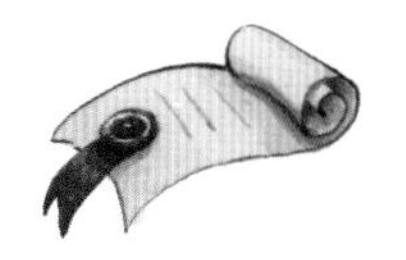

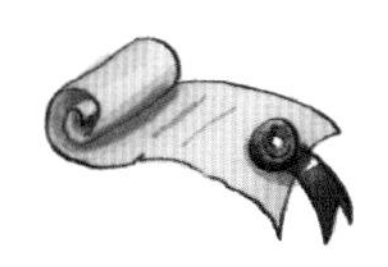

Jack and the Beanstalk

By Joseph Jacobs

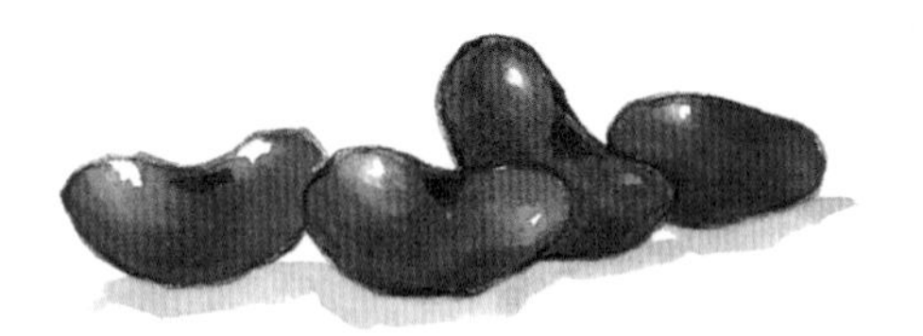

This is the story of how Jack did a silly thing, but all was well in the end. Jack and his mother were very poor and there came a sad day when there was no more money left, so Jack was told to take

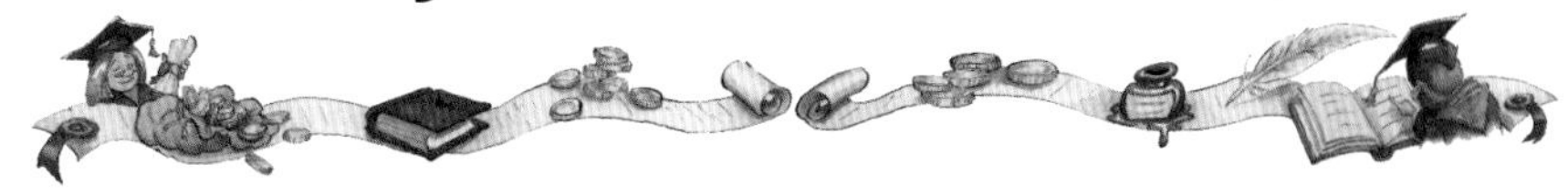

the cow to market to sell her.

As Jack led the cow to market, he met a funny little man with a tall feather in his hat.

"And where might you be going with that fine-looking cow?" the funny little man asked.

Jack explained and the little man swept off his hat and shook out five coloured beans.

"Well, I can save you a journey. I will give you these five magic beans in exchange for your cow."

Once Jack heard the word 'magic' he didn't stop to think. He took the beans at once, gave the funny little man the cow and ran off home to his mother.

"Jack, you are a fool! You have exchanged our fine cow for five worthless beans!"

She flung the beans out of the window, and sent Jack to bed without any supper.

When he woke in the morning, Jack couldn't understand why it was so dark in the cottage. He rushed outside to find his mother staring in amazement at an enormous beanstalk that reached right up into the clouds.

"I told you they were magic beans," smiled Jack, and he began to climb the beanstalk. He climbed until he could no longer see the ground below. At the top there stood a castle. Jack knocked on the door, and it was opened by a HUGE woman!

"My husband eats boys for breakfast so you had better run away," she told Jack. But before Jack could reply, the ground started to shake.

"Too late!" said the giant's wife. "You must hide," and she bundled Jack into a cupboard. Jack peeped through the keyhole, and saw the most colossal

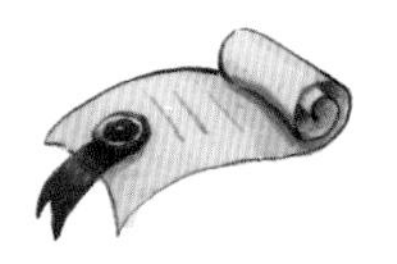

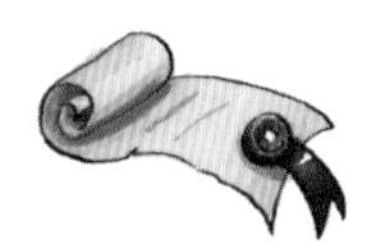

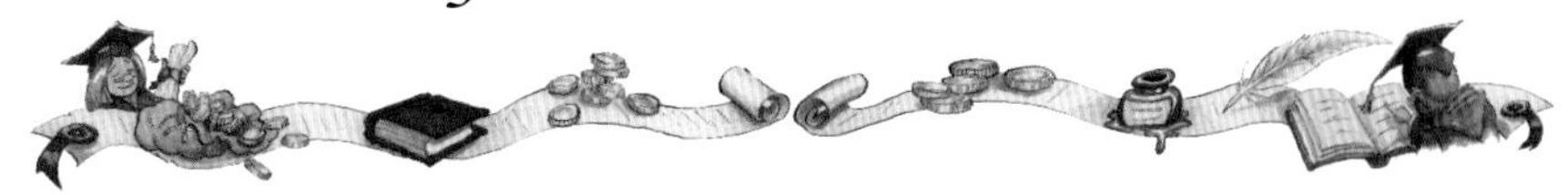

man. "Fee fi fo fum! I smell the blood of an Englishman!" he roared.

"Don't be silly, dear. You can smell your breakfast," said the giant's wife, placing a plate piled high with fat, juicy sausages in front of him. The giant did not seem to have very good table manners, and had soon gobbled the lot. Then he poured a great bag of gold onto the table, and with a smile on his big face, he soon fell asleep.

Jack darted out of the cupboard,

grabbed the bag of money, ran out of the kitchen and slithered down the beanstalk.

Jack's mother bought two cows and they were very content. But after a while Jack decided he would like to climb the beanstalk again. The giant's wife was not pleased to see him.

"My husband lost a bag of gold when you were here," she muttered. But the ground began to shake, so Jack hid in the cupboard.

"Fee fi fo fum! I smell the blood of an Englishman!"

"Don't be silly, dear. You can smell your breakfast," said the giant's wife, placing a plate piled high with thirty-eight chickens in front of

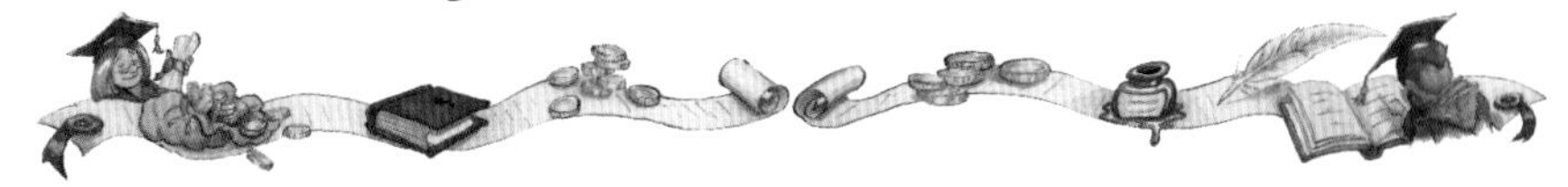

him. The giant had soon gobbled the lot. Then he lifted a golden hen onto the table. With a smile on his big face he fell asleep, snoring loudly.

Jack darted out of the cupboard, grabbed the golden hen, ran out of the kitchen and slithered down the beanstalk.

Jack's mother bought a herd of cows, lots of new clothes, and they were very content. But after a while Jack decided he would like to climb the beanstalk one last time. The giant's wife was not pleased to see him.

"My husband lost a golden hen when you were here." she grumbled. But then the ground began to tremble. This time Jack hid under the table.

The giant stomped into the kitchen. "Fee fi fo fum! I smell the blood of an Englishman!"

"I would look in the cupboard," said the giant's wife, but it was empty. They were both puzzled.

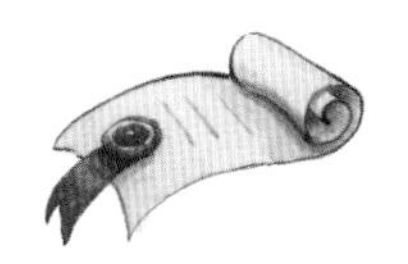

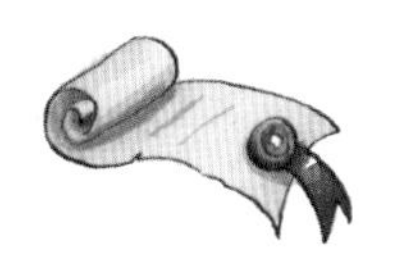

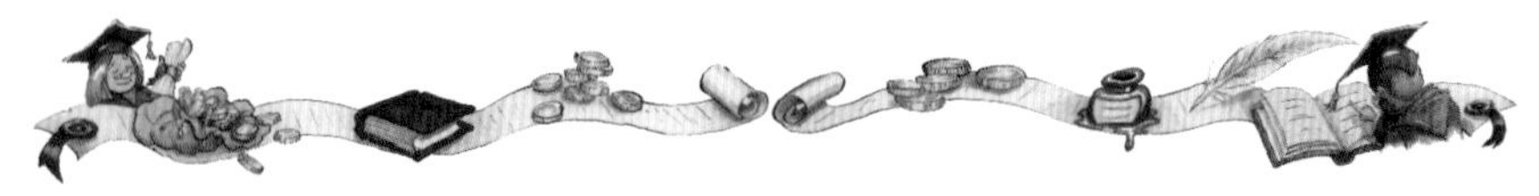

"Eat your breakfast. I have cooked you ninety-two fried eggs," said the giant's wife, placing a plate in front of him. The giant had soon gobbled the lot. Then he lifted a golden harp onto the table, and was soon fast asleep, snoring loudly.

Jack crept out and grabbed the golden harp, but the harp called "Master!" and the giant awoke. He chased Jack who scrambled down the beanstalk as fast as he could with the harp in his arms. As soon as Jack reached the ground, he chopped through the beanstalk with an axe. Down tumbled the beanstalk and the giant. That was the end of them both and Jack and his mother lived happily for the rest of their days.

Trickery and Mischief

The Giant who Counted Carrots

A German fairytale

High upon a mountainside there was once a giant who was always very sleepy, and when he went to sleep, he would sleep for hundreds of years at a time. So every time he awoke things had changed a great deal. He spent time as a herdsman, but he did not like being poor. So he went back to sleep. On another visit he spent time as a rich farmer, but he found his servants cheated him so he went back to sleep. When he eventually

awoke again he wandered down the mountainside to see what he could see.

He came upon a rock pool where a waterfall tumbled down the rocks. A group of laughing girls were sitting dangling their toes in the water. The giant hid and watched. One of the girls was quieter than the others, but to the giant she was the prettiest. Her name was Elizabeth and she was to be married in a few days to the young duke. She and her friends chattered about the forthcoming celebrations as they paddled in the pool, and all the while the giant watched. When they skipped away, his heart grew sad. He realized just how very lonely he was.

He decided to try to win Elizabeth's heart. All through the night he worked. He covered the steep stone under the waterfall with white marble so it sparkled in the clear water. He lined the pool with silver, and filled it with darting golden fish. He covered the banks with rich green grass, planted with sweetly smelling violets and forget-me-nots and deep blue hyacinths. Then he hid himself again.

When the girls arrived they were astonished, but Elizabeth looked thoughtful. She knew that some powerful enchantment had been at work. She wandered to the edge and looked deep into the silver pool, full of the golden fish. And as she looked she heard a voice, whispering, whispering to her to step into the pool. There was a sudden splash, and as her friends looked round in alarm, Elizabeth slipped into the pool. The girls ran over to the pool and looked into the silver depths. In

vain they tried to find her. When they went home and told the young duke, he came with all haste to the pool. All the giant's adornments had vanished. The waterfall fell over steep and black rocks, the silver lining and the golden fish had disappeared from the pool, and there was not a single flower to be seen. Sadly, the duke went back to the palace and nothing would cheer him.

Meanwhile Elizabeth found herself in the giant's garden. He begged her to stay with him and be his queen, but she told him she loved the duke and would not forsake him. The giant hoped she would forget the duke, but as the days passed he saw

that she grew pale and sad. He wondered how he could cheer her, and change her mind. Then he remembered his magic staff. Whatever it touched would turn into any animal he wished for. He gave the staff to Elizabeth and for a few hours she was happy. First a kitten, then a dog, then a canary appeared thanks to the staff. But it was not long before she grew silent again.

Now the giant grew very good carrots, and he was very proud of them. He pulled up some for supper and Elizabeth said she had never tasted such delicious carrots in all her life,

which was true. So the next day, the giant took Elizabeth out into the fields round the castle where the carrots grew. As far as the eye could see there were carrots, row upon row of them.

Elizabeth asked the giant how many there were, but he couldn't tell her that at all. So she begged him to count at least one row, and as he began counting she quickly drew the staff out from under her cloak and touched a black stone that lay on the ground. It turned into a black horse with great hooves that pounded the earth as Elizabeth mounted its back and fled down the valley, away from the giant.

The very next day, Elizabeth married her duke and they lived happily ever after. The lonely giant went slowly back to his garden, and fell into a deep sleep. Many hundreds of years passed and still the giant never awoke. In time grass and plants and

trees grew over the slumbering giant, and still he slept on. Over the years the mound that was the sleeping giant became known as Giant Mountain, and so it is still called today. So beware if you see great rows of carrots on a mountain side, you might be very near a sleeping giant!

How the Rhinoceros got his Skin

By Rudyard Kipling

Once upon a time, on an uninhabited island on the shores of the Red Sea, there lived a Parsee from whose hat the rays of the sun were reflected in oriental splendour. And the Parsee lived by the Red Sea with nothing but his hat and his knife and a cooking stove of the kind that you must particularly never touch. And one day he took flour and water and currants and plums and sugar and things, and made himself one cake that

was two feet across and three feet thick. It was indeed a superior dish, and he put it on the stove because he was allowed to cook on that stove, and he baked it and he baked it till it was all brown and smelt most delicious. But just as he was going to eat it there came down to the beach from the Altogether Uninhabited Interior one rhinoceros with a horn on his nose, two piggy eyes and few manners. In those days the rhinoceros' skin fitted him quite tight. There were no wrinkles in it anywhere. He looked exactly like a Noah's ark rhinoceros, but of course much bigger. All the same, he had no manners then, and he has no manners now, and he never will have any manners. He said, "How!" and the Parsee left that cake and climbed to the top of a palm tree with nothing on but his hat, from which the rays of the sun were always reflected in oriental splendour.

And the rhinoceros upset the oil stove with his nose and the cake rolled on the sand, and he spiked that cake on the horn of his nose and he ate it, and he went away waving his tail, to the desolate and Exclusively Uninhabited Interior that is next to the islands of Mazanderan, Socotra and Promontories of the Larger Equinox. Then the Parsee came down from his palm tree and put the stove on its legs and recited the following poem, which, as you have not heard, I will now proceed to relate:

"Them that takes cakes
Which the Parsee man bakes
Makes dreadful mistakes."

And there was a great deal more in that than you would think. Because, five weeks later, there

was a heatwave in the Red Sea, and everybody took off all the clothes they had. The Parsee took off his hat but the Rhinoceros took off his skin and carried it over his shoulder as he came down to the beach to bathe. In those days it buttoned underneath with three buttons and looked like a waterproof. He said nothing whatever about the Parsee's cake, because he had eaten it all, and he never had any manners, then, since, or henceforward. He waddled straight into the water and blew bubbles through his nose, leaving his skin on the beach.

Presently the Parsee came by and found the skin, and he smiled one smile that ran all round his face two times. Then he danced three times round the skin and rubbed his hands. Then he went to his camp and filled his hat with cake crumbs, for the Parsee never ate anything but

cake, and never swept out his camp. He took that skin, and he shook that skin, and he scrubbed that skin, and he rubbed that skin just as full of dry, stale, tickly cake crumbs and some burnt currants as ever it could possibly hold. Then he climbed to the top of his palm tree and waited for the rhinoceros to come out of the water and put it on.

And the rhinoceros did. He buttoned it up with the three buttons, and it tickled like cake crumbs in bed. Then he wanted to scratch, but that made it worse, and then he lay down on the sands and rolled and rolled and rolled,

and every time he rolled the cake crumbs tickled him worse and worse and worse. Then he ran to the palm tree and rubbed and rubbed and rubbed himself against it. He rubbed so much and so hard that he rubbed his skin into a great fold over his shoulders and another fold underneath, where the buttons used to be (but he rubbed the buttons off) and he rubbed some more folds over his legs. And it spoiled his temper, but it didn't make the least difference to the cake crumbs. They were inside his skin and they tickled. So he went home, very angry indeed and horribly scratchy, and from that day to this every rhinoceros has great folds in his skin and a very bad temper.

But the Parsee came down from his palm tree, wearing his hat, from which the rays of the sun were reflected in oriental splendour, packed up his cooking stove and went away.

Under the Sun

By Juliana Horatia Gatty Ewing

There once lived a farmer who was so greedy and miserly, and so hard in all his dealings that, as folks say, he would skin a flint. It is needless to say that he never either gave or lent.

Now, by scraping, and saving, and grinding for many years, he had become almost wealthy, though, indeed, he was no better fed and dressed than if he had not a penny to bless himself with. But what bothered him sorely was that his next

neighbour's farm prospered in all matters better than his own, even though he was very generous.

Now on the lands of the generous farmer (whose name was Merryweather) there lived a fairy or hillman, who made a bet that he would both beg and borrow from the envious farmer, and out-bargain him as well. So he went one day to his house, and asked him if he would kindly give him half a stone of flour to make a pudding, adding, that if he would lend him a bag to carry it, this should be returned clean and in good condition.

"Look you, wife," said he, "this is no time to be saving half a stone of flour when we may make our fortunes at one stroke. I have heard my grandfather tell of a man who lent a sack of oats to one of the fairies, and got it back filled with gold pieces. And as good a measure as he gave of oats,

he got back of gold." Saying which, the farmer took a canvas bag to the flour bin, and began to fill it.

Meanwhile the fairy sat in the larder window and cried, "Give us good measure, neighbour, and you shall have anything under the sun."

When the farmer heard this he was nearly out of his wits with delight, and his hands shook so that the flour spilled all about the larder floor.

"Thank you, dear sir," he said, "It's a bargain, and I agree to it. My wife hears us, and is witness. Wife! Wife!" he cried, running into the kitchen, "I am to have anything under the sun. I think of asking for neighbour Merryweather's estate, but I should like to make a wise choice."

"You will have a week to think it over in," said the fairy, who had come in behind him. "I must be off now, so give me my flour, and come to the hill

behind your house seven days hence at midnight."

"Not for seven days, did you say, sir? Then I expect something over and above the exact amount. Interest we call it, my dear sir."

"What do you expect?" asked the fairy.

"Oh, dear sir, I leave it to you," said the farmer.

With that the fairy shouldered the flour-sack, and went on his way.

For the next seven days, the farmer had no peace for thinking and scheming how to get the most out of his one wish. His wife made many suggestions to which he did not agree, but he was careful not to quarrel with her.

And so, after a week of sleepless nights and anxious days, he came back to his first thought, and resolved to ask for his neighbour's estate.

At last the night came. It was full moon, and the farmer looked anxiously about, fearing the fairy

might not be true to his appointment. But at midnight he appeared, with the flour bag neatly folded in his hand.

"You hold to the agreement," said the farmer, "I am to have anything under the sun."

"Ask away," said the fairy.

"I want neighbour Merryweather's estate," said the farmer.

"What, all this land below here, that joins on to your own?"

"Every acre," said the farmer.

"Farmer Merryweather's fields are under the moon at present," said the fairy, coolly, "and thus not within the terms of the agreement. You must choose again."

But the farmer could choose nothing that was not then under the moon. He soon saw that he had been tricked, and he was angry at the fairy.

"Give me my bag," he screamed, "and the string – and the extra gift that you promised. For half a loaf is better than no bread," he muttered.

"There's your bag," cried the fairy, clapping it over the miser's head, "it's clean enough for a nightcap. And there's your string," he added, tying it tightly round the farmer's throat. "And, for my part, I'll give you what you deserve." Saying which he gave the farmer such a hearty kick that he kicked him straight down from the top of the hill to his own back door.

The Fairy Fluffikins

By Michael Fairless

The Fairy Fluffikins lived in a warm woolly nest in a hole down an old oak tree. She was the sweetest, funniest little fairy you ever saw. She wore a little, soft dress, and on her head a little woolly cap. Fairy Fluffikins had red hair and the brightest, naughtiest brown eyes imaginable.

What a life she led the animals! Fairy Fluffikins was a sad tease. She would creep into the nests where the fat baby dormice were asleep in bed

while mamma dormouse nodded over her knitting and papa smoked his little pipe, and she would tickle the babies until they screamed with laughter.

One night she had fine fun. She found a little dead mouse in a field, and an idea struck her. She hunted about till she found a piece of long grass, and then she took the little mouse, tied the piece of grass round its tail, and ran away with it to the big tree where the ancient owl lived. There was a little hole at the bottom of the tree and into it Fairy Fluffikins crept, leaving the mouse outside in the moonlight.

Presently she heard a gruff voice in the tree saying, "I smell mouse, I smell mouse." Then there was a swoop of wings, and Fairy Fluffikins promptly drew the mouse into the little hole and stuffed its tail into her mouth so that she might not be heard laughing, and the gruff voice said angrily, "Where's that mouse gone?"

She grew tired of this game after a few times, so she left the mouse in the hole and crept away to a

new one. She really was a naughty fairy.

Next she took to tormenting the squirrels. She used to find their stores of nuts and carry them away and fill the holes with pebbles, and this, when you are a hard-working squirrel with a large family to support, is very trying to the temper. Then she would tie acorns to their tails, and she would clap her hands to frighten them, and pull the baby squirrels' ears, till at last they offered a reward to anyone who could catch Fairy Fluffikins and bring her to be punished.

No one caught Fairy Fluffikins – but she caught herself, as you shall hear.

She was poking about round a haystack one night, trying to find something naughty to do, when she came upon a sweet little house with pretty wire walls and a wooden door standing open. In hopped Fluffikins, thinking she was going

to have some new kind of fun. There was a little white thing dangling from the roof, and she laid hold of it. Immediately there was a bang, the wooden door slammed, and Fluffikins was caught.

How she cried and stamped and pushed at the door, and promised to be a good fairy and a great many other things! But all to no purpose, the door was tight shut, and Fluffikins was not like some fortunate fairies who can get out of anywhere.

There she remained, and in the morning one of the labourers found her, and, thinking she was some kind of dormouse, he carried her home to his little girl, and if you call on Mary Ann Smith you will see Fairy Fluffikins there still in a little cage. There is no one to tease and no mischief to get into, so if there is a miserable little fairy anywhere it is Fairy Fluffikins, and I'm not sure it doesn't serve her quite right.

The Pot of Gold

An Irish folk tale

Niall O'Leary was sitting on a gate in the sunshine, day-dreaming quite happily, when – TIC! TIC! TIC! – he became aware of a sharp sound coming from the field behind him.

"Now what on earth can that be?" Niall wondered to himself. "It's too loud to be a grasshopper . . . and it's too quiet to be a bird."

TIC! TIC! TIC! it went.

Niall O'Leary swung his legs over the gate and

turned around. He blinked in astonishment. There in the long grass of the field was the tiniest man Niall had ever seen, no higher than his boot. The tiny man had his back to Niall, but Niall could see that he was dressed all in green, with a long white feather in his cap. A tiny leather shoe lay before him on a rock, and he was banging away at it with a tiny stone hammer.

Niall's eyes lit up. A leprechaun! A real, live leprechaun! Niall licked his lips greedily. Every tiny leprechaun had a huge pot of gold hidden somewhere. And as everybody knew, if you caught hold of a leprechaun and squeezed him tightly enough, he would have to tell you where his treasure was buried.

Quietly, Niall O'Leary got down from the gate. TIC! TIC! TIC! went the leprechaun's hammer.

Quietly, Niall O'Leary crept through the grass.

TIC! TIC! TIC! went the leprechaun's hammer.

Quietly, Niall O'Leary reached out with his large, meaty hands...

"GOTCHA!" cried Niall O'Leary, and he squeezed and squeezed the wriggling leprechaun with all his might.

"Oooooof!" cried the leprechaun. "Let me go, you big bully!"

"Tell me where your gold is and I will!" boomed Niall.

"I can't tell you anything while you're squeezing the breath out of me," the leprechaun gasped, looking rather purple.

"Oops, sorry!" blustered Niall, and relaxed his grip.

"That's better," wheezed the leprechaun, taking gulps of air. "Now put me down and I promise I'll

show you where my gold is hidden."

A broad grin spread across Niall's face as he lowered the leprechaun back down to the grass. "A leprechaun can't break his promise!" he chuckled.

"No," grumbled the leprechaun rather crossly, "and my gold is buried under here." He leapt a few steps into the middle of the field and pointed at a clump of dandelions. "You'll need a spade, mind," the leprechaun added thoughtfully. "You'll have to dig quite a way down."

Niall's face fell. "But I haven't got a spade with me," he said, glumly. "What shall I do?"

"Why don't you tie your handkerchief around the dandelions so you don't forget where the gold is buried," the leprechaun suggested. "Then hurry back home and fetch a spade. I promise on my word of honour that I won't untie the handkerchief."

Niall's face brightened once again. "What a great idea!" he beamed. He fumbled in his pocket, brought out a rather grubby red silk handkerchief, and tied it around the clump of dandelions. It waved at him in the breeze like a cheerful flag. "Thank you Mr Leprechaun," Niall remembered to say politely. "You've been mighty helpful." Then in a few strides, he was back over

the gate and away home, humming merrily.

As soon as Niall had grabbed the biggest spade he could find in the garden shed, he set off back to the field at once. All the way down the lane, he day-dreamed of what he would do with the gold. But when Niall O'Leary reached the gate, he stopped stone-still and his mouth hung open. He dropped the spade and scratched his head. "Well, blow me down," gasped Niall. All over the field, thousands of red silk handkerchiefs were tied onto clumps of dandelions and fluttering in the breeze. And Niall could hear the sound of leprechaun laughter floating over the grass on the wind.

So Niall O'Leary never got his pot of gold after all. But that is how he came to own the most successful silk handkerchief shop in Ireland.

The Ogre's Bride

By Juliana Horatia Gatty Ewing

There was once an ogre who kept a whole town in the grip of fear without anyone daring to challenge him. Over the years, the ogre had become very rich, and although he had huge cellars full of gold and jewels, and big barns groaning with the weight of stolen goods, the richer he grew the more greedy he became.

What he took from the people was not their biggest worry. Even to be killed and eaten by him

was not what they feared most. The worst was this – he would keep getting married and he only liked short wives. And as his wives always died very soon, he always needed new ones.

Some said he tormented his wives, some said he ate them, others said he worked them to death. The ogre only cared for two things in a woman – for her to be little, and a good housewife.

Now, it was when the ogre had just lost his twenty-fourth wife that these two qualities were joined in the daughter of a certain poor farmer. Everybody felt sure that Managing Molly must now be married to the ogre.

And sure enough, the giant came to the farmer and wanted to take Molly. The farmer did not know what to say and the ogre invited himself to supper at the farm later that week.

Managing Molly was not distressed at the news.

"Do what I ask you, and say as I say," said she to her father. First, he fetched a large number of hares, and then a barrel of white wine, on which he spent every penny he had. On the day of the ogre's visit, Molly made a delicious hare stew, and the wine barrel was set near the table.

When the ogre came, Molly served the stew, and the ogre sat down, his head just touching the kitchen rafters. The stew was perfect, and there was plenty of it. The ogre was very pleased, and said politely, "I'm afraid, my dear, that

you have been put to great trouble and expense."

"Don't mention it," said Molly. "The fewer rats there are, the more corn. How do you cook them?"

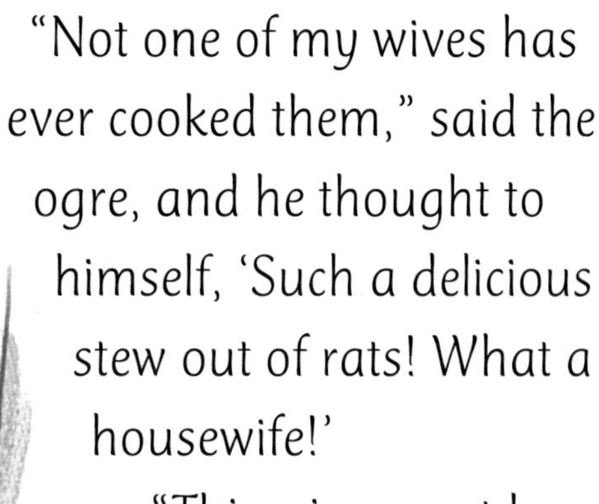

"Not one of my wives has ever cooked them," said the ogre, and he thought to himself, 'Such a delicious stew out of rats! What a housewife!'

"This wine must have cost you a great deal, neighbour," said he, drinking to the farmer.

"I don't know that rotten apples could be better used," said the farmer, "but I leave all that to Molly."

The ogre was now in a hurry to arrange the match, and asked what the farmer would pay.

"I should never dream of paying for someone to take Molly," said the farmer, boldly. "In fact, I shall expect payment from whoever takes her."

The ogre named a large sum of money, but the farmer told him to double it. Angrily he named a larger sum, which the farmer agreed to.

"Bring it in a sack tomorrow morning," said he to the ogre, "and then you can speak to Molly."

The next morning the ogre appeared, carrying a sack, and Molly came to meet him.

"There are two things," said she, "I would ask of any husband of mine: a new farmhouse and a feather bed of fresh goose feathers, filled when the old woman plucks her geese."

So, to save the expense of labour, the ogre built it himself, and worked hard under Molly's orders.

"Now for the feather bed," said Molly. When it snows, they say the old woman up in the sky is plucking her geese, and so at the first snow storm Molly sent for the ogre.

"You see the feathers falling," said she, "fill the bed with them."

The ogre carried in shovelfuls of snow to the bed, but as it melted as fast as he put it in, his labour never seemed done. Towards night the room got so cold that the snow would not melt, and the bed was soon filled.

Molly hastily covered it with sheets and blankets, and said, "Pray, rest here tonight, and tell me if the bed is not comfort itself. Tomorrow we will be married."

So the tired ogre lay down on the bed he had filled, but, do what he would, he could not get warm.

"The sheets must be damp," said he, and in the morning he woke with such horrible pains that he could hardly move, and half the bed had melted away. "It's no use," he groaned, "she's a very managing woman, but to sleep on such a bed would be the death of me."

And he went off home as quickly as he could, before Molly could call upon him to be married.

Iktomi and the Ducks

By Zitkala-sa

Iktomi is a spider fairy. He wears brown deerskin leggings with long soft fringes on either side. His long black hair is parted in the middle and wrapped with red, red bands. He even paints his funny face with red and yellow, and draws big black rings around his eyes. He wears a deerskin jacket, sewed with bright coloured beads.

Iktomi lives alone in a cone-shaped wigwam upon the plain. One day he sat hungry within his

teepee. Suddenly he rushed out, dragging after him his blanket. Quickly spreading it on the ground, he tore up dry tall grass with both his hands and tossed it into the blanket. Tying all the four corners together in a knot, he threw the light bundle of grass over his shoulder and leapt away.

Soon he came to a hilltop, where he paused for breath. Shading his eyes from the western sun, he peered far away into the lowlands.

"Ah ha!" grunted he, satisfied with what he saw.

A group of wild ducks were dancing and feasting in the marshes. Within the ring, beating a small drum, sat the chosen singers, nodding their heads and singing a merry dance-song.

Following a winding footpath, he made his way towards the ducks.

"Ho! Who is there?" called out a curious old duck, still bobbing up and down in the dance.

"Ho, Iktomi! Old fellow, pray tell us what you carry in your blanket. Do not hurry off! Stop! Halt!" urged one of the singers.

"My friends, I must not spoil your dance. Oh, you would not care to see what is in my blanket. Sing on! Dance on! I must not show you what I carry on my back," answered Iktomi. Now all the ducks crowded about Iktomi.

"We must see what you carry! We must know what is in your blanket!" they shouted in both his ears. Some even brushed their wings against the mysterious bundle.

Nudging himself again, wily Iktomi said, "My friends, it is only a pack of songs I carry in my blanket."

"Oh, then let us hear your songs!" cried the curious ducks.

At length Iktomi agreed to sing his songs, and

with great delight all the ducks flapped their wings and cried together, "Hoye! Hoye!"

Iktomi, with great care, laid down his bundle on the ground. "I will build first a round straw house, for I never sing my songs in the open air," said he.

Quickly he bent green willow sticks, planting both ends of each pole into the earth. These he covered with reeds and grasses.

Soon the straw hut was ready. One by one the fat ducks waddled in through a small opening, which was the only entrance.

In a strange low voice Iktomi began to sing his queer tunes. These were the words he sang:

"Istokmus wacipo, tuwayatunwanpi kinhan ista nisasapi kta."

This means: 'With eyes closed you must dance. He who dares to open his eyes, forever red eyes shall have.'

Up rose the circle of seated ducks and holding their wings close against their sides, they began to dance to the rhythm of Iktomi's song and drum.

With eyes closed they did dance! Iktomi began to sing louder and faster. He seemed to be moving about in the center of the ring. No duck dared blink a wink. Each one shut his eyes very tight and danced even harder.

One of the dancers could close his eyes no longer and peeped at Iktomi.

"Oh! Oh!" squawked he in awful terror! "Run! Fly! Iktomi is twisting your heads and breaking your necks! Run out and fly! Fly!" he cried.

Hereupon the ducks opened their eyes. There beside Iktomi's bundle of songs lay half of their crowd – flat on their backs.

Out they flew through the opening. But as they soared high into the blue sky they cried to one another, "Oh! Your eyes are red-red!"

"And yours are red-red!" For the warning words had proven true.

"Ah ha!" laughed Iktomi, untying the four corners of his blanket, "I shall not be hungry anymore." Homeward he trudged along with nice fat ducks in his blanket.

A French Puck

By Paul Sébillot

Among the mountain pastures and valleys that lie in the centre of France there dwelt a mischievous spirit called Puck, whose delight it was to play tricks on everybody, particularly on the shepherds. They never knew when they were safe from him, as he could change himself into a man, woman or child, a stick or a goat. Indeed, there was only one thing whose shape he could not take, and that was a needle. At least, he could transform

himself into a needle, but he never was able to imitate the hole, so every woman would have found him out at once, and this he knew.

One day he was told of a young couple who were going to the nearest town to buy all that they needed for setting up house. Quite certain that they would forget something that they could not do without, Puck waited patiently till they were jogging along in their cart on their return journey, and changed himself into a fly in order to overhear their conversation. For a long time it was very dull – all about their wedding day next month, and who were to be invited. This led the bride to her dress, and she gave a scream.

"Oh! I have forgotten to buy the coloured reels of cotton to match my clothes!"

"Oh dear!" exclaimed the man. "That is unlucky."

And then she gave another little scream, which

had quite a different sound from the first. "Look!" The bridegroom looked, and on one side of the road he saw a large ball of thread of all colours – of all the colours, that is, of the dresses that were tied on to the back of the cart.

"Well, that is a wonderful piece of good fortune," cried he, as he sprang out to get it. "One would think a fairy had put it there on purpose."

"Perhaps she has," laughed the girl, and as she spoke she seemed to hear an echo coming from the horse, but of course that was nonsense.

The dressmaker was delighted with the thread that was given to her. It matched the clothes so perfectly, and never tied itself in knots, or broke, as most thread did. She finished her work quickly and the bride said she was to be sure to come to the

church and see her in her wedding dress.

There was a great crowd assembled to witness the ceremony. The doors were opened, and the bride could be seen from afar.

"What a beautiful girl!" exclaimed the men. "What a lovely dress!" whispered the women. But just as she entered the church and took the hand of the bridegroom, who was waiting for her...

Crick! Crack! Crick! Crack! The wedding dress fell to the ground.

Not that the ceremony was put off for a little thing like that! Cloaks were offered to the young bride, but she was so upset that she could hardly stop the tears. One of the guests, more curious than the rest, stayed behind to examine the dress, to find out the cause of the disaster. But search as she would, she could find none. The thread had vanished! Mischievous Puck!

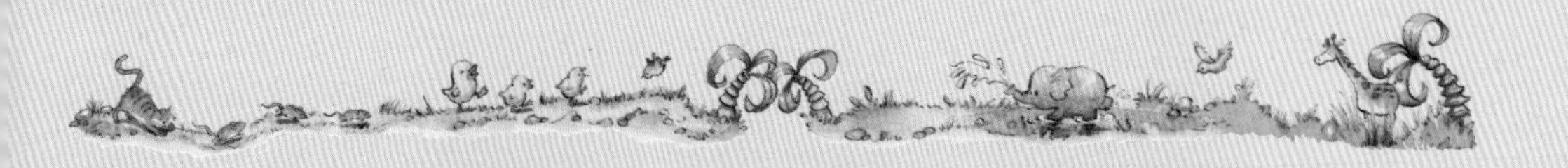

Animal Antics

The Cat and the Mouse

By the Brothers Grimm

Now this is the tale of a wily cat and a foolish mouse. The mouse lived in a bare mouse hole under the pulpit in the church. The cat lived on an old cushion in the vestry. They had met on several occasions, the mouse usually whisking herself away very fast to the safety of her hole. She did not like the look of the cat's claws.

One day, the cat called on the mouse at home.

"Miss mouse," a purry voice said, "why don't you

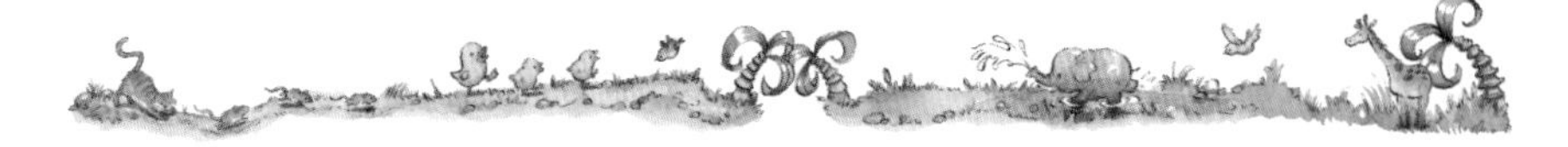

and I set up home together? We could live in the bell tower and look after each other. We could share our food, too."

The mouse thought about this carefully. She had never been fond of cats ever since her great grandfather had been supper for the farm tom cat one cold, frosty night. But she could see that there would be benefits. The cat had a nice smile on his face. So she agreed.

They put their savings together and bought a pot full of fat for the winter. The cat said he would hide it away safely under the altar where no one ever went, and so it was done. They both promised not to touch it until the weather became really bad.

The mouse went about her business, quite happy in her new home, although she found the stairs wearisome. But the cat could not stop thinking about the pot of fat. So he thought up a plan.

"My cousin has just had a kitten," he told the mouse. "And she wants me to be godcat. I should like to go to the christening, would you mind?"

"Not at all, Mister cat," said the mouse. "I have plenty to do today."

But the wicked Cat went straight to the pot of fat and ate the top off. Then he went to sleep for the rest of the day. When it was evening, he stretched and strolled back up to the bell tower.

"Did you have a nice time?" asked the mouse

"Oh yes, very nice," said the not-very-nice cat.

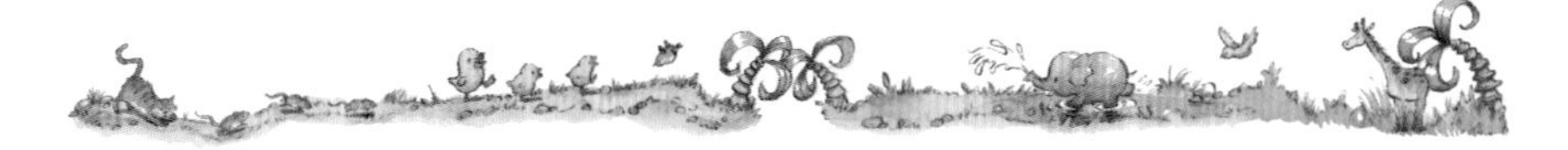

"And what is the kitten called?"

"Topoff," replied the cat.

"Topoff?" asked the mouse. "That is a very strange name. Still I suppose cats have different family names," and she went on with her work.

All was quiet for a few days but then the cat had great longings for the pot of fat again so he went to the mouse.

"I find I have another new godkitten. Would you mind if I went to the christening?" said the cat, his green eyes half closed.

"Another godkitten?" said the mouse. "My, my you do have a big family."

And the beastly cat slunk off and ate up half the pot of fat. When he sauntered back up the stairs that night the mouse was waiting.

"Well, how did it all go?" she said. "What is this kitten to be called?"

"Halfempty," replied the cat.

"Halfempty?" said the mouse. "I have never heard such a thing before."

But the cat was asleep, a smile twitching his whiskers.

Well, as you can imagine, it was not long before that greedy cat wanted some fat again.

"Miss mouse, just imagine! I have yet another godkitten. I should really go to this christening too," he said.

Miss mouse thought it all very strange but she was a kindly creature so she waved the cat off to yet another christening. The cat, of course, just scuttled downstairs, slid under the

altar and licked the pot of fat quite clean. He came back very late that night.

"What strange name did your family give this new kitten?" asked the mouse crossly. She had a headache from all the noise in the tower when the bells rang.

"Allgone," said the cat.

"Topoff, Halfempty and now Allgone!" the mouse said in disbelief. "Well, I am glad I am not a member of your family. I couldn't be doing with such weird names," and she went to sleep with her paws over her ears.

There were no more christenings. The weather became colder, and the mouse began to think of the pot of fat hidden under the altar.

"Mister cat," she said one frosty morning, "I think it is time we collected our pot of fat. I am looking forward to a lick."

'We'll see about that', thought the cat, but he padded downstairs behind the mouse. She reached under the altar and brought out the pot, but of course when she looked in, it was all empty.

"What a foolish mouse I have been!" she cried. "Now I see what a wicked cat you have been. Topoff, Halfempty and Allgone indeed!"

"Such is the way of cats," said the cat, and he grabbed at her with his paw. But she was too quick for him, and dived back into her dear little mouse hole.

Never ever again did she trust cats.

The Ugly Duckling

By Hans Christian Andersen

The mother duck was waiting for her eggs to hatch. Slowly the first shell cracked. A tiny bill and a little yellow wing appeared. Then with a rush, a bedraggled yellow duckling fell out. He stretched his wings and began to clean his feathers. Soon he stood beside his mother, watching as his sisters and brothers all pushed their way out of their shells.

Only one shell was left. It was the largest, and the mother duck wondered why it was taking longer

than the others. She wanted to take her babies down to the river for their first swimming lesson. There was a loud crack, and there lay the biggest, ugliest duckling she had ever seen. He wasn't even yellow – his feathers were brown and grey.

"Oh dear," said the mother duck.

She led the family down to the river, the ugly duckling trailing along behind the others. They all splashed into the water, and were soon swimming gracefully – all except the ugly duckling who looked large and ungainly even on the water.

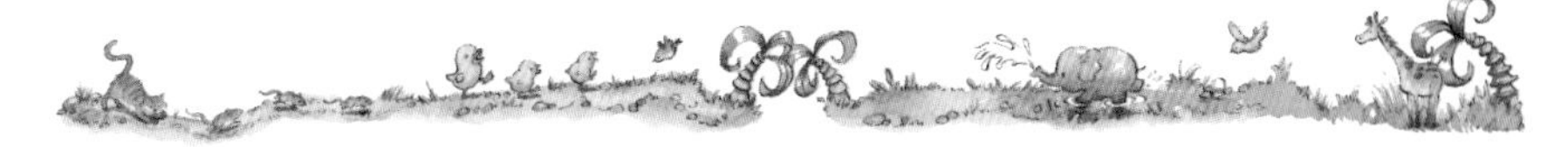

"Oh dear," said the mother duck.

The whole family set off for the farmyard where they were greeted with hoots and moos and barks and snorts from all the other animals.

"Whatever is that?" said the rooster, pointing rudely at the ugly duckling. All the other ducklings huddled round their mother and tried to pretend the ugly duckling was not with them.

"Oh dear," said the mother duck.

The ugly duckling felt very sad and lonely. No one seemed to like him, so he ran away from the farmyard and hid in some dark reeds by the river. Some hunters came by with their loud noisy guns and big fierce dogs.

The ugly duckling paddled deeper into the reeds, trembling with fear. Only later in the day, as it was growing dark, did he stir from his hiding place.

All summer he wandered over fields and down rivers. Everywhere he went people laughed and jeered at him, and other ducks just hissed at him or tried to bite his tail. As well as being ugly, the duckling was very lonely and unhappy. Soon winter came and the rivers began to freeze over. One day the duckling found himself trapped in the ice. He tucked his head under his wing, and decided that his short life must have come to an end.

He was still there early the next morning when a farmer came by on his way to feed the cows in the fields. The farmer broke the ice with his shoe, wrapped the ugly duckling in his jacket and carried him home to his children. They put the poor frozen ugly duckling in a box by the fire, and as he thawed

out they fed him and stroked his feathers. And there the ugly duckling stayed through the winter, growing bigger all the time.

Now the farmer's wife had never had much time for the ugly duckling. He was always getting under her feet in the kitchen, and he was so clumsy that he kept knocking things over. He spilt the milk in the bucket from the cow. He put his great feet in the freshly churned butter. He was just a nuisance, and one day the farmer's wife had enough. So, in a rage, she chased him out of her kitchen, out of the farmyard and through the gate down the lane.

It was a perfect spring day. The apple trees were covered in blossom and the air was filled with the sound of birdsong. The ugly duckling wandered down to the river, and there he saw three magnificent white swans. They were so beautiful and graceful as they glided towards the bank where

he stood. He waited for them to hiss at him and beat the water with their wings to frighten him away, but they didn't do any such thing. Instead they called him to come and join them. At first he thought it was a joke, but they asked him again.

He bent down to get into the water, and there looking back at him was his own reflection. But where was the ugly duckling? All he could see was another great and magnificent swan. He was a swan! Not an ugly duckling, but a swan. He lifted his long elegant neck, and called in sheer delight, "I am a swan! I am a SWAN!" and he sailed gracefully over the water to join his real family.

The Three Billy Goats Gruff

A European folk tale

In a mountain valley beside a rushing river, there lived three billy goats. One was very small, one was middle-sized and one was huge, and they were called the Three Billy Goats Gruff. Every day they would eat the lush green grass by the river, and they were very content.

One day, however, the Three Billy Goats Gruff decided they would like to cross the river and see if the grass was any greener on the other side. The

grass was actually no greener, nor was it any tastier, but they all felt they would like a change. First they had to find a way to cross the rushing river. They trotted a good way upstream before they found a little wooden bridge. After a supper of lush green grass, they decided to wait until next morning before crossing the wooden bridge, so they settled down for the night.

Now, what the Three Billy Goats Gruff did not know was that under the little wooden bridge there lived a very mean and grumpy troll. He could smell the Three Billy Goats Gruff, and he thought they smelled good to eat. So the next morning when the Three Billy Goats Gruff had eaten a breakfast of lush green grass, the troll was hiding under the little wooden bridge, waiting for his chance to have breakfast too.

"That little wooden bridge does not look too strong," said the very small Billy Goat Gruff. "I will go across first to see if it is safe," and he trotted across the little wooden bridge. But when he was only halfway across, the mean and grumpy troll leapt out of his hiding place.

"Who is that trit-trotting across my bridge?" he roared. "I am going to eat you up!"

But the very small Billy Goat Gruff wasn't ready

to be eaten up just yet, so he bravely said to the mean and grumpy troll, "You don't want to eat a skinny, bony thing like me. Just wait till my brother comes across, he is much bigger." And with a skip and a hop, the very small Billy Goat Gruff ran across the bridge to the lush green grass on the other side.

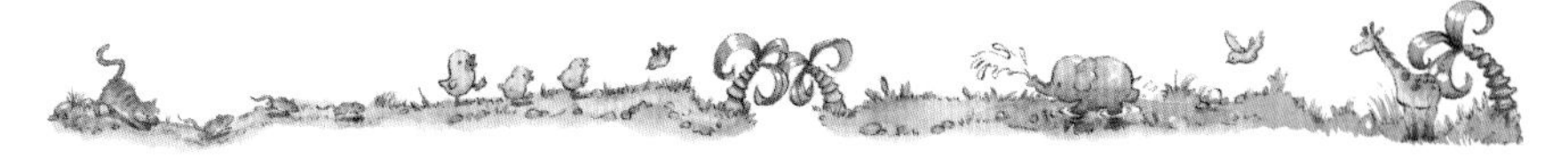

The middle-sized Billy Goat Gruff started to cross the little wooden bridge, but when he was only halfway across, the mean and grumpy troll roared at him, "Who is that trit-trotting across my bridge? I am going to eat you up!"

But the middle-sized Billy Goat Gruff wasn't ready to be eaten up just yet either, so he bravely said to the mean and grumpy troll, "You don't want to eat a skinny, bony thing like me. Wait till my brother comes across, he is even bigger." And with a skip and a hop, the middle-sized Billy Goat Gruff ran across the bridge to the lush green grass on the other side.

Now, the huge Billy Goat Gruff had been watching all the time. He smiled to himself and stepped onto the little wooden bridge. By this time the troll was very hungry , and he was even meaner and grumpier when he was hungry. He didn't bother to hide, but stood in the middle of the bridge looking at the huge

Billy Goat Gruff who came trotting up to him.

"Who is that trit-trotting across my bridge?" he roared. "I am going to eat you up!"

"Oh no, you won't!" said the huge Billy Goat Gruff, and he lowered his head and with his huge horns he biffed the mean and grumpy troll into the rushing river. The water carried him far away down the river, and he was never seen again. The Three Billy Goats Gruff lived happily for many more years eating the lush green grass, and they were able to cross the river whenever they wanted!

The Seven Little Kids

By the Brothers Grimm

There was once a mother goat who had seven little kids. One day she had to go into the wood to fetch food for them, so she called them to her.

"Dear children," said she, "While I am gone, watch out for the wolf. If he gets in he will eat you up. He often disguises himself, but he may always be known by his hoarse voice and black paws."

"Mother," said the kids, "you need not be afraid, we will take care of ourselves."

Soon the kids heard knocking at the door, and a voice cried, "Open the door children, your mother has returned, and brought each of you something."

But they knew it was the wolf by the hoarse voice.

"We will not open the door," they cried, "you are not our mother. She has a delicate and sweet voice, and your voice is hoarse – you must be the wolf!"

The wolf went to a shop and bought a big lump of chalk, and ate it up to make his voice soft. Then he came back, knocked at the door and cried, "Open the door children, your mother has returned, and brought each of you something."

But the wolf had put his black paws up against the window, and the kids cried out, "We will not open the door, our mother has no black paws – you must be the wolf!"

The wolf ran to a baker. "Baker," said he, "I have hurt my feet, pray spread some dough over them."

When the baker had done so, the wolf ran to the miller and said, "Cover my paws with white flour." The miller refused, thinking the wolf must wish to harm someone.

"If you don't," cried the wolf, "I'll eat you up!"

And the miller was afraid and did as he was told.

Now the wolf arrived at the door again and knocked. "Open children!" cried he, "Your mother has returned, and brought each of you something."

"Show us your paws," said the kids.

The wolf put his paws up to the window, and when the kids saw that they were white they opened the door.

When the door opened and he entered they saw it was the wolf. The kids tried to hide. One ran under

the table, the second got into bed, the third into the oven, the fourth in the kitchen, the fifth in the cupboard, the sixth under the sink and the seventh in the clock-case.

But the wolf found them, and swallowed them all – all but the youngest, hidden in the clock-case. Having eaten his fill, the wolf strolled into the meadow, lay himself down under a tree, and fell asleep.

When the mother goat returned, a horrible sight met her. The door was open, table and chairs were thrown about, and dishes were broken. Her children were nowhere to be seen. She called to them but none answered, until she came to the youngest.

"Here I am, mother," a little voice cried, "Here, in the clock-case."

She helped him out and heard how the wolf had come, and eaten all the rest. How she cried for the loss of her dear children! At last she left her house, the youngest kid with her. When they came to the meadow they saw the wolf lying under a tree, snoring. The mother goat looked at him carefully on all sides and she noticed how something inside him was moving and struggling.

'Dear me!' thought she, 'can it be that my poor children are still alive?' And she sent the little kid back to the house for a pair of shears, a needle and some thread. Then she cut the wolf open – no sooner had she made one snip than out came the head of one of the kids. One after another the six little kids all jumped out alive and well, for in his greediness the rogue had swallowed them whole.

"Now fetch some hard stones," said the mother, "and we will fill his body with them while he sleeps."

They put the stones inside him, and the mother sewed him up quickly so that he was none the wiser.

When the wolf awoke, the stones inside him made him very thirsty. As he was going to the brook to drink, they rattled against each other. He cried out,

"What is this I feel inside me
Knocking hard against my bones?
How should such a thing betide me!
They were kids, and now they're stones."

He came to the brook and stooped to drink, but the heavy stones weighed him down, and he fell into the water and was drowned.

The little kids saw him fall. "The wolf is dead!" they cried, and they danced all about the place.

The Sagacious Monkey and the Boar

By Yei Theodora Ozaki

Long ago, in the province of Shinshin in Japan, there lived a travelling monkey man. He earned money by taking round a monkey and showing off its tricks. One day he came home very cross and told his wife to send for the butcher in the morning.

His wife was bewildered and asked her husband, "Why do you wish me to send for the butcher?"

"It's no use taking that monkey round any longer, he's old and he forgets his tricks. I beat him with my

stick, but he won't dance properly. I must now sell him to the butcher and make what money out of him I can. There is nothing else to be done."

The woman felt sorry for the poor animal, and pleaded for her husband to spare the monkey, but her pleading was in vain, the man was determined.

Now the monkey was in the next room and he had overheard every word. He understood that he was to be killed, and he said to himself, "Barbarous, indeed, is my master! Here I have served him faithfully for years, and instead of allowing me to end my days comfortably, he is going to let me be cut up by the butcher, and my poor body is to be roasted and stewed and eaten? What am I to do? Ah! A thought has struck me! There is a wild boar living in the forest nearby. I have often heard tell of his wisdom. Perhaps if I tell him the strait I am in he will give me his counsel. I will go and try."

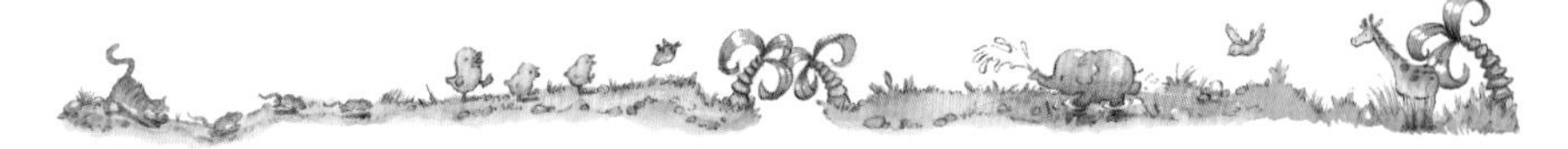

The monkey slipped out of the house and ran to find the boar. The boar was at home, and the monkey told his tale of woe. "Mr Boar, I have heard of your wisdom. I am in great trouble. I have grown old in the service of my master, and because I now cannot dance he intends to sell me to the butcher. What do you advise? I know how clever you are!"

The boar thought for a while and then said, "Has your master a baby?"

"Oh, yes," said the monkey, "he has a baby son."

"Does it lie by the door in the morning? Well, I will come round early, seize the baby and run off with it."

"What then?" said the monkey.

"You must run after me and rescue the child and take it home safely to its parents. When the butcher comes they won't have the heart to sell you."

The monkey thanked the boar and went home.

In the morning he was the first up, waiting

anxiously for what was to happen. It seemed to him a very long time before his master's wife began to move about and open the shutters.

Luckily, everything happened as the boar had planned. The mother placed her child near the porch as usual while she got the breakfast ready.

The child was crooning happily in the morning sunlight, dabbing on the mats at the play of light

and shadow. Suddenly there was a noise in the porch and a loud cry from the child. The mother called her husband from the inner room where he was still sleeping soundly, and they both ran to the porch door just in time to see the boar disappearing with their child. Then they saw the monkey running after the thief as hard as his legs would carry him.

Both the man and wife were moved to admiration at the plucky conduct of the sagacious monkey, and their gratitude knew no bounds when the faithful monkey brought the child safely back to their arms.

"There!" said the wife. "This is the animal you want to kill – if the monkey hadn't been here we should have lost our child forever."

"You are right, wife," said the man as he carried the child into the house. "You may send the butcher back when he comes, and now give us all a good breakfast and the monkey too."

When the butcher arrived he was sent away with an order for some boar's meat for the evening dinner, and the monkey was petted and lived the rest of his days in peace, nor did his master ever strike him again.

How the Camel got his Hump

By Rudyard Kipling

In the beginning of years, when the world was new-and-all, and the animals were beginning to work for man, there was a camel. He lived in the middle of a desert because he did not want to work. He ate sticks, thorns and tamarisks, milkweed and prickles. He was most idle, and when anybody spoke to him he said "Humph!"

Presently the horse came to him on Monday morning, with a saddle on his back and a bit in his

mouth, and said, "Camel, come and trot like the rest of us."

"Humph!" said the camel, and the horse went away and told the man.

Presently the dog came to him with a stick in his mouth, and said, "Camel, come and fetch and carry like the rest of us."

"Humph!" said the camel and the dog went away to tell the man.

Presently the ox came to him, with the yoke on his neck and said, "Camel, come and plough like the rest of us."

"Humph!" said the camel, and the ox went away and told the man.

At the end of the day the man called the horse

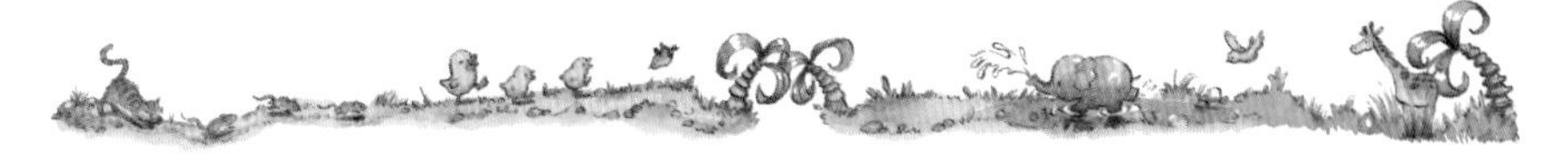

and the dog and the ox together, and said, "Three, I'm sorry for you, but that thing in the desert can't work. You must work double to make up for it."

That made the Three angry (with the world so new-and-all), and they held a palaver and a pow-wow on the edge of the desert, and the camel came and laughed at them. Then he said "Humph!" and went away again.

Presently there came along the djinn in charge of All Deserts, and he stopped to palaver and pow-pow with the Three.

"Djinn of All Deserts," said the horse, "is it right to be idle, with the world so new-and-all?"

"Certainly not," said the djinn.

"Well," said the horse, "there's a thing in the middle of your desert with a long neck and long legs, and he hasn't done a stroke of work since Monday morning. He won't trot."

"Whew!" said the djinn, whistling, "that's my camel! What does he say about it?"

"He says Humph!" said the dog, "And he won't fetch and carry."

"Does he say anything else?"

"Only Humph! And he won't plough," said the ox.

"Very good," said the djinn. "I'll humph him if you will kindly wait a minute."

The djinn found the camel looking at his own reflection in a pool of water.

"My long and bubbling friend," said the djinn, "what's this I hear of you doing no work, with the world so new-and-all?"

"Humph!" said the camel.

The djinn sat down, with his chin in his hand, and began to think a great magic. "You've given the Three extra work ever since Monday morning, all on account of your idleness," said the djinn.

"Humph!" said the camel.

"I shouldn't say that again if I were you," said the djinn, "You might say it once too often. Bubbles, I want you to work."

And the camel said "Humph!" again, but no sooner had he said it than he saw his back, that he was so proud of, puffing up into a great big humph.

"Do you see that?" said the djinn. "That's your very own humph that you've brought upon your very own self by not working. Today is Thursday, and you've done no work since Monday, when the work began. Now you are going to work."

"How can I," said the camel, "with this humph on my back?"

"That's made on purpose," said the djinn, "all because you missed those three days. You will be able to work now for three days without eating, because you can live on your humph, and don't

you ever say I never did anything for you. Come out of the desert and go to the Three, and behave."

And the camel humphed himself, humph and all, and went away to join the Three. And from that day to this the camel always wears a humph (we call it 'hump' now, not to hurt his feelings) but he has never yet caught up with the three days that he missed at the beginning of the world, and he has never yet learned how to behave.

The Husband of the Rat's Daughter

By Andrew Lang

Once upon a time there lived in Japan a rat and his wife who came of an old and noble race. They had one daughter, the loveliest girl in all the rat world. Her parents were very proud of her. There was not another young lady in the whole town who was as clever as she was in gnawing through wood, or who could drop from such a height onto a bed, or run away so fast if anyone was heard coming. Great attention, too, was paid to her appearance,

and her skin shone like satin, while her teeth were as white as pearls, and beautifully pointed.

Of course, with all these advantages, her parents expected her to make a great marriage, and, as she grew up, they began to look for a suitable husband.

But here a difficulty arose. The father was a rat from the tip of his nose to the end of his tail, and desired that his daughter should wed among her own people. She had no lack of suitors, but her father's hopes rested on a fine young rat, with moustaches that almost swept the ground, whose family was nobler and more ancient than his own. But the mother had other views for her child. She was one of those people who always despised their own family and surroundings, and take pleasure in thinking they are made of finer material than the rest of the world. "My daughter should never marry a mere rat," she declared, holding her head high.

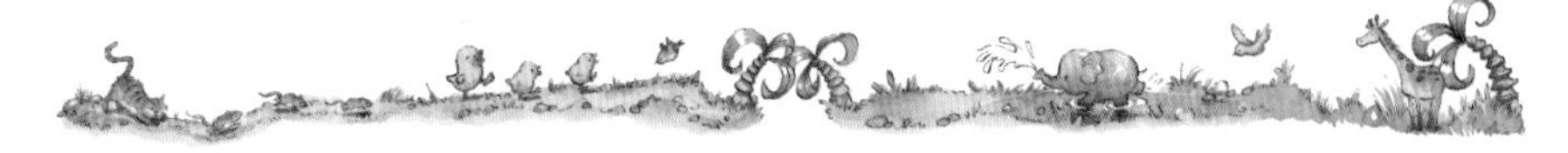

"With her beauty and talents she has a right to look for someone a little better than that."

So she talked to anyone that would listen. What the girl thought about it all nobody knew or cared.

The old rat and his wife had many quarrels upon the subject. "Reach up to the stars is my motto," cried the lady one day, when she was in a greater passion than usual. "My daughter's beauty places her higher than anything upon earth, and I will not accept a son-in-law who is beneath her."

"Better offer her in marriage to the sun," her husband answered impatiently. "As far as I know there is nothing greater than he."

"I was thinking of it," replied the wife, "and as you are of the same mind, we will pay him a visit."

The next morning the two rats, having spent hours making themselves smart, set out to see the sun, leading their daughter between them.

The journey took some time, but at length they came to the golden palace where the sun lived.

"Noble king," began the mother, "behold our daughter! She is so beautiful that she is above everything in the whole world. Naturally, we wish for a son-in-law who, on his side, is greater than all. Therefore we have come to you."

"I feel very much flattered," replied the sun, who had not the least wish to marry anybody. "You do me honour by your proposal. But you are mistaken. There is something greater than I am, and that is the cloud. Look!" And as he spoke a cloud spread itself over the sun's face, blotting out his rays.

"Oh, we will speak to the cloud," said the mother. And turning to the cloud she repeated her proposal.

"Indeed I am unworthy of anything so charming," answered the cloud, "but you make a mistake again in what you say. There is one thing

that is even more powerful than I, and that is the wind. Ah, here he comes, you can see for yourself."

And the mother did see, for catching up the cloud as he passed, the wind threw it on the other side of the sky. Then, tumbling father, mother and daughter down to the earth again, he paused for a moment beside them, his foot on an old wall.

When she had recovered her breath, the mother began her little speech once more.

"The wall is the proper husband for your daughter," answered the wind, whose home was a cave, which he only visited when he was not rushing about elsewhere, "you can see for yourself that he is greater than I, for he has power to stop me in my flight." And the mother turned at once to the wall.

Then something unexpected happened. "I won't marry that ugly old wall," sobbed the girl, who had not uttered one word all this time. "I would have

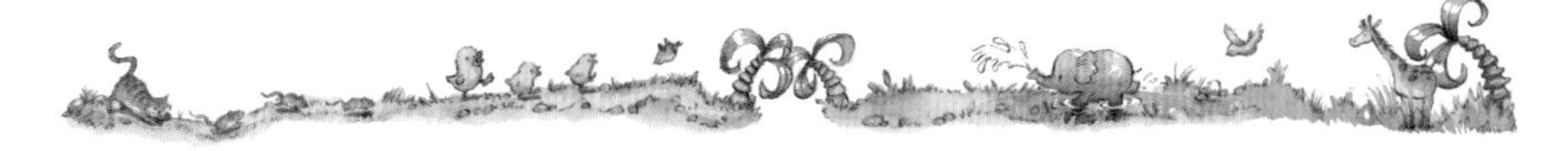

married the sun, or the cloud, or the wind, because it was my duty, although I love the handsome young rat, and him only. But that horrid old wall – I would sooner die!"

And the wall, rather hurt in his feelings, declared that he had no claim to marry so beautiful a girl.

"It is quite true," he said, "that I can stop the wind who can part the clouds who can cover the sun, but there is someone who can do more than all these – the rat. It is the rat who passes through me, and can reduce me to powder with his teeth. If, therefore, you want a son-in-law who is greater than the whole world, seek him among the rats."

"What did I tell you?" cried the father. And his wife, though angry at losing, soon thought that a rat son-in-law was what she had always desired.

So all three returned happily home, and the wedding was celebrated three days after.

Why the Swallow's Tail is Forked

By Florence Holbrook

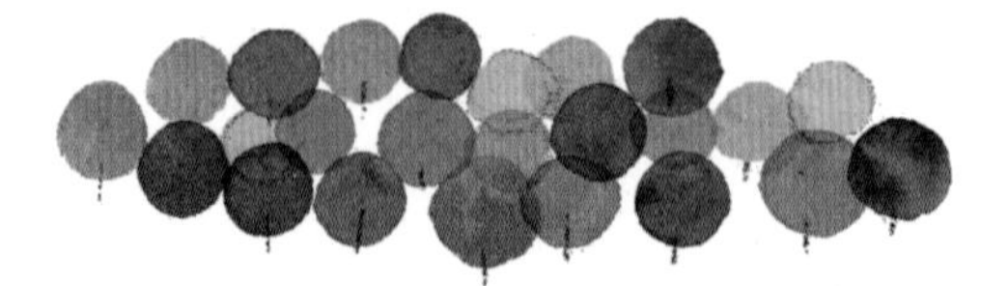

This is the story of how the swallow's tail came to be forked. One day the Great Spirit asked all the animals that he had made to come to his lodge. Those that could fly came first – the robin, the bluebird, the owl, the butterfly, the wasp and the firefly. Behind them came the chicken, fluttering its wings and trying hard to keep up. Then came the deer, the squirrel, the serpent, the cat and the rabbit. Last of all came the bear, the beaver and the

hedgehog. Each travelled as swiftly as he could, for each wished to hear the words of the Great Spirit.

"I have called you together," said the Great Spirit, "because I often hear you scold and fret. What do you wish me to do for you? How can I help you?"

"I do not like to hunt so long for my food," said the bear.

"I do not like to build nests," said the bluebird.

"I do not like to live in the water," said the beaver.

"I do not like to live in a tree," said the squirrel.

At last man stood before the Great Spirit and said, "O Great Father, the serpent feasts upon my blood. Will you not give him some other food?"

"And why?" asked the Great Spirit.

"Because I am the first of all the creatures you have made," answered man proudly.

Then every animal in the lodge was angry to hear the words of man. The squirrel chattered, the wasp

buzzed, the owl hooted and the serpent hissed.

"Hush, be still," said the Great Spirit. "You are, man, the first of my creatures, but I am father of all. Each has his rights, and the serpent must have food. Mosquito, you are a great traveller. Fly away and find what animal's blood is best for the serpent. You must all come back in a year and a day."

The animals straightway went to their homes. Some went to the river, some to the forest and some to the prairie, to wait for the day when they must meet at the lodge of the Great Spirit.

The mosquito travelled over the earth and stung every creature that he met to find whose blood was the best for the serpent. On his way back to the lodge of the Great Spirit he looked up into the sky and there was the swallow.

"Good day, swallow," called the mosquito.

"I am glad to see you, my friend," sang the

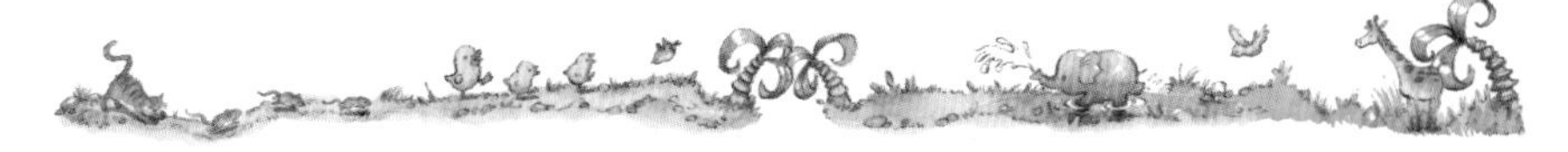

swallow. "Are you going to the Great Spirit? Have you found out whose blood is best for the serpent?"

"The blood of man," answered the mosquito.

The mosquito did not like man, but the swallow had always been man's friend. 'What can I do to help man?' he thought. Then he asked the mosquito, "Whose blood did you say?"

"Man's blood," said the mosquito, "that is best."

"This is best," said the swallow, and he tore out the mosquito's tongue.

The mosquito buzzed angrily and went quickly to the Great Spirit.

"All the animals are here," said the Great Spirit. "Whose blood is best for the serpent?"

The mosquito tried to answer, "The blood of man," but he could not say a word. He could make no sound but "Kss-ksss-ksssss!"

"What do you say?"

"Kss-ksss-ksssss!" buzzed the mosquito angrily.

Then said the swallow, "Great Father, the mosquito is timid and cannot answer you. I met him earlier, and he told me whose blood it was."

"Then let us know at once," said the Great Spirit.

"It is the blood of the frog," answered the swallow quickly. "Is it not so, friend mosquito?"

"Kss-ksss-ksssss!" hissed the angry mosquito.

"The serpent shall have the frog's blood," said the Great Spirit. "Man shall be his food no longer."

Now the serpent was angry with the swallow – he did not like frog's blood. As the swallow flew by him, he seized him by the tail and tore away a little of it. That is why the swallow's tail is forked, and it is why man always looks upon the swallow as his friend.

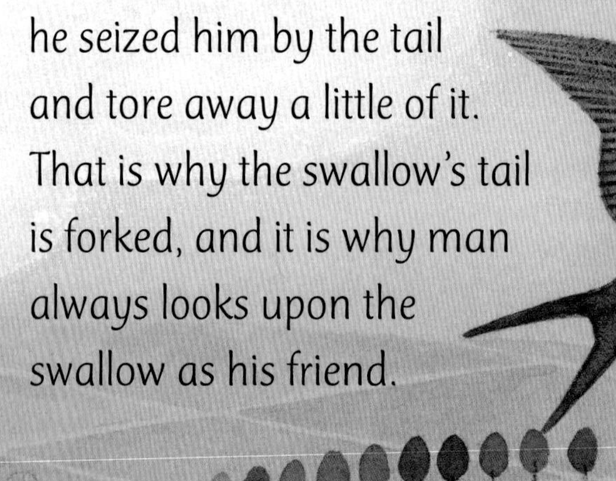

The Old Woman and her Pig

A traditional folk tale

Long ago, an old woman found a bright, shining sixpence and went to market to buy a pig. She set off home with the pig trotting quite happily at her side. But when they were nearly there, they came to a stile and the pig wouldn't jump over it.

So the old woman went on a little further. She met a dog and said, "Dog! Dog! Bite pig. Pig won't jump over the stile, so I won't get home tonight." But the dog wouldn't.

So the old woman went on a little further. She met a stick and said, "Stick! Stick! Beat dog. Dog won't bite pig, and pig won't jump over the stile, so I won't get home tonight." But the stick wouldn't.

So the old woman went on a little further. She met a fire and said, "Fire! Fire! Burn stick. Stick won't beat dog, dog won't bite pig, and pig won't jump over the stile, so I won't get home tonight." But the fire wouldn't.

So the old woman went on a little further. She met some water and said, "Water! Water! Put out fire. Fire won't burn stick, stick won't beat dog, dog won't bite pig, and pig won't jump over the stile, so I won't get home tonight." But the water wouldn't.

So the old woman went on a little further. She met a horse and said, "Horse! Horse! Drink water. Water won't put out fire, fire won't burn stick, stick won't beat dog, dog won't bite pig, and pig won't

jump over the stile, so I won't get home tonight." But the horse wouldn't.

So the old woman went on a little further. She met a rope and said, "Rope! Rope! Lasso horse. Horse won't drink water, water won't put out fire, fire won't burn stick, stick won't beat dog, dog won't bite pig, and pig won't jump over the stile, so I won't get home tonight." But the rope wouldn't.

So the old woman went on a little further. She met a rat and said, "Rat! Rat! Gnaw rope. Rope won't lasso horse, horse won't drink water, water won't put out fire, fire won't burn stick, stick won't beat dog, dog won't bite pig, and pig won't jump over the stile, so I won't get home tonight." But the rat wouldn't.

So the old woman went on a little further. She met a cat and said, "Cat! Cat! Scare rat. Rat won't gnaw rope, rope won't lasso horse, horse won't drink water, water won't put out fire, fire won't burn stick, stick won't beat dog, dog won't bite pig, and pig won't jump over the stile, so I won't get home tonight."

"All right," said the cat, " – if you get me some milk." The old woman was highly surprised and fetched a saucer of milk at once.

The cat scared the rat, so the rat gnawed the rope,

so the rope lassoed the horse, so the horse drank the water, so the water put out the fire, so the fire burnt the stick, so the stick beat the dog, so the dog bit the pig, so the pig jumped over the stile – and that's how the old woman got home that night!

Why the Manx Cat has no Tail

A myth from the Isle of Man

The rain was falling in torrents, and there were great storm clouds building up. The rivers were overflowing and the fields looked like lakes. Noah decided that the time had come to fill his ark with two of every animal that lived. He called his sons Shem and Ham and Japeth and they began rounding up the animals and leading them onto the ark. First came the big beasts, the giraffes and lions and elephants. Then came the cows, the sheep and

the pigs. Then came the foxes and the rabbits (but not together of course). Then came the birds, the grasshoppers and the ants, who were rather nervous of the elephants' feet. Finally came the dogs, but only one cat – a big ginger tom cat.

The she-cat, who was a stripy tabby, had decided that she would like to go mousing one last time, as she realized she would not be able to eat a fellow passenger when they were all cooped up in the ark.

Mrs Noah called and called her, but still she did not come. Cats are always contrary and she was no exception. Noah looked at the rising water and told Mrs Noah that he would have to pull up the gangplank as the ark would soon be afloat.

All the other animals were settling in to their various stalls, and what a noise there was! Roaring and mooing, trumpeting and baaing, snorting and squawking. Toes and flippers and trotters and paws got stood on, fur and feathers were ruffled and horns and long tails got stuck, but eventually everyone was in place. Noah began to pull the great door of the ark to, and just as he was about to shut it fast, up pranced the she-cat, soaking wet but licking her lips. She managed to slip through the gap in the nick of time but her great plume of a tail was caught in the door as it slammed shut. She turned round and her entire tail was cut off! The cat

was cross, but Noah told her it was entirely her own fault and she would have to wait until they found land again before she could have her tail mended.

Forty days and forty nights later, the flood was over and Noah opened the great door of the ark once more. First out was the she-cat, and she ran and ran until she found the Isle of Man, and there she stopped, too ashamed for anyone else to see her. Ever since then, the cats from the Isle of Man have had no tails. Nowadays they are rather proud to be different.

Girls and Boys

Peter and the Wolf

Original libretto by Sergei Prokofiev

Peter lived with his grandfather at the edge of the forest. Peter used to play with the wild birds and animals in the garden, but his grandfather always warned him not to go into the meadow in case the wolf crept out of the forest.

I am afraid Peter did not always do as he was told, so one day he slipped through the garden gate and into the meadow when he met a duck swimming in the middle of the pond.

"You must watch out for the wolf," said Peter to the duck but she was busy enjoying herself and did not listen. A little bird flew down and the duck tried to persuade her to come into the pond as well. But as the little bird stood talking to the duck, Peter saw the cat sneak up behind her.

"Look out!" shouted Peter and the bird flew up to safety in the tree.

"Thank you, Peter," she said. The cat was not so pleased. Just then Peter's grandfather came out and saw the open garden gate.

"Peter! How many times do I have to tell you? Come back into the garden at once," he shouted and Peter walked slowly back in.

Meanwhile, at the far side of the meadow, near the forest, a grey shape slunk from under the trees. It was the wolf! The little bird flew up into the tree, and the cat joined her – but on a lower branch.

But the duck was too busy swimming to see what was happening and in a flash the wolf grabbed her and swallowed her whole!

Peter saw it all from the garden. "I am going to catch that old wolf," he said to himself.

He found a piece of rope and climbed up a tree whose branches overhung the meadow. He made a loop in the rope and hung it out of the tree. Then he called to the little bird, "Can you tempt the wolf this way by flying round his head, please? I am going to catch him!"

The brave little bird darted down very close to the wolf's nose. The wolf snapped his fierce teeth, and only just missed the little bird. Closer and

closer they came to the tree where Peter was hiding. The wolf was so busy trying to catch the bird that he did not see the rope. Peter looped it over the wolf's tail, and there he was, dangling from the branch of the tree!

Peter's grandfather came out and he was astonished to see the wolf. Then some hunters came out of the forest.

"Well done," they cried, "you have caught the wolf. We have been after him for a long time."

And they all went off in a joyful procession to the zoo. Peter led the wolf at the front, the little bird flew overhead, and the cat padded alongside. The hunters came up in the rear with Peter's grandfather. And from inside the wolf's tummy, the duck quacked loudly, just to remind everyone that she was there!

The Selfish Giant

By Oscar Wilde

Once there was a beautiful garden in which the children used to play every day on their way home from school. The children didn't think that the beautiful garden belonged to anyone in particular. But one day a huge giant strode in and boomed, "What are you all doing here? This is MY garden. Get lost!" Seven years ago, the giant had gone to visit his friend the Cornish ogre. Now he was back and he wanted his garden all to himself.

Of course, the children ran away at once. But the giant wasn't satisfied. He put up a high fence all the way around his garden with a noticeboard outside which read 'TRESPASSERS WILL BE PROSECUTED'. He really was a very selfish giant.

Now the poor children had nowhere to play. But the giant didn't give any thought to that. He was too busy wondering why the blossom had fallen from the trees, why the flowers had withered, and why all the birds had flown away. Surely it is meant to be the springtime, the giant thought to himself as he looked out of the window and saw huge flakes of snow tumbling from the sky. Frost painted the trees silver. A blanket of ice chilled the ground and hardened the plants into stiff, lifeless spikes. Day after day, the north wind roared around the giant's garden, zooming around his roof and howling down his chimney pots. And the

hail came too, battering on the giant's windows until he bellowed with annoyance and clapped his hands over his ears against the noisy rattling.

Then one Saturday, the giant woke to a sound he had almost forgotten – it was a bird, chirruping in his garden. A beautiful perfume tickled the giant's nose... the scent of flowers! "Spring has come at last!" the giant beamed, and he pulled on his clothes and ran out into his garden.

The giant couldn't believe what he saw. The snow had melted, the frost was gone, the sky was blue and the breeze was gentle. And there were children everywhere. They had crept back into his garden through a hole that had worn away in the fence. Now children were sitting in trees heavy with ripe fruit. Playing among flowerbeds filled with nodding blossoms. Running over emerald green grass scattered with daisies and buttercups. And

the sound of their happy laughter filled the air.

Only in one corner of the garden was it still winter. A little boy was standing in a patch of snow, looking up at the bare branches of a chestnut tree and crying because he couldn't reach it.

The giant's heart ached as he watched. "Now I know what makes my garden beautiful," he said. "It is the children. How selfish I have been!"

The giant strode through the garden towards the sobbing little boy. He scooped him up gently

and set him among the icy boughs of the chestnut tree.

At once, leaves appeared all over the branches. It was spring. The little boy's face brightened into a huge smile and he reached his arms up around the giant's neck and hugged him.

"It is your garden now, little children," laughed the giant. The giant took his axe, knocked down the fence and had more fun than he had ever had before, playing with them all day. Only one thing spoiled the giant's new happiness. He looked all over his garden for the little boy whom he had helped into the tree, but he was nowhere to be found. The giant loved the little boy the best,

because he had hugged him, and he longed more than anything to see his friend again.

Many years passed and the children came every day to play in the garden. The giant became old and creaky. Eventually he could no longer run about and let the children climb over him as he had done. He sat in a special armchair so he could watch the children enjoying themselves. "My garden is beautiful," he would say to himself, "but the children are the most beautiful things of all." Sometimes the giant's grey head would nod and he would begin to snore, and the children would creep away quietly so they didn't disturb him.

One afternoon, the giant woke from a little doze to see an astonishing sight. In the far corner of his garden was a golden tree he had never seen before. The giant's heart leapt for joy, for standing underneath it was the boy he had loved.

The giant heaved himself up from his armchair and shuffled across the grass as fast as his old legs would take him. But when he drew near the boy, his face grew black as thunder – there were wounds on the little boy's palms and on his feet. "Who has dared to hurt you?" boomed the giant. "Tell me, and I will go after them with my big axe!"

"These are the marks of love," the little boy smiled. He took the giant's hand. "Once, you let me play in your garden," he said. "And today, you shall come with me to mine, which is in Paradise."

And when the children came running to play that afternoon, they found the giant lying dead under the beautiful tree, covered with a beautiful blanket of snowy-white blossoms.

The Red Shoes

By Hans Christian Andersen

There was once a woman who was so poor that she couldn't afford to buy her daughter Karen any shoes. The woman often wept to see Karen's feet all rough and blistered. She would have been overjoyed to know that the shoemaker's wife felt so sorry for Karen that she was making her a pair of red shoes from some leftover leather. But the woman never found out. She died the very day that the red shoes were finished and Karen wore

them for the first time as she walked behind her mother's coffin on the way to church.

The shoemaker's wife couldn't sew very well and the shoes had turned out to be rather clumsy and misshapen. But Karen thought that her soft, red shoes were the most wonderful things in the world.

But the old lady who kindly took Karen in said, "You can't possibly go walking around in those odd things. Whatever will people think?" She threw the red shoes onto the fire and bought Karen a pair of sensible, sturdy black ones.

It was the sensible, sturdy black shoes that Karen was wearing when the old lady took her to the palace to see the parade for the little princess's birthday. The king and queen stood with the little princess on the balcony, waving and smiling. But Karen didn't look at the gracious expressions on their faces, or their fine, rich robes. Karen couldn't

take her eyes off the red shoes on the feet of the princess. They were made of satin, not leather, so they shone like rubies. Those really are the most wonderful things in all the world, thought Karen.

From that moment, whenever Karen buckled on her sensible, black shoes, she thought of the little princess's beautiful red ones. Whenever Karen took off her sensible, black shoes, she thought of the princess's beautiful red ones. And she longed for those beautiful red shoes with all her heart.

One day, the old lady who looked after Karen

looked at her sensible, black shoes and tutted, "My, my! Those are looking rather old and shabby – and they're too small for you now. We can't have you going along to church in those tomorrow." The old lady handed her a purse full of money. "Buy yourself some new ones," she smiled.

Karen walked all the way to the shoe shop with a thumping heart. First, she tried on some sensible, sturdy black shoes – but none fit her. Then she tried on some smart, lace-up brown shoes – but they either slopped up and down or cramped her toes. Then Karen peered up at a high shelf and saw a red pair exactly like the ones the little princess had worn. They fitted her perfectly. Karen held her breath as she handed over her money and stepped out of the shop. Her feet gleamed and twinkled in the sunlight. She could hardly believe it. Her dream had come true.

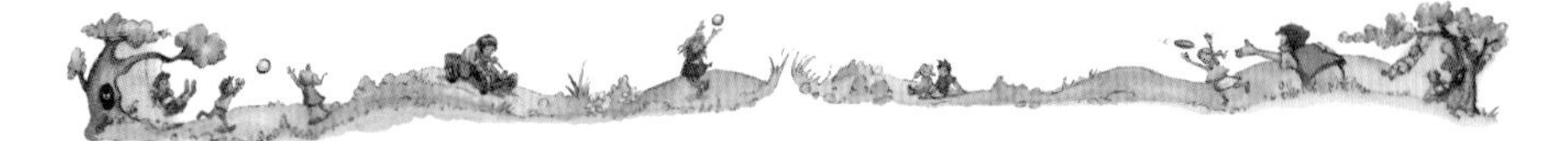

Karen knew full well that the old lady wouldn't approve at all of her choice. But luckily for her, the old lady's eyesight wasn't what it was, and the colour of Karen's new shoes was just a dark blur. Karen kept quiet, saying nothing of the truth.

Next day, Karen's heart nearly burst with excitement as she slipped on her shoes. She tripped gaily to church, and even though there were many finely dressed people about, she had eyes for no one and nothing except the red shoes. She hoped that everyone would see them.

Even as Karen sat in her church pew, she couldn't take her eyes off her red shoes.

Even when the priest was praying, she couldn't take her eyes off her red shoes. Even when the organist began to strike up a hymn of praise, she couldn't take her eyes off her red shoes. The statues of the angels and saints seemed to frown down sternly upon her, but Karen didn't notice. She still couldn't take her eyes off the red shoes.

As the choir started to sing and their voices filled the air, Karen felt a strange sensation in her feet. Her toes began to twitch inside the red satin. Her heels began to quiver. Suddenly, Karen's feet began to dance. Right there and then in church, her red shoes forced her to stand up and leap and turn and skip. With the eyes of everyone upon her, the red shoes danced her down the aisle and out into the sunlight. "Help me!" she cried, but no one knew what to do. The red shoes danced Karen all around the graveyard and out of the church gate.

Then they danced her round and round the churchyard wall and off down the street...

By day and by night, the enchanted red shoes carried Karen along, twinkling wickedly. They danced her in and out of houses and up and down stairs. They danced her through the city gates, across the fields and into the dark forest. They danced her out of the trees and through meadows, until Karen had forgotten how long she had been dancing... and still they made her dance. "Forgive me!" the sobbing girl cried out. "Forgive me for thinking of these foolish things above everything else!" At last, the red shoes were still. Utterly exhausted, Karen collapsed into a heap and closed her eyes. And when her soul reached heaven, she never had to dance or think about red shoes ever again.

Cap o' Rushes

By Joseph Jacobs

There was once a rich gentleman who had three daughters. He thought he'd see how fond they were of him, so he said to the first, "How much do you love me?"

"Why," said she, "as I love my life."

He said to the next, "How much do you love me?"

"Why," said she, "better than all the world."

He said to the last, "How much do you love me?"

"I love you as fresh meat loves salt," said she.

Her father was angry. "You don't love me," said he, "and in my house you will stay no more." And he drove her out there and then.

She went away till she came to a fen. She made some rushes into a cloak with a hood, to hide her fine clothes. Then she came to a great house.

"Do you want a maid?" said she. "I ask no wages, and do any sort of work."

"Well," said they, "if you would like to wash the pots and scrape the saucepans you may stay."

So she stayed and did all the dirty work. She gave no name so they called her 'Cap o' Rushes'.

One day there was to be a dance a little way off. The servants were allowed to go, but Cap o' Rushes said she was too tired. But when the others had left, she took off her cap and went to the dance.

Well, who should be there but her master's son, and what should he do but fall in love with her?

He would dance with no one else.

Next morning the other maids said, "You missed a sight, Cap o' Rushes! The most beautiful lady you ever saw, dressed so grand. The master never took his eyes off her."

"I should have liked to have seen her," she replied.

"There's another dance this evening. Perhaps she'll come."

But in the evening, Cap o' Rushes said she was too tired to go.

When they were gone, she took off her cap and went to the dance. The master's son danced with no one else, and never took his eyes off her.

Next day the other maids said again, "Cap o' Rushes, you should ha' been there to see the lady. There she was, gay and grand. There's a dance again tonight. You must go with us."

Well, come that evening, Cap o' Rushes said she was too tired to go, and do what they would she stayed at home. But when they were gone, she took off her cap and went to the dance.

The master's son gave her a ring and told her if he didn't see her again he should die. But before the dance was over, she slipped away again.

The next day, the master's son tried to find out where the lady had gone, but no one knew. He got worse for the love of her till he had to stay in bed.

"Make some gruel for the master," they said to the cook. The cook set about making it when Cap o' Rushes came in.

"What are you doing?" said she.

"I'm going to make some gruel for the master," said the cook, "for he's dying for love of the lady."

"Let me make it," said Cap o' Rushes.

Cap o' Rushes made the gruel, and slipped the ring into it before the cook took it upstairs.

The young man drank it and saw the ring at the bottom. "Who made this gruel here?" said he.

"'Twas Cap o' Rushes," said the cook.

"Send Cap o' Rushes here," said he.

So Cap o' Rushes came.

"Did you make my gruel?" said he.

"Yes, I did," said she.

"Where did you get this ring?" said he.

"From him that gave it me," said she.

"Who are you, then?" said the young man.

"I'll show you," said she. She took off her cap o' rushes, and there she was in her beautiful clothes.

They married soon after and everyone was

asked to the wedding – even Cap o' Rushes' father. But she never said who she was.

Before the wedding, she asked the cook to dress every dish without a grain of salt.

"That'll be nasty," said the cook.

"That doesn't matter," said she.

The wedding day came, and they were married, and everyone sat down to dinner. The meat was so tasteless they couldn't eat it. Cap o' Rushes' father burst out crying.

"What is the matter?" asked the master's son.

"I had a daughter," said he, "and I asked her how much she loved me. She said, 'As much as fresh meat loves salt.' I turned her from my door, thinking she didn't love me. Now I see she loved me best of all. She may be dead for all I know."

"No, father, I am here!" Cap o' Rushes put her arms round him. They were all happy ever after.

The Sorcerer's Apprentice

A German folk tale

The sorcerer lived in a dusty room at the top of a tall gloomy tower. His table was covered with bottles and jars full of strange-coloured potions, and bubbling mixtures filled the air with horrible smells. The walls of the tower were lined with huge old books. These were the sorcerer's spell books and he would let no one else look inside them.

The sorcerer had a young apprentice called Harry – a good but lazy boy who longed to do

magic himself. The sorcerer had promised to teach him, but only when Harry was ready.

One day the sorcerer had to visit a friend. He had never left Harry alone in the tower before and he did not entirely trust him. Looking fierce, the sorcerer gave Harry his instructions.

"I have an important spell to conjure up when I return. I need the cauldron full of water from the well," he said. "When you have filled the cauldron, you can sweep the floor and light the fire."

Harry was not pleased. It would take many trips to the well to fill the cauldron, and he would have many steps to climb each time. The sorcerer climbed onto his small green dragon and said, "Touch nothing!" before flying off in a cloud of smoke and flame from the dragon.

Harry watched until the sorcerer was safely out of sight. Then he took one of the spell books and

turned the pages until he found what he was looking for – a spell to make a broomstick obey orders. He read the spell out loud.

The broomstick quivered and then stood up. It grabbed a bucket and jumped off down the stairs. Soon it was back, the bucket full of water. It tipped the water into the cauldron and set off down the stairs again. Harry was delighted. On and on the broomstick went and the cauldron soon was full.

"Stop, stop!" shouted Harry, but

the broomstick just carried on, and on. Soon the floor was awash and bottles and jars were floating around the room. Nothing Harry could say would stop the broomstick. In desperation, he grabbed the axe that lay by the fireside and chopped the broomstick into bits. To his horror, all the pieces turned into new broomsticks and set off to the well, buckets appearing magically in their hands.

By now the water was nearly up to the ceiling

and Harry gave himself up for lost. Suddenly there was a clatter of wings and a hiss of steam as the dragon flew into the tower. The sorcerer was back! He ordered the broomsticks to stop. They did. Then he ordered the water back into the well. It all rushed back down the stairs. Then he ordered the dragon to dry everything with its hot breath. Then he turned to look at Harry. Harry could see that the sorcerer was very angry. The sorcerer looked as if he might turn Harry into a frog, but then he sat down on a soggy cushion.

"Right, I think it is time I taught you how to do magic PROPERLY!" And he did.

Hansel and Gretel

By the Brothers Grimm

At the edge of a forest lived a poor woodcutter and his wife – a spiteful woman – and their two children, Hansel and Gretel. They were very poor so there was often very little food on the table.

One day there was no food at all. Everyone went to bed hungry. That night, Hansel heard his mother tell his father, "Husband, there are too many mouths to feed. You must leave the children in the forest tomorrow."

"Wife, I cannot abandon our children, there are wolves in the forest!" said the poor woodcutter.

But his wife made him agree to her evil plan. Hansel felt his heart grow icy cold. But he was a clever boy and so he slipped out of the house and filled his pockets with shiny white stones.

The next morning they all rose early and the children followed their father deep into the forest.

He lit them a fire and told them he was going to gather wood and would be back to collect them. He left them, tears falling down his face.

The day passed slowly. Hansel kept their fire going but when night fell, it grew very cold and they could hear all kinds of rustling under the shadowy trees. Gretel could not understand why their father had not come back to collect them, so Hansel had to tell her that their mother had told the woodcutter to leave them there deliberately.

"But don't worry, Gretel," he said, "I will lead us home," and in the moonlight he showed her the line of shiny white stones that he had dropped from his pocket, one by one, as their father had led them into the forest. They were soon home where their father greeted them with great joy. But their mother was not pleased.

Some time passed. They managed to survive

with very little to eat but another day came when Hansel heard his mother demanding that the woodcutter leave them in the forest again. And when Hansel went to collect some more pebbles, he found the door locked and he couldn't get out.

In the morning, their father gave them each a piece of bread, and led them even deeper into the forest than before. All day long, Hansel comforted Gretel and told her that this time he had left a trail of breadcrumbs to lead them safely back home. But when the moon rose and the children set off there was not a breadcrumb to be seen. The birds had eaten every last one. There was nothing to do but go to sleep and wait until the morning.

The next day they walked and walked, but they saw nothing but trees. And the next day was the same. By this time they were not only cold and hungry but deeply frightened. It looked as if they

would never ever be able to find a way out of the forest.But just as it was getting dark, they came to a clearing, and there stood a strange house.

The walls were made of gingerbread, the windows of fine spun sugar and the tiles on the roof were brightly striped sweets. Hansel and Gretel could not believe their luck and were soon breaking off bits of the house to eat. Then a little voice came from inside.

"Nibble, nibble, little mouse,
Who is that eating my sweet house?"

Out of the front door came a very old woman. She smiled sweetly at the children and said, "Dear ones, you don't need to eat my house. Come inside and I will give you lots to eat and you shall sleep in warm beds." Hansel and Gretel needed no second asking. They were soon tucked up, warm and full of hot milk, ginger biscuits and apples. They both fell asleep quickly. Little did they know they were in worse danger than ever before. The old woman was a wicked witch and she had decided to make Gretel work in the kitchen, and worst of all, she planned to fatten Hansel up so she might eat him!

The very next morning she locked poor Hansel in a cage and gave Gretel a broom and told her to clean the house from top to toe. In the evening, the witch fed Hansel a huge plate of chicken but she only gave Gretel a dry hunk of bread. But once she was asleep, Hansel shared his meal with Gretel.

So they lived for many days. The witch could not see very well, so every morning she made Hansel put his finger through the cage so she could tell how fat he was getting. But clever Hansel poked a chicken bone through the bars so the witch thought he was still too skinny to eat.

After many days, she grew fed up and decided to eat him anyway. She asked Gretel to help her prepare the big oven. The witch made some bread to go with her supper and when the oven was hot,

she put it in to cook. When the bread was ready the witch asked Gretel to lift it out to cool. But Gretel was clever too. She pretended she couldn't reach the tray, and when the witch bent down inside the oven Gretel gave her a great shove and closed the door. And that was the end of the witch!

Gretel released Hansel, and together they set off once more to try to find their way home. After all their adventures, fortune finally smiled on them and they soon found the path home. Their father was simply overjoyed to see them again. And what, you might ask, of their mean mother? Well, the poor woodcutter had not had a happy moment since he left the children in the forest. He had become so miserable that she decided there was no living with him. The day before Hansel and Gretel returned, she had upped sticks and left. That served her right, didn't it?

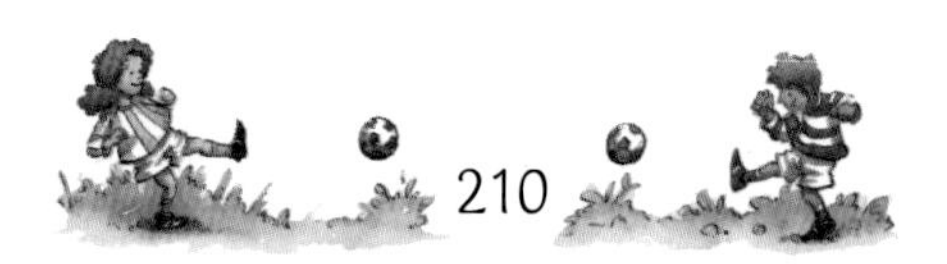

My Own Self

By Joseph Jacobs

In a tiny house in the north country, far from any town or village, there lived a poor widow all alone with her little son, a six-year-old boy.

The door of the house opened straight on to the hillside and all round about were moorlands, huge stones and swampy hollows. Their nearest neighbours were 'ferlies' in the glen below, and 'will-o'-the-wisps' in the long grass along the path.

And many a tale she could tell of the 'good folk'

calling to each other in the oak trees, and the twinkling lights hopping on to her windowsill on dark nights. In spite of the loneliness she lived on from year to year in the little house.

But she did not care to sit up late. When the fire burnt low, no one knew what might be about. After they had had their supper, she would make up a good fire and go to bed.

This, however, was far too early to please her son, so when she called him to bed, he would go on playing beside the fire, as if he did not hear her.

He had always been bad since the day he was born, and his mother did not often cross him. Indeed, the more she tried to make him obey her, the less he did as he was told, so he usually got his own way.

But one night, at the end of winter, the widow did not want to go to bed and leave him by the

fire, for the wind was tugging at the door and rattling the windowpanes, and she knew that on such a night, fairies were bound to be out, and up to mischief. So she tried to coax the boy into going at once to bed.

The more she begged and scolded, the more he shook his head. At last she lost patience and cried that the fairies would surely come and take him, and went off to bed in despair. Her naughty little son sat on his stool by the fire, not at all put out by her crying.

But he had not long been sitting there, when he heard a fluttering sound in the chimney and then down by his side dropped the tiniest girl you could think of. She had hair like spun silver, eyes as green as grass, and cheeks as red as roses.

"Oh!" said the boy, "What do they call you?"

"My own self," she said in a shrill but sweet voice.

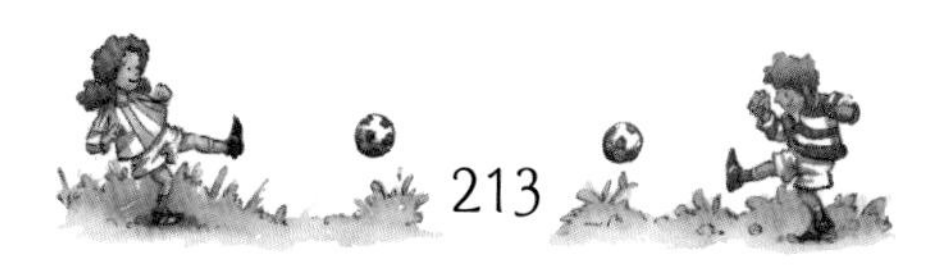

She looked at him too. "What do they call you?"

"Just my own self too!" he answered, and with that they began to play together.

She made moving animals out of ashes, and tiny houses with walking people an inch high in them.

The little boy stirred the coals to make them blaze, and out jumped a red-hot cinder, which fell on the fairy child's tiny foot.

She squealed so loudly that the boy clapped his hands to his ears. He bolted to bed, and hid under the blankets to listen in fear.

Then a sharp voice came from the chimney:

"Who's there, and what's wrong?" it said.

"It's my own self," sobbed the fairy, "and my foot's burnt. Ooh!"

"Who did it?" said the voice angrily, and the boy, peeping from under the clothes, could see a white face looking out from the chimney-opening.

"Just my own self too!" said the fairy.

"If you did it your own self," cried the elf-mother, "what's the use of making all this fuss about it?"

With that she stretched out, caught the creature by its ear, and pulled it up the chimney.

Next evening, the boy's mother was surprised to find that he was happy to go to bed when she asked.

"He's taking a turn for the better at last!" she said to herself, but he was thinking that when next a fairy came to play with him, he might not get off quite so easily as he had done this time.

The Little Matchgirl

By Hans Christian Andersen

It was New Year's Eve and bitterly cold. Snow lined the streets like an untrodden white carpet, for all the people were indoors, preparing to bring in the New Year. All alone in the windy square by the fountain, the poor girl who sold matches shivered. She pulled her ragged shawl closer around her thin dress. She rubbed her hands together and stamped her feet, but freezing snow came swamping through the holes in her boots.

The little matchgirl hadn't sold one box of matches all day and she was too frightened to go home, for her father would be very angry.

"Someone must pass this way and buy soon," she told herself. "If only I could light one of my matches; that would warm me a little." Her fingers stiff with cold, the little matchgirl falteringly took out one of her matches and struck it.

The match blazed into a bright flame and the little girl cupped her hands over it, craving its warmth. As she stared into the centre of the flame, she saw herself standing in front of a stove giving out heat that warmed her from the tips of her toes to the top of her head. Suddenly, the match's flame went out and the vision died with it. The little matchgirl somehow felt even colder than before.

She didn't dare light another match for a long time. Then "Just one more," she whispered,

through her chattering teeth. Shaking, the little matchgirl drew out another one and struck it on the wall. The glimmer seemed to light up the stone until it was clear and glassy, like a crystal window. Through the window, she could see a room with a welcoming fire and a table laden with food. She held out her hands to it. Then the match died. The magical room vanished, and huge tears filled the little matchgirl's eyes.

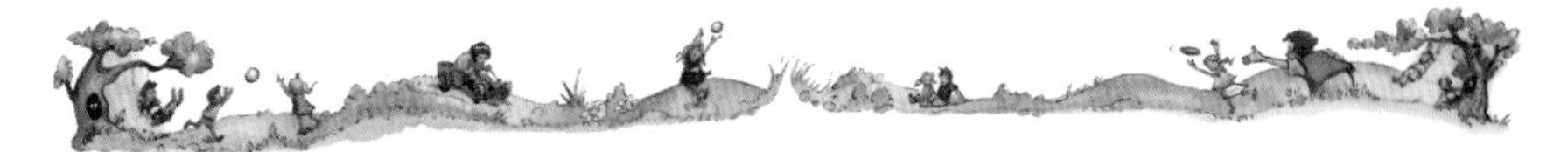

Her numb hands fumbled to light another, and her face lit up with wonder in the glow of the third flame. A magnificent Christmas tree sparkled before her. It shimmered with glassy balls of many colours, and dots of candlelight danced all over its green needles. "How beautiful!" breathed the little matchgirl. Then the match scorched her fingers and she dropped it into the snow. The Christmas tree was gone, but the glimmering lights from its candles were still there, rising up into the night sky until they mingled with the twinkling stars.

Suddenly, one of the lights fell through the darkness, leaving a blazing trail of silver behind it.

"That means someone is dying," the little matchgirl murmured, remembering what her Granny used to say when they saw shooting stars.

As the little matchgirl stood dreaming of her grandmother, she lit up another match – and

there was her granny before her in the light of the flame. As she lit one match after another, so the vision wouldn't fade like all the others. "Let me stay with you!" she begged, and the old lady smiled and held out her arms for the little girl to run into, just as she always had done.

At midnight, the church bells rang to welcome the New Year. People danced, sang and wished each other well. Lying in the snow by the fountain, was a little girl's thin, lifeless body, surrounded by spent matches. For the little matchgirl had left them there when she had gone away with her grandmother. She had no need for matchsticks in the place where they were going: a place without cold, nor hunger, nor pain – just happiness.

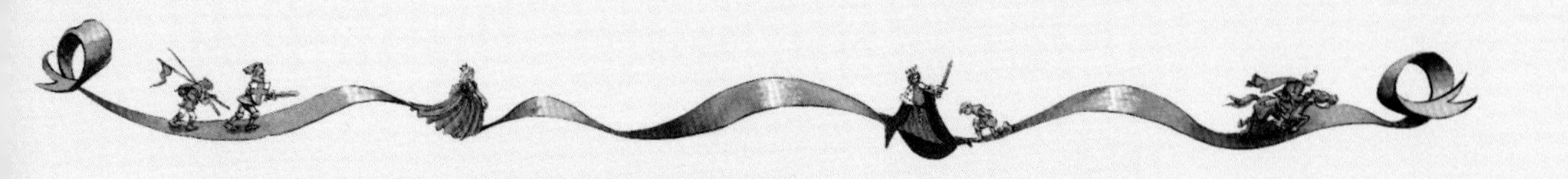

Royal Adventures

The Seven Ravens

A Polish fairytale

There was once a poor widow who had seven sons and a daughter. The daughter, Anne, was a good girl, but the seven brothers were wild as the hills. One day the widow was baking a pie. As she rolled out the pastry the noisy troop came into the kitchen shouting, "Pie! When will it be ready?"

"When it is cooked," she said crossly. "Let me finish then we can all eat." But the boys just ran about the hot kitchen, pushing and shoving and

leaving muddy bootmarks all over the floor.

"Quiet! I wish you were ravens instead of noisy boys," she cried. Her eyes widened in horror – the boys shrank, feathers covered them, their mouths became beaks, and they flew out of the door. Anne rushed to the window, but they were already out of sight. Mother and daughter sat weeping, and not even the smell of burning pie could rouse them.

The next day Anne told her mother that she would find her brothers and bring them home.

She set off with nothing but her needle, thread and scissors. She walked until she came to a strange house in the woods. It was made of silver, and the woman who opened the door was dressed in a long silver robe. "Oh, my husband will be home soon. There is no supper ready, and I have to mend his cloak," she said all in a rush.

"I could mend the cloak," said Anne taking out her needle, "and then you can cook the supper."

The woman was delighted and let her in. Anne sat in the corner and mended the beautiful cloak with the tiny stitches. When the husband came in, also dressed in silver, he invited Anne to join them for a supper of roast chicken.

The silver man asked Anne where she was going so she told them the whole story of her brothers.

"We are the moon's helpers," said the silver man. "I will ask her if she has seen your brothers."

As the wife cleared the table after supper, she gave Anne the chicken bones and said, "Keep these in your pocket – they might come in useful."

When the silver man returned the next morning he told Anne that the moon had seen seven ravens flying round Amber Mountain. Anne thanked them and set off.

After several days she came to a halt at Amber Mountain. Its sides were as steep as glass. Anne remembered the chicken bones. She pushed one into the surface of the mountain and stood on it. Then she put the second bone in and stood on that, and so she slowly climbed to the top of the mountain. There she found seven ravens – her brothers! But an evil old witch was there too.

"Your brothers are under my spell. You can release them by remaining silent for seven years," and with an evil cackle she flew off.

Anne climbed down the mountain, and when

she got home she could tell her mother nothing. Four years passed until one day Anne met a prince who was struck by Anne's quiet ways. He came by every day, and asked her to marry him. She smiled her acceptance but didn't utter a word.

Three more years passed, and the prince and Anne had a baby son. Now the queen had never really approved of her son marrying such a poor girl and so she liked to make mischief. One day she accused Anne of trying to poison the baby. The prince was horrified and when he asked Anne

if she had done such a terrible thing, she was unable to reply. So he sent her to the dungeons.

Three days passed and Anne was brought into the courtyard where everyone waited to see what would happen next. Suddenly there was a great flapping of wings and seven ravens landed in a circle around Anne. In a blink of an eye there stood her brothers, restored to human shape.

Well, you can imagine what a lot Anne had to tell! They talked into the night.The seven brothers went to collect their mother, and when they all came back together, the prince promised her that she would never have to do a day's work again!

The Golden Touch

A myth from ancient Greece

There was once a king called Midas who loved gold more than anything in the world. Each day, he spent hour after hour in his treasure house, running his hands through his sacks of gold coins, admiring his golden jars and statues, and holding up his golden jewellery to the light to watch it gleam and shine. Midas thought that the precious metal was a much more delightful colour than the emerald green of the grass or the

sapphire blue of the sea. He thought it was far more beautiful than the gold of waving fields of wheat, the gold of his wife's hair – even the gold of sunshine.

The king once helped the god Dionysus by taking care of one of his friends who was lost. Dionysus was very grateful and insisted, "Let me repay you for your kindness by granting you a wish! Now think hard... Make it something good! Whatever you like."

Midas knew exactly what he wanted. "I wish for everything I touch to turn to gold!" he declared.

"Are you sure about that?" Dionysus asked. "Are you quite, quite sure?"

"What could be better?" cried Midas, delightedly.

"Very well then," sighed the god. "It is done."

Midas couldn't wait to try out his new powers. He hurried over to a tree and snapped off a twig.

Unbelievable! It immediately grew heavy and bright. It had turned to solid gold. Joyfully, Midas rushed around touching everything in his royal garden. Soon the apples hung on the trees like golden baubles. The flowers hardened into gold sculptures. The fountain froze into a spray of golden glitter and the grass solidified into a gold pavement.

"How wonderful!" laughed Midas, clapping his hands. "Now for my palace!" and he picked up his robes and ran inside. By the time Midas reached the cool of his great chamber, his clothes had stiffened into a fabric woven from pure gold thread. "Ooof!" puffed Midas. "That's a little heavy!" The weight of his golden clothes were dragging him down, slowing him up and making his shoulders ache.

Still, thought Midas, that's a minor botheration compared to how beautiful my robes now look! He set off through the halls and corridors, touching pillars, pictures, doors, furniture, floors… until everything glowed gold.

Phew! It was hungry, thirsty work! Midas sank into one of his new golden chairs at his new golden dining table and called for his servants to bring him his lunch. He wriggled about a bit on his rock hard seat, but couldn't get comfy. "Never mind!" said Midas to himself, as the servants brought in platter after platter of delicious food. "I don't know any other king who is rich enough to eat off gold plates!" And he touched each serving dish and bowl and saw them gleam.

"Amazing!" Midas whooped, and licking his lips, he reached for a juicy chicken leg. "OWWW!" he yelled, biting down on hard metal and breaking a

tooth. He reached for a goblet of wine and took a gulp. "AAARRGH!" Midas roared, as the mouthful of gold got stuck in his throat. The king pushed his chair back, spitting out the hunk of treasure.

"Oh, no!" the king moaned. Suddenly he realized what the god Dionysus had been trying to warn him about. "I'm going to have a whole kingdom full of gold, but I'm not going to be able to eat or drink anything!"

At that very moment, Midas's golden doors swung open and his little daughter came running towards him. Midas backed away in horror – but it was too late. "Daddy!" the little girl cried, flinging her arms happily around him. Suddenly the king's beloved daughter was no more than a lifeless statue. Midas howled with misery and huge tears began to stream from his eyes. "I would gladly give away every piece of gold that I own to have

my little girl back again," he wailed. "How foolish I have been! There must be some way to take back my wish!"

Desperately trying not to touch anything else, Midas hurried to Dionysus and begged him to undo his magic. "Go and wash in the River Pactolus," the god instructed him. As soon as the king had done so, he was hugely relieved to find that his golden touch was gone. All the things Midas had turned into gold were back to normal – including his beautiful little daughter. After that, if the king had had his way, he would never have looked at another nugget of gold as long as he lived. But the god Dionysus turned the sandy bed of the River Pactolus gold for ever more, so that every time Midas walked along its banks, he would remember his greedy mistake.

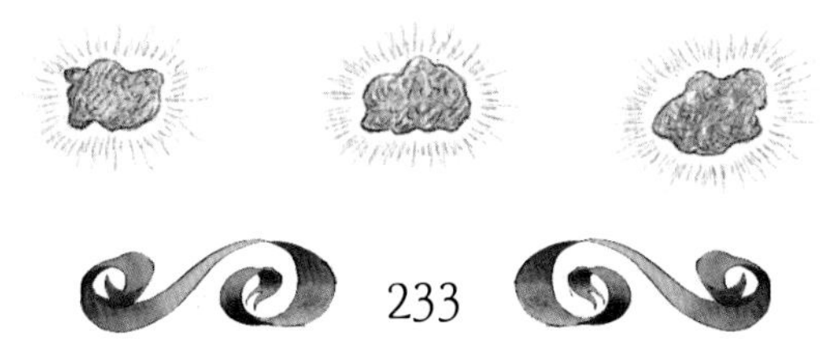

The Sword in the Stone

A Celtic legend

The blacksmith's anvil had suddenly appeared in the courtyard of the cathedral on Christmas morning. No one knew how it had got there. The anvil had a sword stuck into it and stood on a huge stone. Words were carved right round it which read: Whoever pulls out this sword is the rightful king of the Britons.

Many a proud lord had stepped up and tried to pull the sword out of the mysterious anvil. But

even though they had heaved and sweated and grunted and pulled and pulled and pulled, all of them had walked away disappointed. Now almost a week had passed. It was time for the New Year's Eve jousting festival, and still the anvil stood on the stone in the courtyard with the sword sticking out of it.

Every year, bold knights came to the capital city from all over the kingdom to ride against each other in the New Year's Eve jousting festival and show off how brave they were. This year, Sir Ector's son, Sir Kay, would joust for the very first time. Sir Ector's younger son, Arthur, was going along too, as Sir Kay's squire. Sir Ector and his sons lived in the very furthest corner of the kingdom – so far away from the capital city that news of the strange anvil hadn't even reached them. It took them three days of hard riding until

they saw the towering cathedral spire and the bright fluttering flags of the jousting field in the distance. Then a dreadful thing happened. Sir Kay put his hand down by his side to pat his trusty sword – and there was nothing there. "My sword!" Sir Kay gasped. "It's gone!"

Arthur turned quite pale with horror. It was a squire's job to make sure that a knight was properly equipped. "We must have left it at the lodging house we stayed at last night," he groaned. "Don't worry, Kay. I'll dash back and fetch it." Before anyone could argue, Arthur had wheeled his horse around and was galloping at full tilt back down the road. There wasn't a second to lose.

But when Arthur arrived back at the lodging house, there wasn't a sign of Sir Kay's sword anywhere. Arthur raced his horse back to the city

wondering how on earth he was going to break the bad news to his brother. He was very nearly at the jousting field when he galloped past the cathedral courtyard and saw the sword sticking out of the magical anvil on the stone. Arthur reined in his panting horse at once and looked all around him. There was no one about; everyone was at the jousting competition. It certainly didn't look as though the sword would be missed if he borrowed it for a while. "I promise I'll bring it back later," Arthur muttered out loud to no one in particular. He dashed over the snow, jumped up onto the stone and grasped the sword. It slid out of the anvil as easily as a needle pulls through cloth. "Gadzooks!" Arthur breathed, as he gazed

at the mighty, jewelled blade in his hands. "This is the most magnificent weapon I have ever seen!" Then he remembered that the competition was about to begin. He sprinted back to his horse, leapt into the saddle, and arrived at the jousting field just as the fanfares were being trumpeted.

Sir Kay was astonished at the superb weapon that his younger brother handed him. He and his father had just heard all about the mysterious anvil from the other knights at the jousting competition, and he realized at once where the strange sword must have come from. "See, father!" he cried over the crowds, brandishing the sword over his head. "I must be the new king of the Britons!"

Sir Ector came running at once and gasped at the magnificent weapon in Kay's hands. "How have you got this?" he demanded.

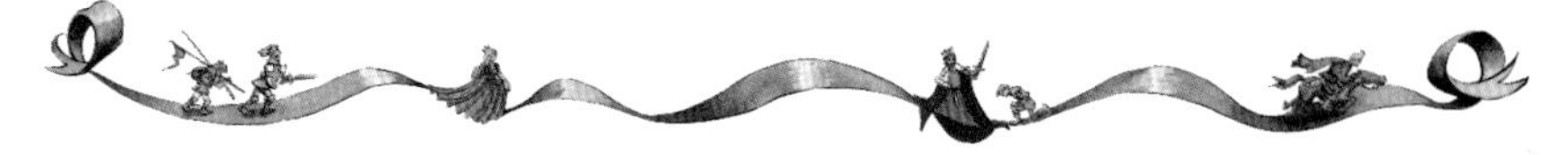

Kay's face fell. "Arthur brought it to me," he mumbled.

Sir Ector's face was grave. "Who pulled this out of the stone and gave it to you?" he quizzed Arthur.

"N-n-o one," stammered Arthur. Quite a few people had gathered around by now and suddenly he felt very nervous. "I pulled it out of the stone myself. I was going to put it back when Kay had finished with it, honest!"

Sir Ector led Arthur back to the cathedral and into the courtyard, with a huge and excited crowd following hot on

their heels. "Put the sword back where you found it, son," he told Arthur.

"All right," shrugged Arthur. He climbed onto the stone and thrust the sword back into the anvil.

First, Sir Ector himself tried to pull it out. Then Sir Kay heaved at it with all his might. The sword didn't budge an inch.

"Now show us how you did it, son," said Sir Ector, his voice trembling slightly.

Everyone held their breath as Arthur stepped up to the anvil. As he pulled the sword out effortlessly, the cheer that went up could be heard all over the capital city and beyond.

And that is how a young boy called Arthur, who wasn't even a knight, was crowned king of the Britons and eventually became the greatest of all the heroes who ever lived in the Celtic lands.

The Princess and the Pea

By Hans Christian Andersen

The prince was very fed up. Everyone in the court, from his father, the king, down to the smallest page, seemed to think it was time he was married. Now the prince would have been very happy to get married, but he did insist that his bride be a princess, a real true and proper princess. He had travelled the land and met plenty of nice girls who said they were princesses, but none, it seemed to him, were really true and proper

princesses. Either their manners were not quite exquisite enough, or their feet were much too big. So he sat in the palace, reading dusty old history books and getting very glum.

One night, there was the most terrible storm.

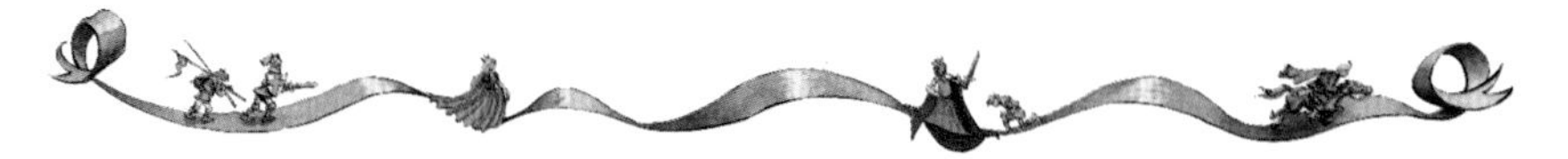

Rain was lashing down, and thunder and lightning rolled and flashed round the palace. The wind kept blowing out the candles, and everyone huddled closer to the fire. Suddenly there was a great peal from the huge front door bell.

And there, absolutely dripping wet, stood a princess. Well, she said she was a princess, but never did anyone look less like a princess. Her hair was plastered to her head, her dress was wringing

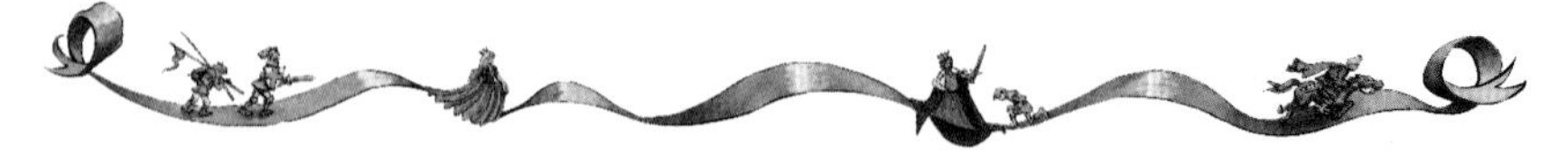

wet and her silk shoes were covered in mud. She was quite alone, without even the smallest maid, and just where had she come from? But she kept insisting she was a princess.

We will see about that, thought the queen. While the dripping girl sat sipping a mug of warm milk and honey, the queen went to supervise the making of the bed in the second-best spare bedroom. She didn't think it necessary to put their late night visitor in the best spare bedroom, after all she might only be a common or garden duchess. The queen told the maids to take all the bedclothes and the mattress off the bed. Then she placed one single pea right on the middle of the bedstead. Next the maids piled twenty mattresses on top of the pea, and then twenty feather quilts on top of the mattresses. And so the girl was left for the night.

In the morning, the queen swept into the bedroom in her dressing gown and asked the girl how she had slept.

"I didn't sleep a wink all night." said the girl. "There was a great, hard lump in the middle of the bed. It was quite dreadful. I am sure I am black and blue all over!"

Now everyone knew she really must be a princess, for only a real princess could be as soft-skinned as that. The prince was delighted, and insisted they got married at once, and they lived very happily ever after. They always slept in very soft beds, and the pea was placed in the museum, where it probably still is today.

The Twelve Dancing Princesses

By the Brothers Grimm

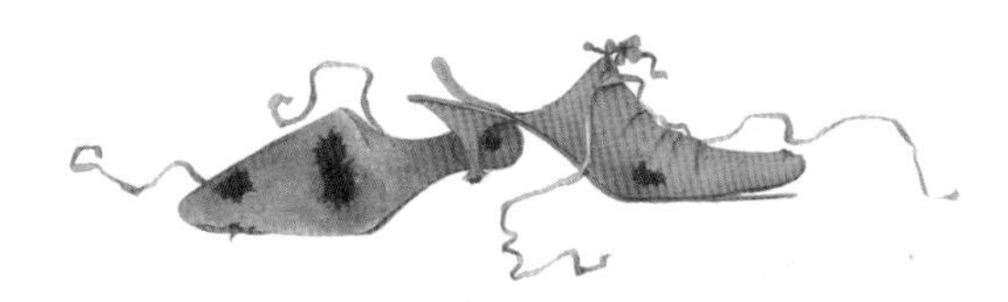

The king was very puzzled. He had twelve daughters, each one as beautiful as the moon and the stars, and he loved them above all the riches in his kingdom. But every morning the princesses would appear yawning and bleary-eyed, and with their shoes quite worn through. Every evening the king would kiss them good night and lock the door behind him. So how did they get out? And where did they go?

Buying new shoes every day was costing him a fortune so the king determined to solve the mystery. The court messenger was sent to all four corners of the kingdom to issue the king's proclamation that he would give the hand of one of his daughters in marriage to any man who could discover the secret. But should he fail after three nights he would be banished forever.

Needless to say there were plenty of young men willing to risk banishment to win such a prize. But they soon found the princesses were too clever by half. Before they realized it, morning had come and there were the sleepy princesses and twelve pairs of worn-out shoes.

Now into the kingdom at this time there wandered a penniless soldier who decided to try his luck when an old woman came slowly down the dusty road. The young man offered her some of his bread and cheese, and as they sat together the old woman asked where he was bound. When he explained, she said, "You must not drink the mead those princesses offer you, for it is drugged. Pretend to be asleep, and you shall see what you shall see. This may help you," and the old woman handed him a cloak.

"Whenever you wear this you will be invisible. Use it well!" and the old woman disappeared. "Well, perhaps I will succeed now I have magic on my side," murmured the young man as he set off for the palace.

The young man bowed deeply to the king and smiled at all the princesses. He ate a hearty supper but when a princess gave him a goblet of mead he only pretended to drink it. Then he yawned loudly and let his head droop as if he had fallen asleep.

The butler and the first footman dumped the young man onto the bed placed across the door of the princesses' bedchamber. He cautiously opened one eye and gazed around the room. The princesses were putting on gorgeous velvet dresses and the brand new jewelled slippers that the shoemaker had only delivered a few hours earlier. The eldest princess clapped her hands three times.

A trap door opened up in the floor and they all swiftly descended down a steeply curving staircase. The young man flung the magic cloak round his shoulders and rushed after them.

He found himself in a wondrous garden where the trees were covered in rich jewels, sparkling in candlelight. Musicians played whirling tunes and

he saw all the princesses dancing with the most handsome princes. The young man was spellbound, but he managed to keep his wits about him. He broke off a branch from one of the jewelled trees and hid it under his cloak. Then he ran back and lay down on his bed.

It was with a weary voice that the king asked the young man at breakfast if he had found out where the princesses went. The king sat up quickly when the young man told his tale and produced the branch from the tree. The king was delighted and the young man chose the youngest sister for his bride. And they all lived happily ever after.

The Frog Prince

By the Brothers Grimm

Once upon a time, there lived a very spoilt princess who never seemed content. The more she had, the more she wanted. And she just would not do as she was told.

One day she took her golden ball out into the woods. She threw it high up into the sky once, twice, but the third time it slipped from her hands and, with a great splash, it fell down, down into a deep well. The princess stamped her foot and

yelled, but this did not help. So she kicked the side of the well and a large frog plopped out.

"Ugh!" said the princess. "A horrible slimy frog," but the frog didn't move. Instead, it said, "What are you making such a fuss about?"

A talking frog! For a moment the princess was speechless, but then she looked down her nose and said, "If you must know, my golden ball has fallen down this well, and I want it back."

With a sudden leap, the frog disappeared down the well. In the wink of an eye, it was back with the golden ball.

The princess went to snatch it up, but the frog put a wet foot rather firmly on it and said,

"Hasn't anyone taught you any manners? I have a special request to make."

The princess looked at the frog in astonishment. No one ever dared talk to her like that. She glared at the frog and said crossly, "May I have my ball back, please, and what is your special request?"

The frog bent closer to the princess. "I want to come and live with you in the palace and eat off your plate and sleep on your pillow, please."

The princess looked horrified, but she was sure a promise to a frog wouldn't count so she said, "Of course you can," and grabbed her ball from frog and ran back to the palace very quickly.

That night at supper the royal family heard a strange voice calling, "Princess, where are you?" and in hopped the frog.

The queen fainted. The king frowned.

"Do you know this frog, princess?" he asked.

"Oh bother!" said the princess again, but she had to tell her father what had happened. He insisted the princess keep her promise.

The frog ate very little, the princess even less. And when it was time to go to bed, the king just looked very sternly at the princess who was trying to sneak off on her own. She picked the frog up by one leg, and when she reached her great four-poster bed, she plonked the frog down in the farthest corner. She did not sleep a wink all night.

The next evening, the frog was back. Supper was a quiet affair. The queen stayed in her room, the king read the newspaper, and the princess tried not to look at the frog. Bedtime came, and once again the frog and the princess slept at opposite ends of the bed.

The third evening, the princess was terribly hungry so she just pretended the frog was not there and ate everything that was placed in front of her. When it came to bedtime, she was so exhausted that she fell in a deep sleep.

The next morning when she woke up, she felt much better for her good sleep until she remembered the frog. But it was nowhere to be seen.

At the foot of the bed, however, there stood a handsome young man in a green velvet suit.

"Hello, princess," he said. "I was the frog who rescued your golden ball. I was bewitched by a fairy who said I was rude and spoilt. The spell could only be broken by someone equally rude being nice to me."

The princess was speechless. The king was most impressed with the man's manners, and the queen liked his fine suit. Everyone liked the fact that the princess had become much nicer and before long, the princess and the young man were married.

The Haughty Princess

By Patrick Kennedy

There was once a very worthy king, whose daughter was the greatest beauty that could be seen far or near, but she was so proud, she wouldn't agree to marry any king or prince. Her father was tired out at last, and invited every king and prince, and duke, and earl that he knew or didn't know to come to his court to give her one more trial. They all came, and the next day after breakfast they stood in a row on the lawn, and the

princess walked along in front of them to make her choice. One was fat, and said she, "I won't have you, beer-barrel!" One was tall and thin, and to him she said, "I won't have you, ramrod!" To a white-faced man she said, "I won't have you, pale death!" and to a red-cheeked man she said, "I won't have you, cockscomb!"

She stopped a little before the last of all, for he was a fine man in face and form. She wanted to find some defect in him, but he had nothing remarkable but a ring of brown curling hair

under his chin. She admired him a little, and then carried it off with, "I won't have you, whiskers!"

So all went away, and the king was so vexed he said to her, "Now to punish you, I'll give you to the first beggar man that calls." And, sure enough, a fellow in rags, with hair to his shoulders, and a bushy red beard all over his face came next morning and began to sing before the window.

When the song was over, the hall door was opened, the singer asked in, the priest brought, and the princess married to Beardy. She roared and she bawled, but her father didn't mind her. "There," said he to the bridegroom," is five guineas for you. Take your wife out of my sight, and never

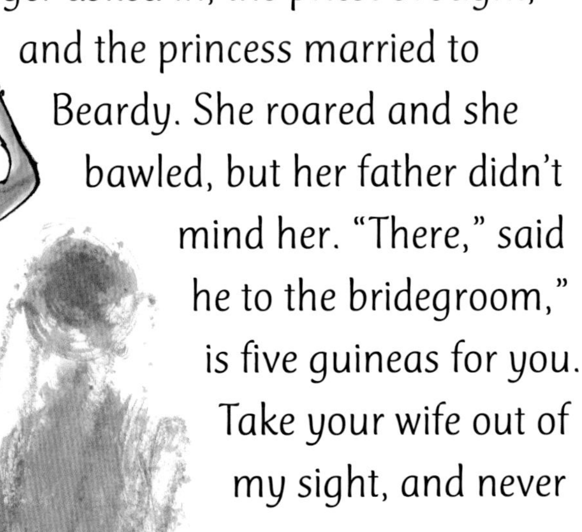

let me lay eyes on you or her again."

Off he led her, and dismal enough she was. The only thing that gave her relief was the tones of her husband's voice and his genteel manners.

"Whose wood is this?" said she, as they were going through one.

"It belongs to the king you called whiskers yesterday." He gave her the same answer about meadows and cornfields, and at last a fine city.

"Ah, what a fool I was!" said she to herself. "He was a fine man, and I might have had him for a husband." At last they were coming up to a poor cabin. "Why are you bringing me here?"

"This was my house," said he, "and now it's yours." She began to cry, but she was tired and hungry, and went in with him. There was neither a table laid out, nor a fire burning, and she was obliged to help her husband to light it, and boil

their dinner, and clean up the place after, and the next day he made her put on a gown and a cotton handkerchief. When she had her house cleaned up, and no business to keep her employed, he brought home willows, peeled them, and showed her how to make baskets. But the hard twigs bruised her delicate fingers, and she began to cry. Well, then he asked her to mend their clothes, but the needle drew blood from her fingers, and she cried again.

He couldn't bear to see her tears, so he got her a kitchen maid's place in the palace. So the poor thing was obliged to stifle her pride once more. She was kept very busy, and she went home to her husband every night, carrying her payment of scraps of leftover food wrapped in papers in her side pockets.

A week after she got the job there was great

bustle in the kitchen. The king was going to be married, but no one knew who the bride was to be. Well, in the evening the cook filled the princess's pockets with cold meat and puddings, and then, said she, "Before you go, let us have a look at the great doings in the big parlour." So they came near the door to get a peep, and who should come out but the king himself, and he was no other but King Whiskers himself.

"Your handsome helper must pay for her peeping," said he to the cook, when he spotted them, "and dance a jig with me."

Whether the princess would or not, he held her hand and brought her into the parlour. The fiddlers struck up, and away went him with her. But they hadn't danced two steps when the meat and the puddings flew out of her pockets. Everyone roared with laughter, and she flew to the

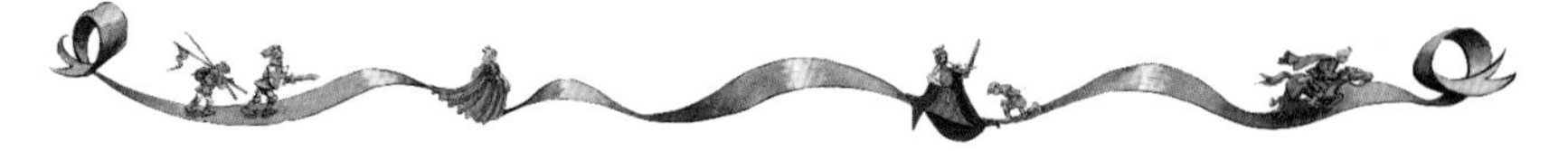

door, crying piteously. But she was soon caught by the king, and taken into the back parlour.

"Don't you know me, my darling?" said he. "I'm King Whiskers, your husband the ballad singer. Your father knew me well enough when he gave you to me, to drive your pride out of you."

Well, she was filled with fright, shame and joy. Love was uppermost anyhow, for she laid her head on her husband's breast and cried like a child. The maids-of-honour soon had her dressed as fine as hands and pins could do. There were her mother and father, too, and while the company were wondering what had happened to the handsome girl and the king, they came in, and such rejoicings and fine doings as there were, none of us will ever see, anyway.

The Twelve Windows

From 'Told Again' by Walter de la Mare

There was once a princess who lived alone with her father the king, the queen having died many years before. The princess was wise and gentle and loved her father very much, so much so that the king dreaded the day when the princess would marry and leave him alone in the empty palace. But she had promised she would never marry until she met a man who would have three chances to hide himself in the palace so cleverly

that she could not see him. Now you might think this was not so difficult but the princess had witch's eyes and she could spy out the smallest thing like an ant or one tiny daisy on the palace lawn. She had a special room at the top of a tower in the palace. It had twelve windows that the princess could look out of to practise her great skill.

Many princes and handsome young men came to court the princess but all failed to hide themselves well enough. Now there was a swineherd who would watch the princes and the handsome young men come and go, and after a while he thought he might just as well try himself to see if he could win the hand of the princess. When he arrived at the palace gate, the guards just laughed at him, but the watchman who was passing at the time thought the young swineherd had an honest face. So he lent him a cloak of

green velvet, and the swineherd was ushered into the princess's rooms.

Straightaway she saw that he had an honest face, but she also saw his poor clothes under the cloak, and she saw his heart beating against his ribs. She wished him luck, and gave him an hour to hide. The swineherd went down, down deep into the palace dungeons and hid himself under a pile

of straw. When the hour was up, the princess climbed up into her special room and looked through the first window. She could see no sign of the swineherd. She looked through the second window. She could see no sign of the swineherd. But then she looked through the third window, and there she could see him, lying under the straw. The princess was sorry as she realized that the young swineherd was the first of the many young men who had come to court her that she actually liked.

The next day, the swineherd went to the palace fish pond and, taking a deep breath, he plunged to the bottom of the pond and hid under the roots of the graceful water lilies. He waited and waited, his lungs bursting.

The princess climbed up into her special room and looked through the first window, then the second, the third, the fourth and the fifth. There was no sign of the swineherd, and the princess found she was pleased. She looked through the sixth and the seventh and the eighth. There was no sign of the swineherd and the princess found she was delighted. But then she looked through the ninth,

and she saw the swineherd crouched in the pond. The princess found she was full of sadness.

That night the young swineherd went to see his friend, the white fox. He told her all about the princess and her witch's eyes. The fox told him to get a good night's sleep. The next morning, the fox touched him with the tip of her tail, and he turned into a beautiful white mountain hare. Then she turned herself into an old woman and, taking the hare in her arms, she walked to the palace.

The princess was walking in the palace gardens. She saw an old woman standing by the garden gate, with a white mountain hare in her arms.

The hare looked so beautiful that the princess could not resist going up to stroke its fur. The old woman who, of course, was really the clever fox, gave the hare who, of course, was really the swineherd, to the princess. Together they climbed the stairs to the room with the twelve windows.

The hare crept round under the princess's hair as she looked out of the first window. There was no sign of the swineherd. She looked out of all the windows until she came to the twelfth. There was no sign of the swineherd. With a beating heart she went to look out of the last window. She so wanted not to see the swineherd. She looked and looked again. She could not see him and so the swineherd had won the hand of the princess. The hare darted down the stairs and ran to where the fox was

waiting. She touched the hare with the tip of her tail and there stood the swineherd once again.

He thanked the fox profusely and than ran back to the palace as fast as ever he could. There he found the princess standing in the garden looking everywhere for him. They went to see the king,
and the whole story came out. The princess and the swineherd said they loved each other. The swineherd said he did not want to live anywhere else in the land. So the king did not lose his daughter. The princess married a man she really liked. The swineherd gained everything from just having a try. The white fox was invited to the wedding, and they all lived happily ever after.

Tattercoats

By Flora Annie Steel

In a magnificent palace by the sea there once dwelt a very rich old lord, who had neither wife nor children living and only one granddaughter, whose face he had never seen. He hated her because at her birth his favourite daughter died.

So he turned his back, and sat by his window looking out over the sea, and wept great tears for his lost daughter, till his hair became white.

Meanwhile, his granddaughter grew up with

no one to care for her, or clothe her. Only the old nurse, when no one was by, would sometimes give her a dish of scraps from the kitchen, or a torn petticoat from the rag-bag, while the other servants of the palace would drive her from the house with blows and mocking words, calling her 'Tattercoats' and pointing to her bare feet and shoulders, till she ran away, crying.

So she grew up, spending her days out of doors, her only companion a gooseherd, who fed his flock of geese on the common. And this gooseherd was a merry little chap, and when she was hungry, or cold, or tired, he would play to her so gaily on his little pipe, that she forgot all her troubles, and would fall to dancing with his flock of noisy geese for partners.

Now one day people told each other that the king was travelling through the land, and was to

give a great ball to all the lords and ladies of the country in the town nearby, and that the prince, his only son, was to choose a wife from amongst the maidens in the company. In due time one of the royal invitations to the ball was brought to the palace by the sea, and the servants carried it up to the old lord, who still sat by his window.

But when he heard the king's command, he dried his eyes and sent for rich clothes and jewels, which he put on, and he ordered the servants to saddle the white horse with gold and silk, so he might ride to meet the king. But he quite forgot he had a granddaughter to take to the ball.

Meanwhile Tattercoats sat by the kitchen door weeping. And when the old nurse heard her crying,

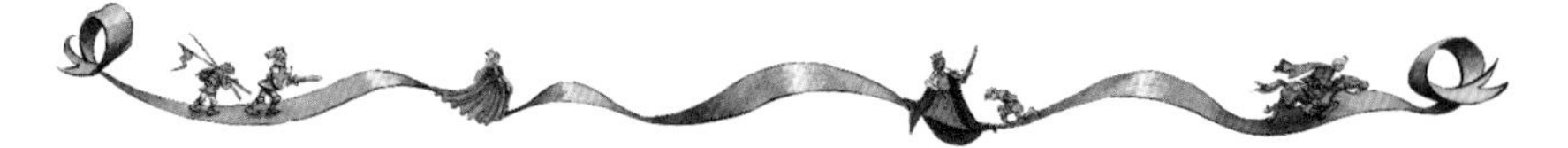

she went to the lord of the palace and begged him to take his granddaughter to the king's ball. But he only frowned and told her to be silent. A second, and then a third time, the old nurse begged him to let the girl go with him, but she was answered only by black looks and fierce words.

The old nurse went to look for Tattercoats, but the girl had gone to see the gooseherd. Now once the gooseherd had listened to her story, he told her to cheer up, and proposed that they should go together into the town to see the king, and all the fine things. He played a note or two upon his pipe, so gay and merry, that she forgot all about her tears and her troubles, and they began dancing towards town.

Before they had gone very far a handsome young man stopped to ask the way to the castle where the king was staying, and when he found

that they too were going, he got off his horse and walked beside them along the road.

"You seem merry folk," he said, "and will be good company."

"Good company, indeed," said the gooseherd, and played a new tune that was not a dance.

It was a curious tune, and it made the strange young man stare at Tattercoats till all he could see was her beautiful face.

Then he said, "You are the most beautiful maiden in the world. Will you marry me?"

Tattercoats laughed. "Not I," said she, "you would be finely put to shame, and so would I

be, if you took a goose girl for your wife! Go and ask one of the great ladies you will see tonight at the king's ball."

But the more she refused him the sweeter the pipe played, and the deeper the young man fell in love, till at last he begged her to come that night at twelve to the king's ball, just as she was, with the gooseherd and his geese, in her torn petticoat and bare feet, and see if he wouldn't dance with her before the king and the lords and ladies, and present her to them all, as

his dear and honoured bride.

So when night came, and the hall in the castle was full of light and music, and the lords and ladies were dancing before the king, just as the clock struck twelve, Tattercoats and the gooseherd, followed by his flock of noisy geese entered and walked straight up the ballroom, while on either side the ladies whispered, the lords laughed, and the king seated at the far end stared in amazement.

But as they came in front of the throne, the man rose from beside the king, and came to meet her. Taking her by the hand, he kissed her thrice before them all, and turned to the king.

"Father!" he said, for it was the prince himself, "I have made my choice, and here is my bride, the loveliest girl in all the land!"

Before he had finished speaking, the gooseherd

had put his pipe to his lips and played a few notes that sounded like a bird singing far off in the woods, and as he played, Tattercoats' rags were changed to shining robes sewn with glittering jewels, a golden crown lay upon her hair, and the flock of geese behind her became a crowd of dainty pages, bearing her long train.

And as the king rose to greet her as his daughter, the trumpets sounded loudly in honour of the new princess, and the people outside in the street said to each other:

"Ah! Now the prince has chosen for his wife the loveliest girl in all the land!"

But the gooseherd was never seen again, and no one knew what became of him, while the old lord went home once more to his palace by the sea, for he could not stay at court, when he had sworn never to look on his granddaughter's face.

The Three Aunts

By George Webbe Dasent

Once upon a time there was a poor man who lived in a hut far away in the wood, and got his living by shooting. He had an only daughter, who was very pretty, and as she had lost her mother when she was a child, and was now half grown up, she said she would go out into the world and earn her bread.

So the girl went off to seek a place, and when she had gone a little while, she came to a palace.

There she stayed and got a place, and the queen liked her so well that all the other maids grew envious of her. So they told the queen that the lassie could spin a pound of flax in four-and-twenty hours.

Now, the poor lassie dared not say she had never spun in all her life, but she only begged for a room to herself. That she got, and the wheel and the flax were brought up to her. There she sat weeping, and knew not how to help herself. She pulled the wheel this way and that, and twisted and turned it, but she knew not what to do.

But all at once, in came an old woman to her.

"What's wrong, child?" she said.

"Ah!" said the lassie, with a deep sigh, "It's no good, for you'll never be able to help me."

"Who knows?" said the old wife. "Maybe I know how to help you after all."

The lassie explained what had happened.

"Well never mind, child," said the old woman, "If you'll call me aunt on the happiest day of your life, I'll spin this flax for you, and so you may sleep." Yes, the lassie was willing enough, and off she went to sleep.

Next morning when she awoke, there lay all the flax spun on the table, so clean and fine – no one had ever seen such even and pretty yarn.

The queen was very glad to get such nice yarn. The others were even more envious,

and agreed to tell the queen how the lassie had said she could also weave the yarn in only four-and-twenty hours. So the queen said she must do it. Again, the lassie dared not say no, but begged for a room to herself, and then she would try. There she sat again, sobbing, when another old woman came in and asked what was wrong.

Again, the lassie explained her grief.

"Never mind. If you'll call me aunt on the happiest day of your life, I'll weave this yarn for you, and so you may sleep." Yes, the lassie was willing enough, so she went to sleep. When she awoke, there lay a piece of linen on the table. So the lassie took it to the queen, who was very glad to get such beautiful linen. But as for the others, they grew more bitter against her.

At last they told the queen the lassie had said she could make up the piece of linen into shirts in

four-and-twenty hours. Again the lassie was shut up in a room by herself, and there she sat in tears. But then a third old wife came, who said she would sew the shirts for her if she would call her aunt on the happiest day of her life. The lassie was only too glad to do this, and then she did as the old wife told her, and went to sleep.

Next morning when she woke she found the piece of linen made up into shirts. When the queen saw the work, she was so glad at the way in which it was sewn, that she clapped her hands, and said:

"Such sewing I never had, nor even saw, in all my born days. Now, you shall have the prince for your husband."

Soon the wedding was upon them. But just as they were going to sit down for the bridal feast, in came an ugly old hag with a long nose. So up got the bride and made a curtsey. "Good day, Auntie.

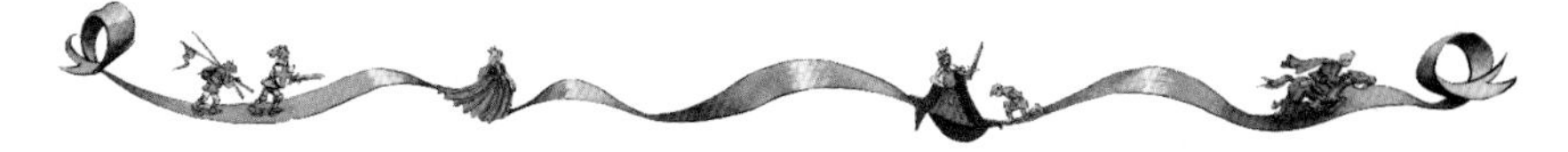

Please sit down with us to the feast."

But just then, in came another ugly old hag with a humped back. Up jumped the bride in a trice, and greeted her with "Good day, Auntie!" She too sat down with them.

But they had scarce taken their seats before another ugly old hag came in, with large, bleary eyes. But up jumped the bride again, and said, "Good day, Auntie."

The prince asked her to sit down, but he wasn't very pleased. He could not keep his thoughts to himself any longer, and asked, "But how, in all the world can my bride, who is such a lovely lassie, have such loathsome misshapen aunts?"

"Ah, I was just as good-looking when I was her age, but my nose got stretched over my spinning."

"And I," said the second, "ever since I was young, I have sat over my loom, and that's how

my back has got so humped."

"And I," said the third, "have sat and stared and sewn, night and day, and that's why my eyes have got so bleary."

"So, so!" said the prince, "'twas lucky I came to know this, for if folk can get so ugly by all this, then my bride shall neither spin, nor weave, nor sew all her life long."

And that was the end of that!

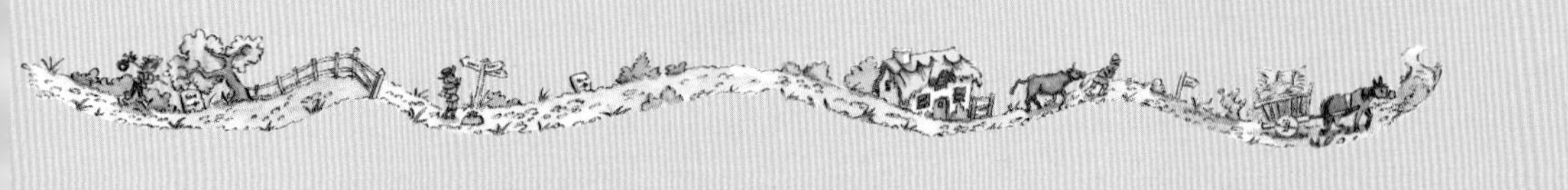

Fantastic Journeys

The Precious Stove

An Austrian folk tale

Peter lived with his mother, father, brothers and sisters in an old wooden cottage, deep in the woods of Austria. They were very poor and the cottage had hardly any furniture, and they might have been very cold in winter were it not for their most treasured possession, a stove. This was no ordinary stove. It was made of white porcelain and it was so tall, the gold crown at the top almost scraped the ceiling. Its feet were carved like lion's

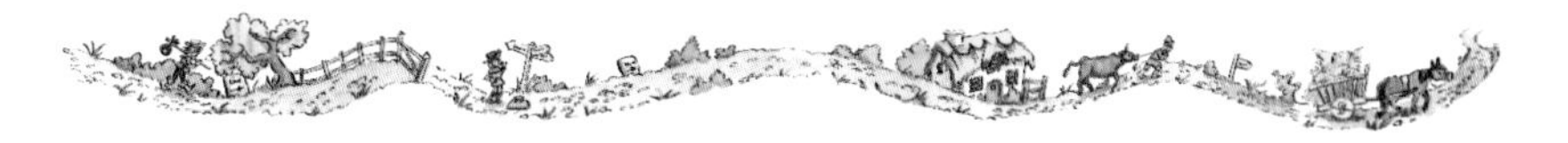

claws, the talons painted gold. The sides of the stove were painted with flowers and rare birds, in glowing colours, and the door was tiled in blue and gold. It looked very out of place in the poor wooden cottage, for it had originally been made for a king's palace. Many years before, Peter's grandfather had rescued it, after a great war, from the ruins of the palace where he used to work. Peter used to draw copies of the flowers and birds on pieces of brown paper with a stub of old pencil.

One evening, as Peter and his sister Gilda lay curled up in the warmth at the foot of the stove, their father came in, shaking the snow from his boots. He looked tired and ill.

"My children, tomorrow the stove will be taken away as I have had to sell it. We have no money, and we need food more than we need a stove."

The children were horrified, but their father would not change his mind. That night, instead of banking up the stove to keep it burning warmly through the night, he let the fire die down so it was quite cold in the morning. The traders arrived and loaded the stove onto a cart. Peter's mother and father looked at the handful of gold coins the traders had given them and shook their heads.

Peter and Gilda whispered together outside behind the wood pile.

"You have to follow the cart, Peter," said Gilda, "so you can see where our stove goes."

So Peter rushed off down the track after the cart, pausing only to grab a couple of apples. The journey into town was slow, but by evening it had

reached the station. Peter crept as close as he dared, and heard the traders arranging for the stove to go to Vienna by train the very next morning. Once the traders had gone to an inn for the night, he clambered inside the stove. He soon fell fast asleep.

When he awoke, the train was moving fast. Peter munched his apples and wondered what his parents would be thinking, just where was he going to end up, and what could he do to keep the stove for his family.

Eventually the train came to a halt and with much banging and clattering all the boxes around the stove were unloaded onto the platform. Then Peter heard a gruff voice.

"That valuable stove is going to the palace. Take care it isn't damaged in any way."

The palace! Peter sat as quiet as a mouse as he felt the stove lifted onto another cart. It clattered through cobbled streets and then came to a halt.

"Truly, it is a very beautiful stove. I did not expect it to be so fine," said a deep important voice. And then the handle of the door turned and light flooded into the stove. Peter tumbled out onto the floor, before looking up at a man dressed in a bright red jacket with great gold tassels and gold buttons. Glittering medals gleamed on his chest and a great silver sword hung by his side. It was the king! Peter was absolutely terrified, but the king kept on smiling.

"Well, my boy, how did you come to be inside my new stove?"

A servant rushed forwards and grabbed Peter by the arm, meaning to drag him away, but the king raised his hand and the man stepped back.

"Let the child speak," said the king.

Well, once Peter found his tongue, he could not stop. He told the king all about the stove. The king listened in silence while Peter told his story.

"Peter, I am not going to give you back your stove for it belongs here in the palace, but I will give your father several bags of gold, for it is a very valuable stove. And perhaps you would like to stay here and look after it for me?" he asked.

Peter was delighted. And he looked after the stove for the king from that day on. His family never wanted for food again, and every summer they would all come to stay at the palace to see Peter – and the stove of course.

The Three Sillies

By Joseph Jacobs

Once upon a time, there was a farmer and his wife who had one daughter. She was to marry a gentleman. Every evening, the gentleman had supper at the farmhouse, and the daughter went down into the cellar to fetch the beer for him.

One evening she went down to fetch the beer, when she looked up at the ceiling and saw a mallet stuck in one of the beams. She thought it was very dangerous to have that mallet there, and said to

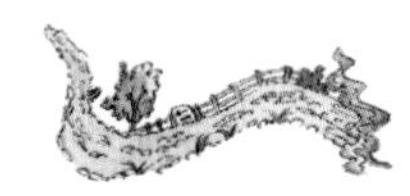

herself, "Suppose him and me were to be married, and we were to have a son, and he was to grow up to be a man, and come down into the cellar to get the beer and the mallet was to fall on his head and kill him!" And she started crying.

Upstairs, they began to wonder why it was taking her so long, so her mother went down to the cellar. She found her daughter crying, with the beer running over the floor. "Whatever is the matter?" said her mother.

"Oh, mother!" said she, "look at that horrid mallet! Suppose we were to be married, and were to have a son, and he was to grow up, and was to come down to the cellar to fetch the beer, and the mallet was to fall on his head and kill him!"

"Dear, dear!" said the mother, and she started crying too. Then after a bit the father began to wonder why they hadn't come back, and he went

down into the cellar to look for them. There the two sat crying, with the beer running all over the floor. "Whatever is the matter?" said he.

"Why," said the mother, "look at that horrid mallet. Just suppose, if our daughter and her sweetheart were to be married, and were to have a son, and he was to grow up, and was to come down into the cellar to fetch the beer, and the mallet was to fall on his head and kill him!"

"Dear, dear!" said the father, and he sat down beside the other two, and started crying.

Now the gentleman got tired of being in the kitchen by himself, and at last he went down into the cellar to see what they were doing. There the three sat crying, with the beer running all over the floor. He turned off the tap and asked, "Whatever are you three doing, sitting crying, and letting the beer run all over the floor?"

"Oh!" said the father, "look at that horrid mallet! Suppose you and our daughter were to be married, and were to have a son, and he was to grow up, and come down into the cellar to fetch the beer, and the mallet was to fall on his head and kill him!"

And then they all started crying worse than before. But the gentleman burst out laughing, and reached up, pulled out the mallet, and said, "I've travelled many miles, and I've never met three

such sillies before. Now I shall start out on my travels again, and if I can find three bigger sillies, then I'll come back and marry your daughter." So he wished them goodbye, and went on his travels.

First, he came to a woman's cottage that had some grass growing on the roof. The woman was trying to get her cow to go up a ladder. The gentleman asked the woman what she was doing.

"Look at all that beautiful grass. I'm going to get the cow on to the roof to eat it. She'll be safe, for I shall tie a string round her neck, and pass it down the chimney, and tie it to my wrist, so she can't fall off without my knowing"

"Oh, you poor silly!" said the gentleman, "you should cut the grass and throw it to the cow!" But the woman thought it was easier to get the cow up the ladder than to get the grass down.

The gentleman went on his way, but he hadn't

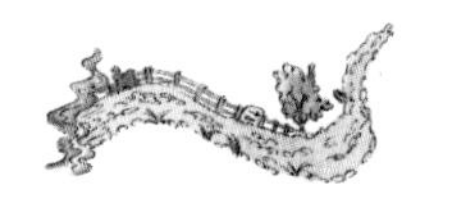

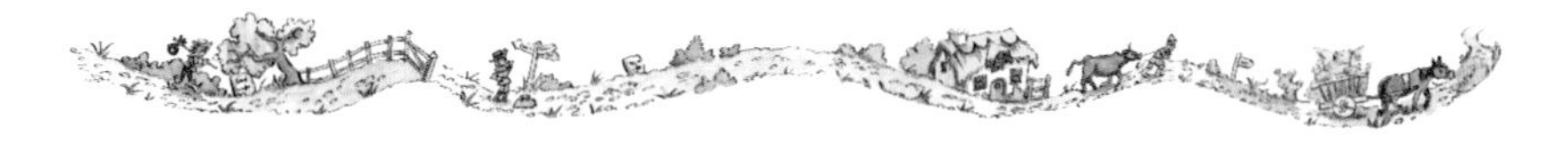

gone far when the cow tumbled off the roof and the weight of the cow pulled the woman up the chimney, where she got stuck, covered in soot. Well, that was one big silly.

The gentleman went on, and stopped the night at an inn, but it was so full that he had to share a room. In the morning, the gentleman was surprised to see the other man hang his trousers on the chest of drawers, run across the room and try to jump into them. At last he stopped. "Oh dear," he said, "It takes me an hour to get into my trousers every morning. How do you manage yours?" The gentleman burst out laughing, and showed him how to put them on. He said that he never would have thought of doing it that way. So that was another big silly.

Then the gentleman went on his travels again, and he came to a village, where there was a crowd of people around a pond. They had rakes and brooms, reaching into the pond. The gentleman asked what was the matter.

"Why," they said, "the moon's tumbled into the pond, and we can't get her out!" So the gentleman burst out laughing, and told them to look into the sky, and that it was only the shadow in the water.

So there were a whole lot of sillies bigger than those three sillies at home. So the gentleman turned back home again and married the farmer's daughter.

The Two Frogs

By Andrew Lang

Once upon a time in the country of Japan there lived two frogs, one of whom made his home in a ditch near the town of Osaka, on the sea coast, while the other dwelt in a clear little stream that ran through the city of Kyoto.

They had never heard of each other, but, funnily enough, the idea came into both their heads at once that they should like to see the world, and the frog who lived at Kyoto wanted to visit Osaka, and

the frog who lived at Osaka wished to go to Kyoto.

So one fine morning, they both set out along the road that led from Kyoto to Osaka, one from one end and the other from the other. Halfway between the two towns there arose a mountain that had to be climbed. It took them a long time and a great many hops to reach the top, but there they were at last, and what was the surprise of each to see another frog before him!

They looked at each other for a moment without speaking, and then told each other why they were there. It was delightful to find that they both wanted to learn a little more of their country.

"What a pity we are not bigger," said the Osaka frog, "then we could see both towns from here, and tell if it is worth our while going on."

"Oh, that's easy," said the Kyoto frog. "We have only got to stand up on our hind legs, hold onto

each other, and then we can look at the towns."

This idea pleased the Osaka frog so much that he at once jumped up and put his front paws on the shoulder of his friend, who had risen also. There they both stood, stretching themselves as high as they could, and holding each other tightly, so that they might not fall down.

The Kyoto frog turned his nose towards Osaka, and the Osaka frog turned his nose towards Kyoto. But they forgot that when they stood up, their eyes lay in the backs of their heads, so looked behind them.

"Dear me!" cried the Osaka frog, "Kyoto is exactly like Osaka. It is certainly not worth such a long journey. I shall go home!"

"If I had had any idea that Osaka was only a copy of Kyoto I should never have travelled all this way," exclaimed the frog from Kyoto. As he spoke he took his hands from his friend's shoulders and they both fell down on the grass. Then they took a polite farewell of each other and set off for home again, and to the end of their lives they believed that Osaka and Kyoto, which are as different as two towns can be, were as alike as two peas in a pod.

Honourable Minu

By William H Barker

One day, a poor man had to travel from his own little village to Accra – one of the big towns on the coast. This man could not speak their language, and they could not speak his.

As he approached Accra he met a great herd of cows. He was surprised at the number of them, and wondered who they belonged to. Seeing a man with them he asked, "Who do these cows belong to?" The man replied, 'Minu,' which means

I do not understand. The poor man, however, thought that Minu was the name of the owner of the cows and exclaimed, "Mr Minu must be very rich."

He then entered the town. Very soon he saw a fine large building, and wondered who it belonged to. The man he asked did not understand his question, so he also answered, "Minu."

"Dear me! What a rich fellow Mr Minu must be!" cried the poor man.

Coming to an even finer building with beautiful

gardens round it, he again asked the owner's name. Again came the answer, "Minu."

"How wealthy Mr Minu is!" said the poor man.

Next he came to the beach. There he saw a magnificent steamer being loaded in the harbour. He asked, "Who does this fine vessel belong to?"

"Minu," replied the man.

"To the Honourable Minu also! He is the richest man I ever heard of!" cried the poor man.

Having finished his business, he set off for home. As he passed down one of the streets, he met men carrying a coffin. He asked the name of the dead person, and received the usual reply, "Minu."

"Poor Mr Minu!" he cried. "He has left all his wealth and died just as a poor person would do! In future, I will be happy with my tiny house and little money." And then he went home quite pleased.

Straw, Coal and Bean

By the Brothers Grimm

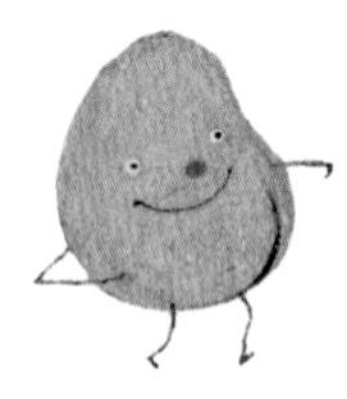

An old woman lived in a village. She had gathered a serving of beans and wanted to cook them, so she prepared a fire in her fireplace. To make it burn faster she lit it with a handful of straw. While she was pouring the beans into the pot, one of them fell unnoticed to the floor, coming to rest next to a piece of straw. Soon afterward a glowing coal jumped out of the fireplace and landed next to them.

The straw said, "Friends, where do you come from?"

The coal answered, "I jumped from the fireplace. If I had not forced my way out, I would have died. I would have burned to ash."

The bean said, "I too saved my skin. If the old woman had gotten me into the pot I would have been cooked to mush."

"Would my fate have been any better?" said the straw. "The old woman sent all my brothers up in fire and smoke. She grabbed sixty at once and killed them. I slipped through her fingers."

"What should we do now?" asked the coal.

"Because we have so fortunately escaped death," answered the bean, "I think that we should join together as comrades. To prevent some new misfortune from befalling us here, let us together make our way to another land."

This pleased the other two, and they set off. They soon came to a small brook. The straw decided to lay across it, so the others could walk across him.

When the coal got to the middle, he stopped, scared to go any further. Then the straw caught fire and fell into the brook. The coal slid after him, hissing as he fell into the water.

The bean who had stayed on the bank laughed until he burst. A wandering tailor was there, resting near the brook. He got out a needle and thread and sewed the bean back together. The bean thanked him and because he used black thread, all beans now have a black seam.

Dick Whittington and his Cat

An English myth

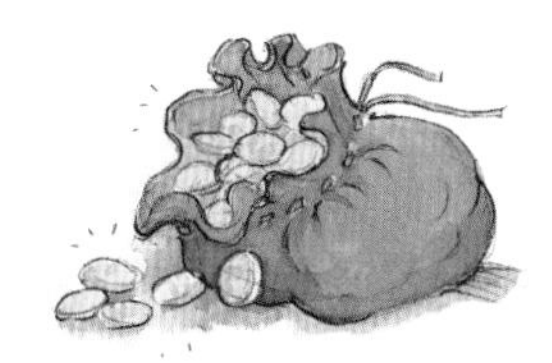

Hundreds of years ago there lived a poor orphan boy called Dick Whittington. His only possession was his cat, but everyone in his village looked after him, so he never wanted for a meal or clothes on his back. In return, he worked hard wherever he was needed. Now Dick's greatest dream was to visit the great city of London where, he had heard, the streets were paved with gold.

One day, a waggoner pulled into the village to

give his two horses a drink. Dick offered to rub the horses down, and before long he was telling the waggoner about his dreams of visiting London.

"Well, you must be in luck," smiled the waggoner, "for that is where I am bound. Why don't you come with me and I will drop you back here again tomorrow?"

This was too good an offer to refuse, so Dick and his cat set off with the waggoner for London. When they arrived, Dick looked round about in astonishment.

Never before had he seen such huge buildings, all crowded so closely together. And there were so many people! Dick set off to explore, promising the waggoner that he would be back in the evening.

The pavements certainly did not appear to be made of gold. But he kept on thinking he should just try round the next corner, and then the next and, before long, Dick realized that he was lost. He stumbled into a doorway, and worn out with hunger and worry, he fell asleep.

Now as luck would have it, Dick had chosen a very good doorway to sleep in. The house belonged to a rich merchant, Mr Fitzwarren, who was kind and willing to help anyone in need. So when he came home later that evening, Mr Fitzwarren took Dick and his cat indoors and told the cook to give him supper.

The next morning, Dick told Mr Fitzwarren the

whole story. Smiling, Mr Fitzwarren told Dick that, as he had found, the streets of London were not paved with gold, and indeed life there was hard.

"But you look like a strong boy, would you like to work for me, Dick?" he asked. "You will have a roof over your head and dinner every day in return for helping in the kitchen and the stables."

Dick was delighted, and soon settled into the household. He worked hard, and everyone liked him, except the cook. She gave him all the horrible jobs in the kitchen and would not let him have a moment's rest.

Whenever one of Mr Fitzwarren's ships went to sea, it was custom for everyone in the household to give something to the ship's cargo for luck. Dick had only his cat. He sadly handed her over.

The ship was at sea for many months before they came to port in China. The captain and crew

went ashore to show the emperor their cargo. The emperor and captain sat down to a banquet before discussing business. But to the emperor's embarrassment, the meal was ruined by the rats that ran everywhere, even over the plates they were eating off. The emperor explained that they had tried everything but nothing could rid the court of the plague of rats. The captain smiled. "I think I have the answer," he said and he sent for Dick's cat. Within moments of her arrival, there were piles of dead rats at the emperor's feet. He was so impressed that he gave the captain a ship full of gold just for the cat.

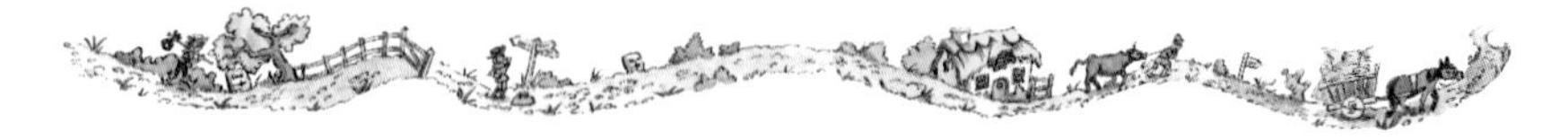

Back in London, Dick's life was a misery. The cook was nastier than ever and he didn't even have his beloved cat, so he ran away. But he had not gone far before he heard the church bells ringing, and they seemed to say, 'Turn again Dick Wittington, Thrice Lord Mayor of London.'

Dick didn't know what the bells meant, but he went back before the cook had even noticed that he was missing. Of course when the ships came home, Mr Fitzwarren gave Dick his fair share. He married Mr Fitzwarren's daughter, Jane, and became Lord Mayor of London three times. He and Jane had many children, and lots of cats!

Rosy's Journey

By Louisa May Alcott

Rosy was a girl who lived with her mother in a small house in the woods. They were very poor, for the father had gone away to dig for gold, and had not come back. When Rosy's mother died, she was left all alone, with no mother, no home and no money. "What will you do?" said the people. "I will find my father," answered Rosy, bravely and days later, she started through the wood on a journey to find him.

One day, as she was resting by a river, she saw a fish on the bank, nearly dead for want of water.

"Poor thing! Go and be happy again," she said, taking him up, and dropping him into the river.

"Thank you, dear child, I'll not forget, but will help you some day," said the fish.

"Why, how can a tiny fish help such a great girl as I am?" laughed Rosy.

"Wait and see," answered the fish, as he swam away with a flap of his little tail.

Rosy went on her way, and forgot all about it. Soon after, as she was looking in the grass for strawberries, she found a field mouse with a broken leg. Rosy took the mouse carefully in her hand and tied up the broken leg with a leaf of spearmint and a blade of grass. Then she carried her to the nest under the roots of an old tree where four

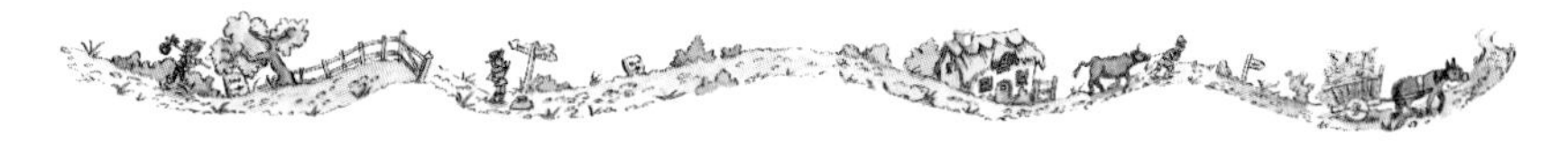

baby mice were squeaking sadly for their mother. She made a bed of thistledown for the sick mouse, and put within close reach all the berries and seeds she could find, and brought an acorn-cup of water from the spring, so they could be comfortable.

"Good little Rosy, I shall pay you for all this kindness some day," said the mouse.

"I'm afraid you are not big enough to do much," answered Rosy, as she continued on her journey.

"Wait and see," called the mouse, and all the little ones squeaked as if they said the same.

Some time after, as Rosy lay up in a tree, waiting for the sun to rise, she heard a great buzzing close by and saw a fly caught in a cobweb. A big spider was trying to spin him up, and the poor fly was struggling to get away.

Rosy put up her finger and pulled down the web, and the spider ran away to hide. But the fly

sat on Rosy's hand, cleaning his wings.

"You've saved my life, and I'll save yours, if I can," said the fly, twinkling his bright eye at Rosy.

"You silly thing, you can't help me," answered Rosy. The fly buzzed away, saying, like the mouse and fish, "Wait and see, wait and see."

Rosy trudged on, till at last she came to the sea. The mountains were on the other side, but how should she get over the water? She sat on the shore, tired and sad, and cried.

"Hello!" called a bubbly sort of voice close by, and the fish popped up his head.

"I've come to help you," said the fish. "I shall call my friend the whale and he will take you over."

Down dived the little fish, and Rosy waited to see what would happen, for she didn't believe such a tiny thing could really bring a whale to help her.

Presently what looked like a small island came

floating through the sea. Rosy was rather scared at this big, strange boat, but she got safely over, and held on fast. So she had a very pleasant voyage, and ran on shore with many thanks to the good whale, who gave a splendid spout and swam away.

Rosy travelled along till she came to a desert, hundreds of miles of hot sand.

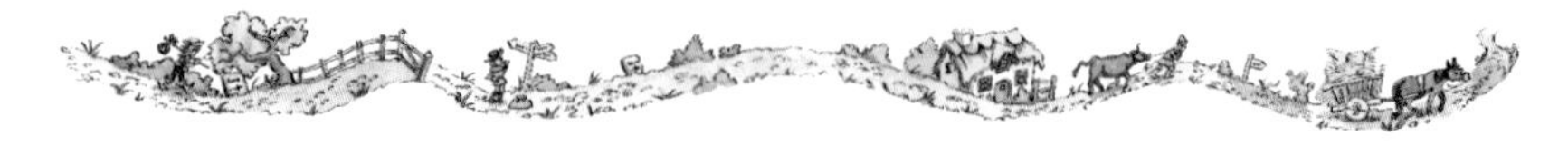

"I never can go that way," she said, "I should starve, and soon be worn out."

"Here I come to help you," said a friendly voice, and there was the mouse.

"Why, you dear little thing, I'm very glad to see you, but I'm sure you can't help me across this desert," said Rosy, stroking its soft back.

"That's easy," answered the mouse, rubbing its paws briskly. "I'll just call my friend the lion."

In a moment a loud roar was heard, and a splendid yellow lion, with fiery eyes and a long mane, came bounding over the sand. He crouched down like a great cat, and Rosy climbed up, and away they went, racing over the sand till her hair whistled in the wind. When they reached the other side, Rosy thanked the beast, and he ran away.

Rosy saw great hills before her, with many steep roads winding up to the top. She started off

bravely, but took the wrong road, and after climbing a long while, she found the path ended in rocks over which she could not go. She was tired, hungry and cold. She lay down on the moss and cried a little, then she tried to sleep, but something kept buzzing in her ear.

"Rosy, don't cry – I'm here to help you all I can," said the fly. "My friend the eagle will carry you right up the mountains and leave you at your father's door," cried the fly.

When a great eagle swooped down and stopped near her, she nestled into the thick brown feathers, and put both arms round his neck, and whiz they went, up, up, up, higher and higher, till the trees

looked like grass, they were so far below.

It was night when they landed, but fires were burning in all the houses, so Rosy went from hut to hut trying to find her father's. At last, in one hung a picture of a pretty little girl on the wall, and under it was written, 'My Rosy'.

Then she knew that this was the right place, and she ate some supper, put on more wood and went to bed, for she wanted to be fresh when her father came in the morning. She was finally home, ready to live happily with her father for the rest of their lives.

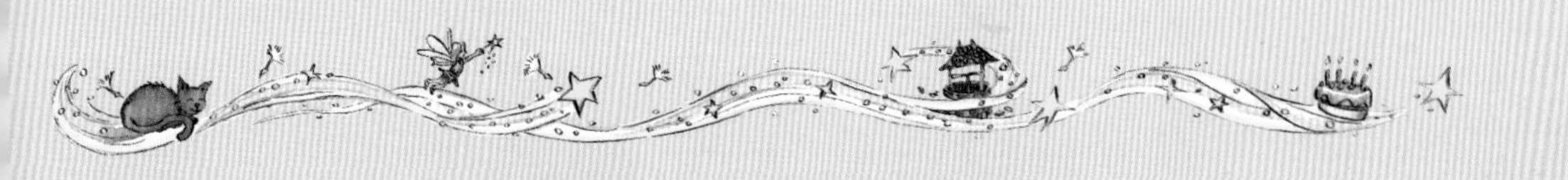

Good Deeds

Hop-Toads and Pearls

A retelling from the original tale by Charles Perrault

Go and fetch the water!" yelled the widow at her younger daughter. "You can finish that sweeping later! And hurry back with it. You've still got to light the fire and peel the potatoes."

The poor girl hurried to rest her broom in the corner and wipe her dusty hands on her tattered apron. She never grumbled about being treated like a slave because she was good and kind and couldn't think badly about anybody. But how she

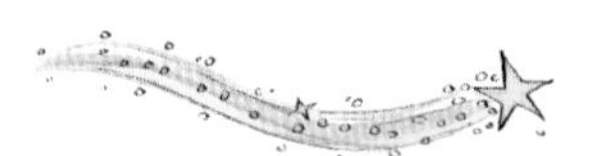

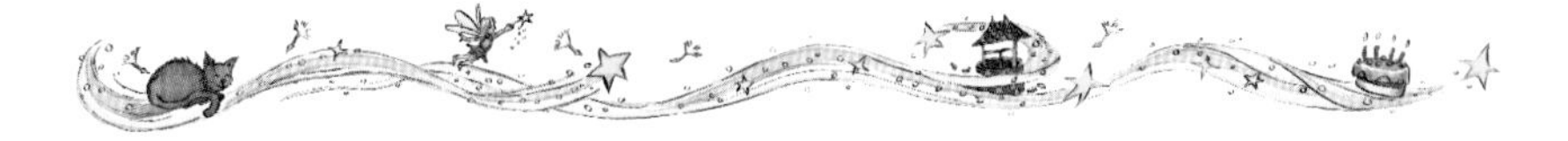

wished that her mother and her sister might help her out with all the housework now and again...

As the exhausted girl stumbled out to the well with the bucket, the widow's elder daughter looked up from her comfy chair and smirked. Fanchon was like her mother in every way: how she looked (very ugly), how she spoke (sharp and nasty) and how she acted (selfish and lazy). This was the reason why her mother adored her so: whenever she looked at Fanchon, she saw herself.

The widow's younger daughter reached the well and heaved up a heavy, full bucket. Suddenly, she noticed that an old beggar-woman had joined her. The toothless crone wheezed, "My dear, I'm hoarse with thirst. Could you spare me a little drink?"

"Of course," the girl said, and hurried to unhook the dripping bucket and help the beggar-woman to a ladleful.

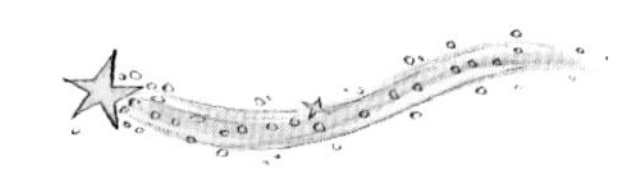

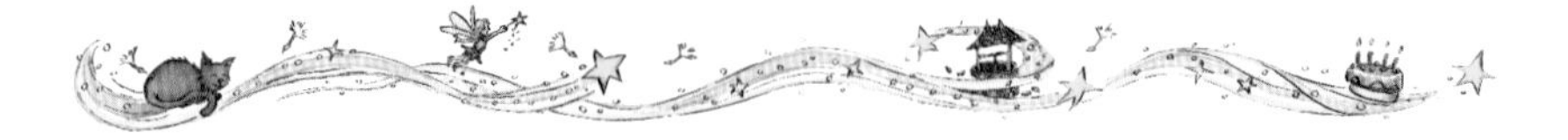

Little did the younger daughter know that the hag who stood in front of her was actually a powerful fairy, who had disguised herself to put the girl to the test. The younger daughter kindly helped the beggar-woman to another ladleful of water and chatted politely to her for a while, before hauling the bucket back home.

How the girl's mother and her sister yelled and screamed and swore at her for taking so long at the well! "I do beg your pardon," the poor girl apologised. "I will be quicker next time."

To everyone's surprise, a shining white pearl dropped from her lips with every word.

The stunned widow woman picked up a pearl from the floor, bit it hard between her teeth, and held it up to the light to examine it.

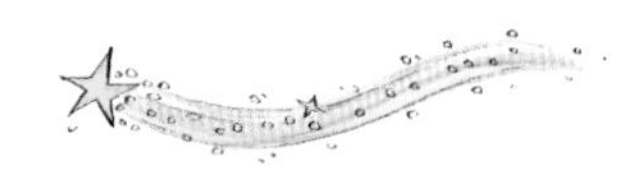

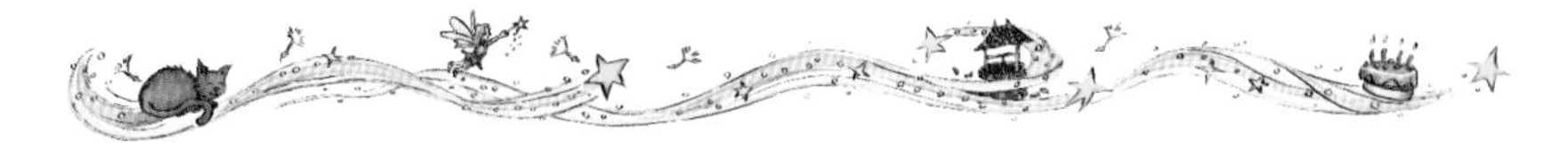

"They're real!" she exclaimed, with a greedy twinkle in her eye. "What on earth happened at the well this evening? Tell me everything, or I'll lock you in the coal cellar all weekend."

The younger daughter was just as amazed as her mother and sister, and truthfully told them that she had done nothing but give a drink to a woman she'd met at the well. Pearls continued to drop from her lips as she spoke, and as fast as they fell, the widow scooped them up greedily into her pockets.

"Did you hear that, Fanchon?" she screeched. "Get yourself down to that well immediately!"

"Get lost!" the rude girl snorted. "I'm not fetching and carrying like a slave for anything!"

"I said GO!" the widow roared, cuffing the horrified Fanchon round the head. "Find that woman and give her a drink, whether she wants

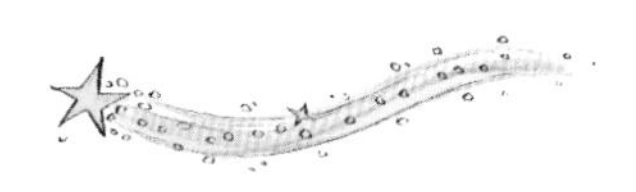

one or not! We're going to be rich, rich, rich!"

Fanchon sulked and pouted, grumbled and cursed with every step that she lugged the splintery bucket – and it was only fear of her mother's temper that made her do it at all. She flung the bucket angrily into the well and moaned and groaned to herself with every wind as she pulled it back up. No sooner had she finished, than she noticed she had been joined by an elegant young woman dressed in fine robes. (It was the fairy, disguised as a princess.) "Good evening," the princess said politely, "would you be so good as to allow me a drink?"

"Oh, it's you, is it?" Fanchon sneered. "You're the reason I've got splinters in my hands, splashes all over my dress, and my arms are killing me. You'd better make it worth my while and give

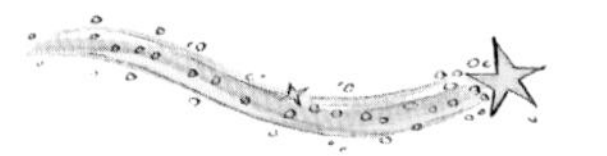

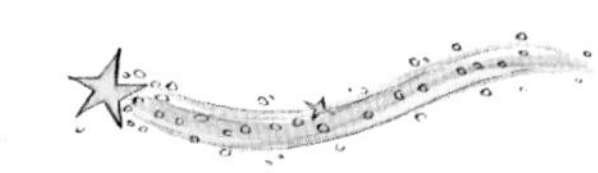

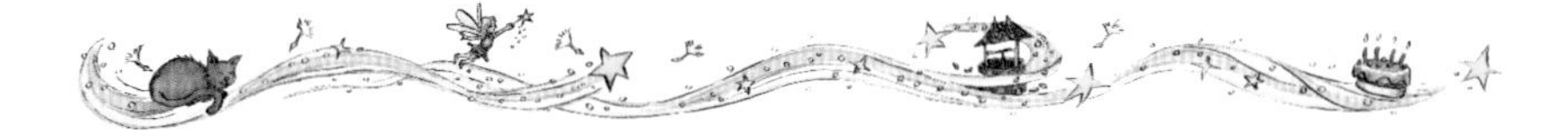

me diamonds instead of pearls, that's all I can say." With that, Fanchon angrily flung the wooden ladle at the princess and dumped the bucket at her feet. "Go on then," she snapped.

No sooner had the princess taken one sip than Fanchon snatched the ladle back and humped the bucket back to the house. "There!" she yelled at her mother. "Happy now?" To everyone's horror, three great hop-toads leapt from her lips and sprang across the floor, croaking. Fanchon clapped her hands over her mouth in alarm.

"Whatever's happened?" cried the widow. "Where are the pearls?"

"I don't know!" wailed Fanchon, and three more hop-toads bounced, bulging-eyed, from her mouth. She began to scream and stamp her feet.

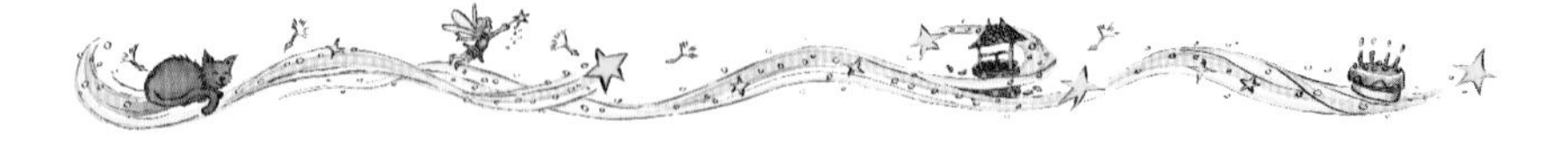

"This is all your fault, you ungrateful wretch!" the widow yelled at her younger daughter. She shoved the girl outside and slammed the door in her face. The poor younger daughter wandered off into the forest, sobbing.

The girl would almost certainly have got lost in the woods forever if the prince hadn't spotted her on his way back from a hunting trip. The prince was fascinated by the pearls that fell from her mouth, but he was even more charmed by the forgiving, kind way in which she spoke of her obviously horrible family. He took the lovely girl back to his palace at once, and after she had got to know and love him, he married her.

As for the nasty elder daughter, even her own mother tired of her moaning. The widow threw the girl out, and they both lived the rest of their lives with only their miserable selves for company.

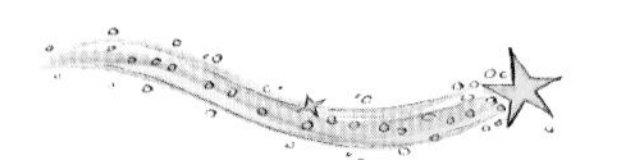

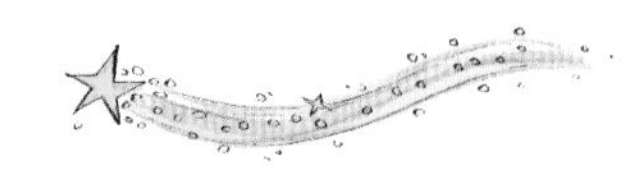

Liam and the Fairy Cattle

An Irish legend

Liam and his mother lived by the sea. They had a small white cottage with a pile of peat for the fire outside, and a row of potatoes to eat with the fish that Liam would catch. They had two cows, and Liam's mother would make butter and cheese from their milk. She baked bread and gathered sweet heather honey from the hives at the bottom of the meadow. They did not have much in life, but they were happy.

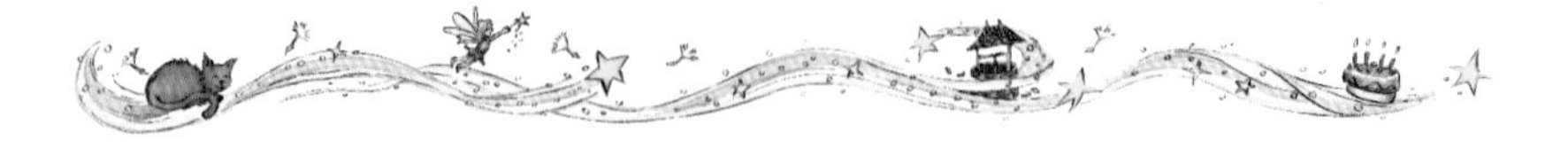

But then there came a time when ill luck fell on the small white cottage. First the two cows died, one after the other, and there was no cheese to eat. Then the shoals of fish swam far out to sea and Liam would come home empty-handed. The potatoes rotted in the ground, and Liam and his mother were hungry all the time.

One day when Liam was wandering along the shoreline he came across two boys throwing stones at a seal. He chased the boys away, but when he went to see if the seal needed help it turned its head once and looked deep into his eyes then slipped away into the sea. As it dived into the waves he saw blood on its head.

Three days later when Liam and his mother were sitting by the fire in the evening there came a knock at the door. There on the doorstep stood an old, old man leaning on a staff. His clothes looked

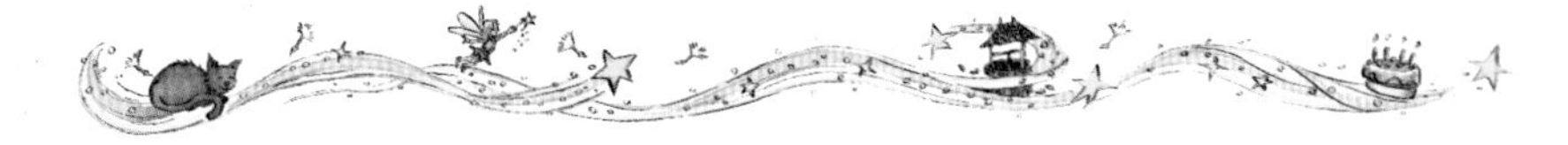

wet through and he had a large cut on his forehead, but his eyes were gentle.

"I am very weary, might I come in and warm myself at your fire?" the old man asked.

Liam opened the door wide, and bid the old man come in. His mother pulled up a stool close to the fire, and warmed up the last of the soup in the pot while she bathed the wound on his head. He thanked her kindly, smiling at Liam, and Liam had the strangest feeling he had looked into those deep brown eyes before. But he

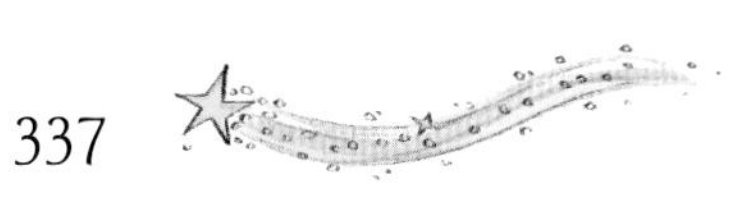

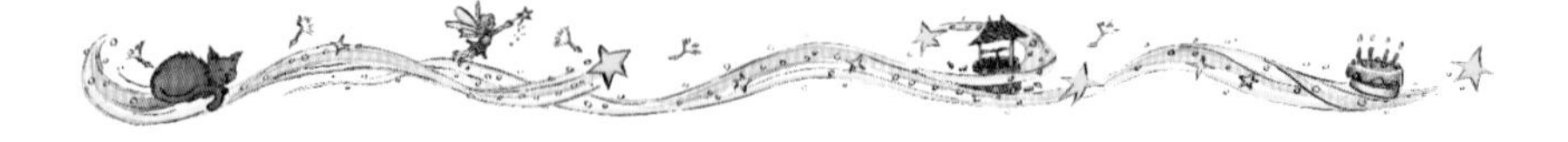

made up the fire for the night and they all slept peacefully until the day.

The old man looked better for his night's shelter, and as he rose to leave he spoke to Liam's mother.

"I have no money to offer you but I would like to thank you for your shelter and food, and I would like to repay the boy here for his kindness," and he turned and looked at Liam with his gentle brown eyes. "I know you have lost your cows so I will tell you where you can find some special cows who will give you milk such as you have never tasted before. Tonight is a full moon and the sea-folk will bring their cattle up out of the sea to graze on the green grass that grows just beyond the shoreline."

Liam's mother laughed. "I have often heard tales of these marvellous cattle, but in all the years I have lived here I have never seen a fairy cow."

"That is because your eyes have not been

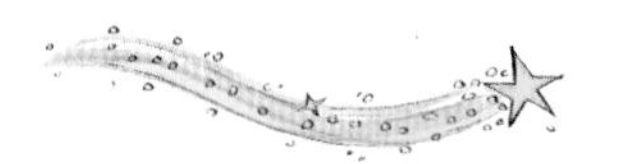

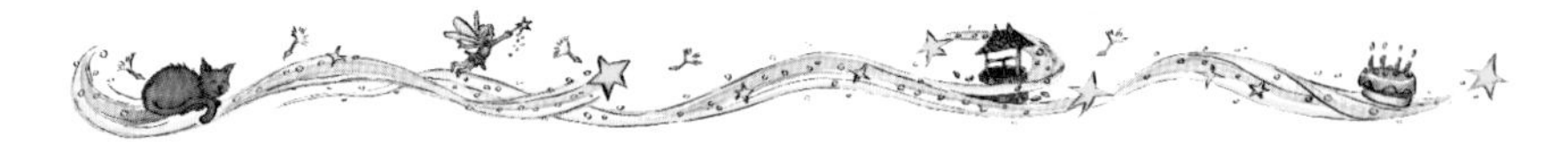

opened by a touch with the heather that grows on the grave of Fionn who died all those years ago," said the old man and there in his hand he held out a sprig of heather. "Will you let me touch your eyes, and the boy's too? Then you shall see."

Well, Liam's mother felt she had nothing to fear from this kindly old man and so both she and Liam let him touch their eyes with the heather.

"Now," he said, "you must gather seven handfuls of earth from the churchyard, and then tonight go to the meadow just beyond the shoreline. There you will see the fairy cattle. Choose the seven you like the best and throw the earth onto each one. They will all run back to the sea, save the seven that you have chosen. Bring those seven back home and look after them in your kindly way and they will be with you always. Now I must return from whence I came. Liam, will you

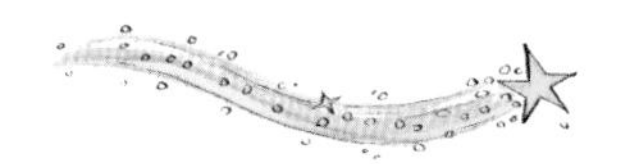

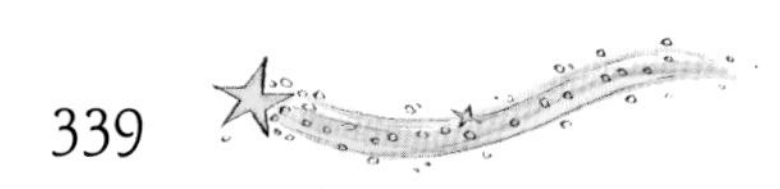

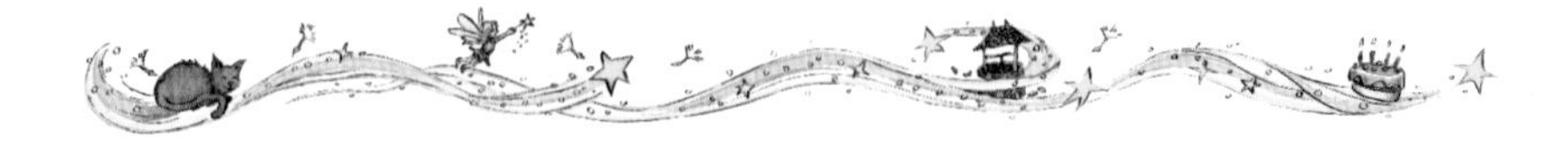

walk with me to the sea?" and the old man looked at Liam with those gentle eyes once again.

So Liam and the strange old man walked to the shoreline. One moment they were together on the sand, the next Liam was alone. But when he looked out to sea, there was a seal, looking at him. Then with a ripple, it was gone under the waves.

That night, Liam and his mother did as the old man had bid. They gathered the earth from the churchyard and made their way quietly down to the meadow. There indeed was the herd of fairy cattle. They were small, no bigger than a sheepdog, and all colours. Liam and his mother choose three black, three white and a brindled one, and Liam crept up behind them and threw the earth onto their backs. The

rest of the herd scattered back down to the shore and ran into the waves where they quickly disappeared. But the seven in the meadow stood quietly and showed no fear as Liam and his mother led them home.

From that day on, Liam and his mother had a plentiful supply of creamy milk. The little fairy cattle would low gently in the byre and were well content with their life on land. But Liam would never let them out to graze when there was a full moon in case the sea-folk came to get them back.

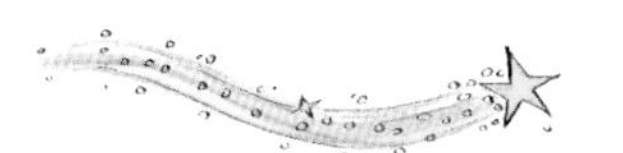

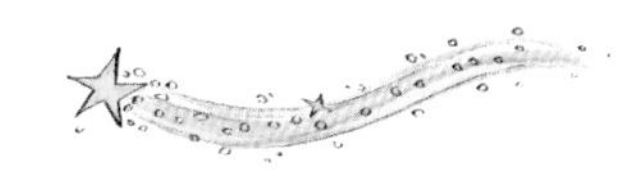

Androcles and the Lion

A retelling from the Fables of Phaedrus

Many thousands of years ago there lived a poor slave called Androcles. Life was very miserable for slaves. They barely had enough to eat, and if they didn't work hard enough they were sent to Rome to be thrown to the lions.

One day, Androcles had a chance to escape. He ran and ran, until he was utterly exhausted. Then he crawled into a forest to hide until he regained his strength. He was just settling down to sleep

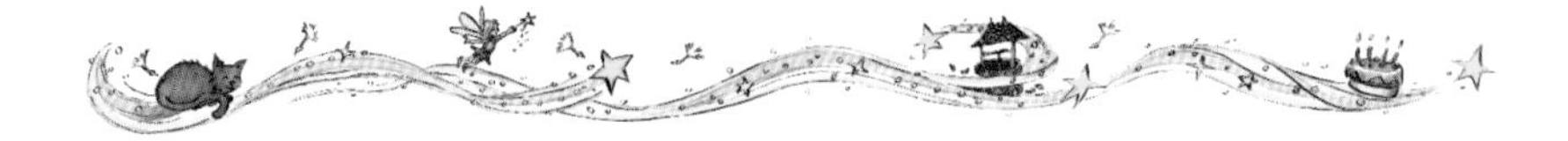

when a great lion hobbled out from behind a tree. At first, Androcles was petrified, but he soon realized the lion was not about to jump on him, but was holding out his paw helplessly. Androcles stepped cautiously towards the lion. The paw was all swollen and bleeding, and when Androcles looked closely he could see a huge thorn stuck in-between the claws.

Androcles pulled the thorn out, and cleaned the wound before wrapping it in leaves to keep it dry. The lion licked Androcles with his rough tongue and then lay down beside him and went to sleep. He kept Androcles warm all night. In the morning the lion slipped away very early and Androcles continued on his way.

Years passed. But one day Androcles' luck ran out and he was captured and sent into the arena to fight. The trapdoor was opened and a huge lion came bounding up to Androcles. He closed his eyes, waiting for death. But then he felt a rough tongue licking his face. It was his lion! The crowds cheered, and the emperor made Androcles tell the story of the thorn in the lion's paw. The emperor decided to free Androcles and the lion.

Androcles kept the lion's paws free of thorns, while the lion kept Androcles warm at night, and so they both lived to a very ripe old age together.

The Lion and the Mouse

A retelling from Aesop's Fables

The lion was very hungry. As he padded through the tall grass, something rustled by his feet. He reached out a great paw, and there was a squeak. He had caught a tiny mouse by the tail.

"Oh please let me go, dear lion," cried the tiny mouse. "I should be no more than a single mouthful for you. And I promise I will be able to help you some day."

The lion roared with laughter. The thought of a

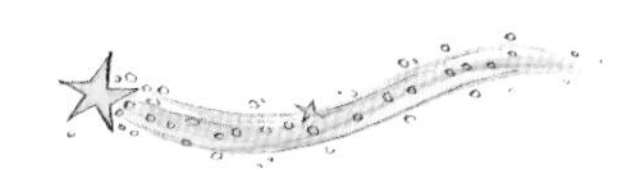

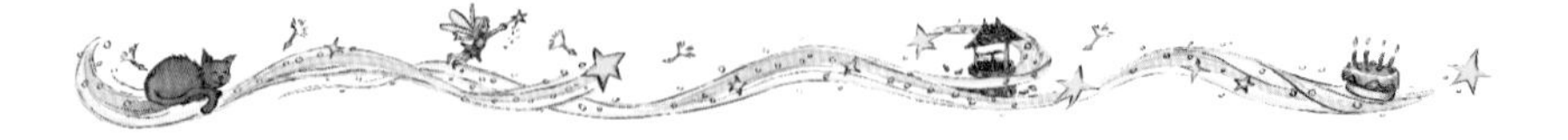

tiny mouse being able to help such a huge creature as himself amused him so much that he did let the mouse go.

"He would not have made much of a meal anyway," smiled the lion.

The mouse scuttled away, calling out to the lion, "I shall not forget my promise!"

Many days and nights later the lion was padding through the grass again when he fell into a deep pit. A net was flung over him, and he lay there helpless, caught by some hunters. He twisted and turned but he could not free himself. The hunters just laughed at his struggles and went off to fetch a cart to carry the great lion back to their village.

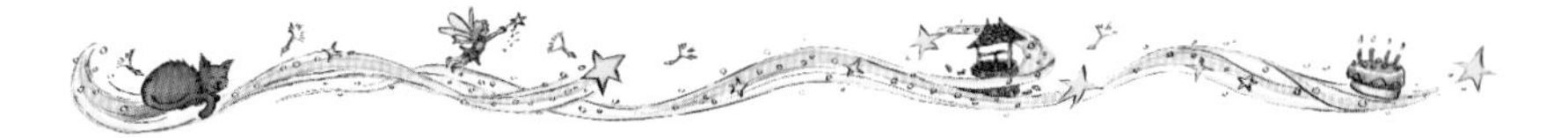

As he lay there, the lion heard a tiny voice.

"I promised I'd be able to help you one day."

It was the tiny mouse! And straight away he began to gnaw through the rope that held the lion fast. He gnawed and chewed, and chewed and gnawed, and eventually he chewed and gnawed right through the rope and the lion was free. With a great bound, he leapt out of the pit and then reached back, very gently, to lift the tiny mouse out too.

"I shall never forget you, mouse. Thank you for remembering your promise and saving me," purred the great lion.

So the tiny mouse was able to help the great lion. One good turn deserves another, you see?

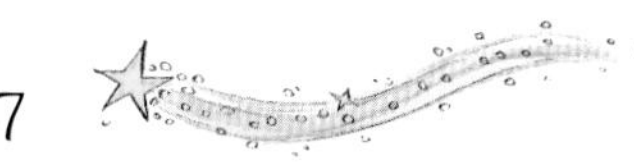

Whippety Stourie

Anon

There was once a gentleman that lived in a very grand house, and he married a young lady who had been delicately brought up. In her husband's house she found everything that was fine – fine tables and chairs, fine looking-glasses, and fine curtains, but then her husband expected her to be able to spin twelve balls of thread every day, besides attending to her house, and, to tell the truth, the lady could not spin a bit. This made her

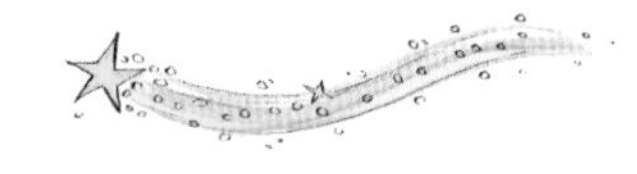

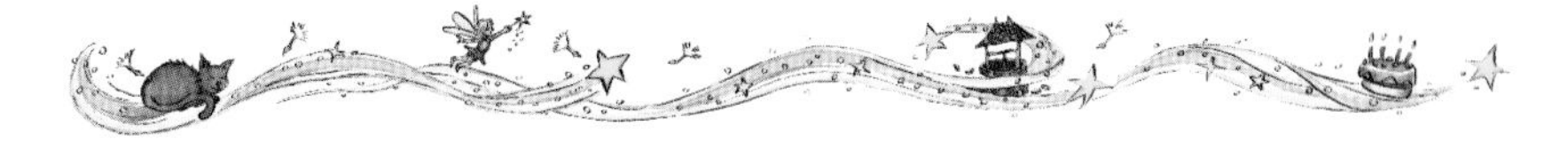

husband cross with her, and, before a month had passed, she found herself very unhappy.

One day the husband went away upon a journey, after telling her that he expected her, before his return, to have not only learned to spin, but to have spun a hundred balls of thread. Quite downcast, she took a walk along the hillside, till she came to a big flat stone, and there she sat down and cried. By and by she heard a strain of fine music, coming as it were from underneath the stone, and, on turning it up, she saw a cave below, where there were sitting six wee ladies in green gowns, each one of them spinning on a little wheel, and singing:

"Little knows my dame at hame
That Whippety Stourie is my name."

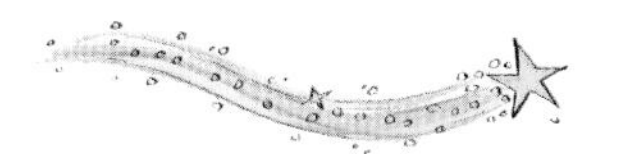

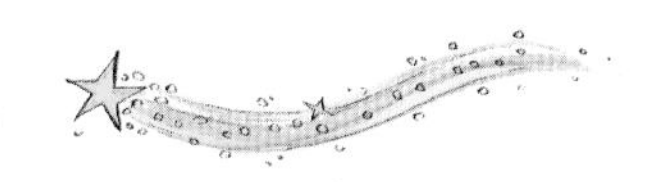

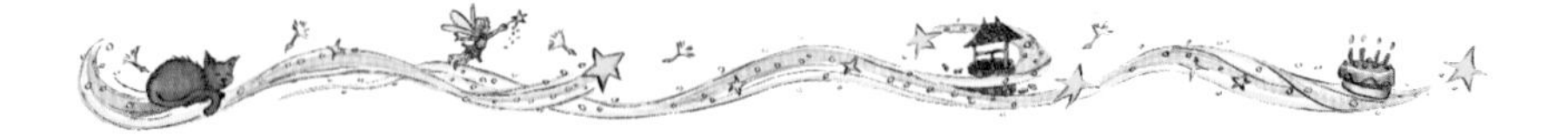

The lady walked into the cave, and was kindly asked by the wee bodies to take a chair and sit down, while they still continued their spinning. She observed that each one's mouth was twisted away to one side, but she did not venture to guess the reason. They asked why she looked so unhappy. She told them that she was expected by her husband to be a good spinner, when the plain truth was that she could not spin at all, and found herself quite unable for it, having been so delicately brought up. Neither was there any need for it, as her husband was a rich man.

"Oh, is that all?" said the little wifies, speaking out of their cheeks alike.

"Yes," said the lady, her heart like to burst with distress.

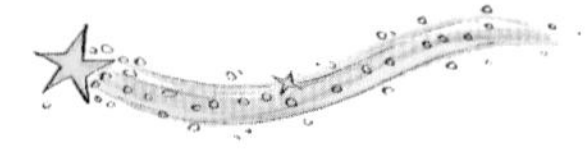

"We could easily quit ye of that trouble," said the wee women. "Just ask us all to dinner for the day when your husband is to come back. We'll then let you see how we'll manage him."

So the lady asked them all to dine with herself and her husband, on the day when he was to come back.

When the good man came home, he found the house so occupied with preparations for dinner, that he had no time to ask his wife about her thread, and, before ever he had once spoken to her on the subject, the company was announced at the hall door. The six fairy ladies all came in a coach-and-six, and were as fine as princesses, but still wore their gowns of green. The gentleman was very polite, and showed them up the stairs with a pair of wax candles in his hand. And so they all sat down to dinner, and conversation went on very

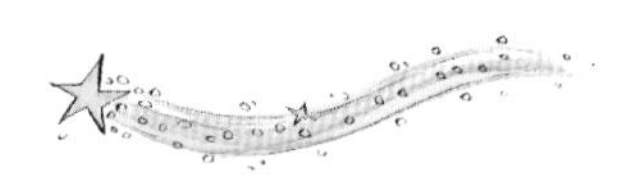

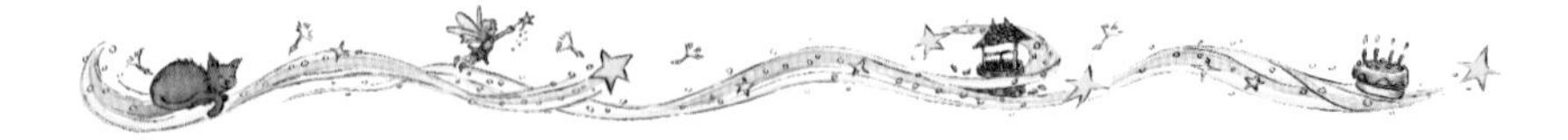

pleasantly, till at length the husband, becoming familiar with them, said:

"Ladies, if it be not an uncivil question, I should like to know how it happens that all your mouths are turned away to one side?"

"Oh," said each one at once, "it's with our constant spin-spin-spinning."

"Is that the case?" cried the gentleman. "Then, John, Tam, and Dick, make haste and burn every rock, and reel, and spinning-wheel in the house, for I'll not have my wife to spoil her bonnie face with spin-spin-spinning."

And so the lady lived happily with her good man all the rest of her days.

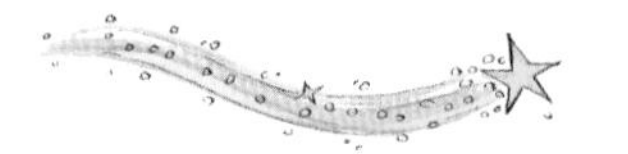

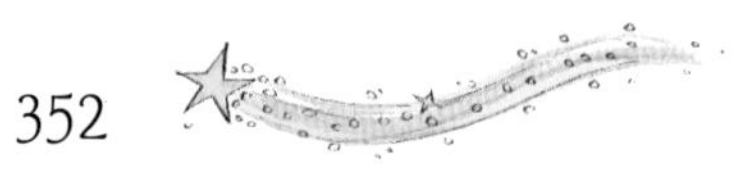

The Elves and the Shoemaker

By the Brothers Grimm

Once there was a shoemaker who worked hard from morn to night. The shoes he made were of the finest leather, but business was slow. One night he found he only had enough leather left for one more pair of shoes. With a heavy heart, he cut the leather carefully and left the pieces ready on his work bench to sew the next morning. He blew out the candle, and crossed the yard from his little shop into the house.

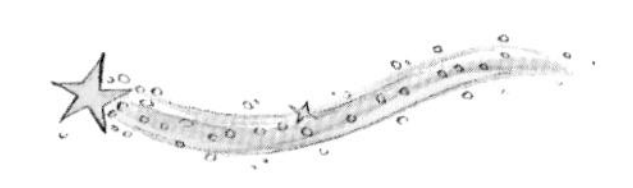

The next day the shoemaker was up early as usual. When he pulled back the shutters in the shop, you can imagine his surprise when he saw not pieces of leather ready to sew on the bench, but a fine pair of ladies' shoes with delicate pointed toes. The stitching was so fine you would think it had been done by mice. He put the shoes in the window of the shop, and before long a rich merchant came in and bought the shoes for his new wife, paying the poor shoemaker double the usual price. The shoemaker was delighted at this

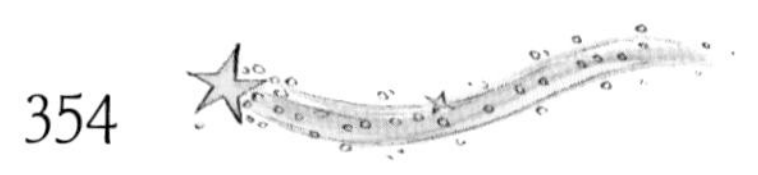

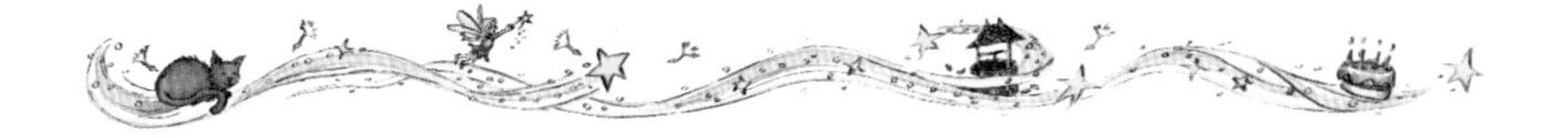

turn in his fortunes, and bought enough leather to make two new pairs of shoes. Once again, he cut the leather, and left the pieces on his work bench to sew the next day.

The next day the shoemaker was up even earlier than usual. His wife came with him as he went into the shop, and pulled back the shutters.

"Oh husband," she gasped, for there on the bench stood two pairs of the finest shoes she had ever seen. There was a green pair with red heels, and a pair so shiny and black the shoemaker could see his face in them. He put the shoes in the window, and very quickly in came a poet who bought the green pair with red heels, and not far behind him there was a parson who bought the shiny black pair. And both paid him a great deal of money for the splendid shoes with stitching so fine you would think it had been done by mice.

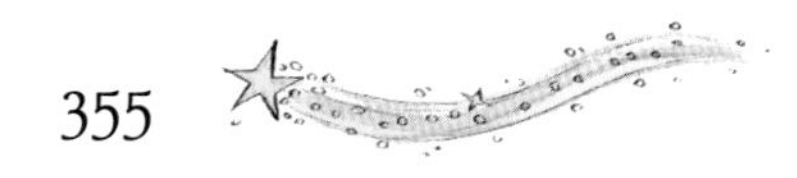

This continued for many days. The shoemaker would buy new leather and leave the pieces cut ready on his bench at night, and when he came back in the morning there would be the most exquisite shoes. The shoemaker's reputation spread, and his shop was soon full of customers. Before long the shoemaker and his wife were no longer poor, but they still lived simply as they had little wish for the luxuries of life.

One day, the wife said,"Husband, I think we must see who has given us this good fortune so we may thank them."

The shoemaker agreed, so that night after laying out the cut leather pieces, he and his wife hid behind the door of the shop. As the town hall clock struck midnight, they heard a scampering of tiny feet and little voices, laughing. Two elves slid out from behind the skirting board and climbed

onto the bench where they were soon hard at work, stitching away with tiny stitches that were so fine they might have been done by mice. The elves sang as they stitched, but oh! They looked poor. Their trousers were ragged, their shirts were threadbare and their feet looked frozen as they had neither socks nor shoes.

Soon the leather was gone, and on the bench stood more shoes. The elves slipped away.

The next day, the shoemaker took some green-and-yellow leather and made two little pairs of boots, yellow with green heels. The wife took some

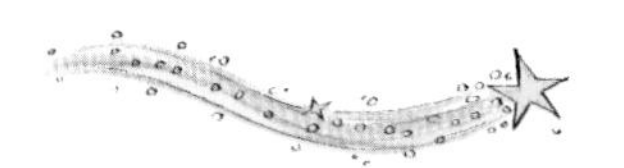

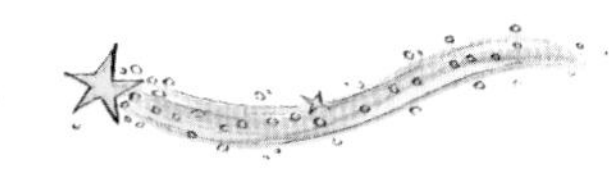

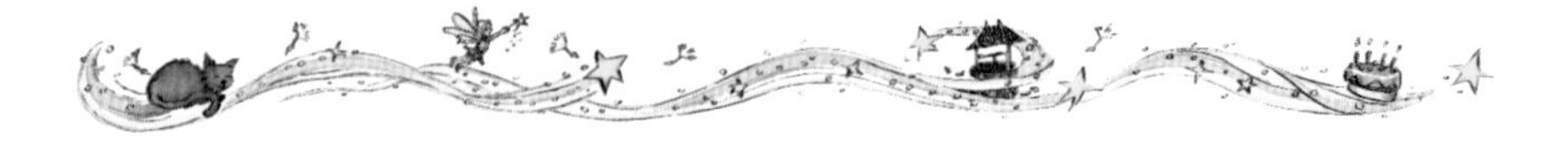

cloth and made two little pairs of red trousers and two green jackets with silver buttons. She knitted two little pairs of socks. That night, they laid out the clothes and boots, and hid behind the shop door.

As the town hall clock struck midnight, the two elves slid out from behind the skirting board and climbed onto the bench. When they saw the gifts, they clapped their hands in delight, flung off their old rags and tried on their new clothes and the boots. They looked splendid. Then they slipped behind the skirting board, and the shoemaker and his wife never saw them again.

But once a year when the shoemaker opened the shop in the morning, on his bench he would find a pair of shoes with stitching so fine you would think it had been done by mice.

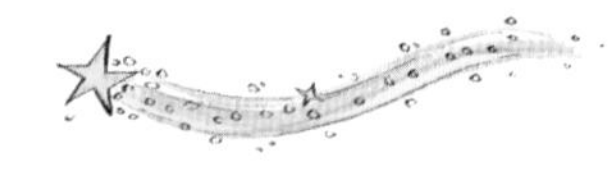

The Fairy Cure

By Patrick Kennedy

For nearly a year, Nora's daughter, Judy, had been in bed with a sore leg. There was nothing that anyone could do.

Nora was a midwife, and one night she was whisked away to a magnificent palace to help a lady about to have a child. In the hall she saw an old neighbour, who warned Nora not to take any refreshments or reward. She could, however, take a cure for a fairy disease.

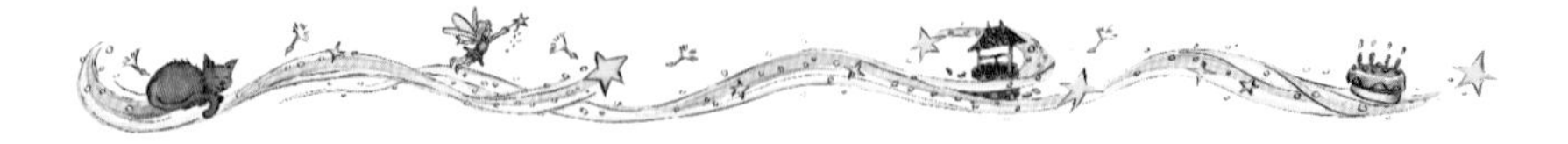

She found the lady of the castle in a bed and in a short time she gave birth to a beautiful little girl. "I am so pleased with you," said the lady. "Please take as much gold, silver and jewels out of the next room as you can carry."

Out of curiosity, Nora stepped in and saw piles of gold and silver coins, and baskets of diamonds and pearls, lying about on every side, but she remembered her caution.

"I'm much obliged to you, my lady," said she, "but if I took jewels home, no one would ever call on me again to help his wife, and I'd be sitting and doing nothing but drinking tea. I'd be dead before a year'd gone by."

"Oh dear!" said the lady, "What an odd person you are! At any rate, sit down at that table, and help yourself to food and drink."

"I'm not hungry, thank you ma'am."

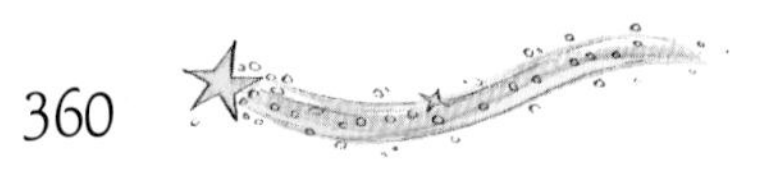

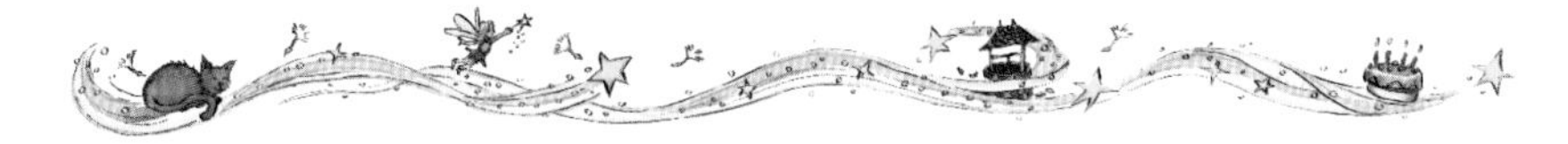

"Alas! Is there any way in which I can show you how grateful I am for your help and skill?"

"Indeed is there, ma'am. My girl, Jude, has had a sore leg for twelve months, an' I'm sure that the lord or yourself can make her as sound as a bell if you only say the word."

"Ask me anything but that."

"Oh, lady, dear, that's giving me everything but the thing I want."

"You don't know the offence your daughter gave to us, or you would not ask me to cure her. You know that all the fairy court enjoy their lives in the night only, and we frequently go through the country, and hold our feasts where the kitchen, and especially the hearth, is swept up clean. About a twelvemonth ago, myself and my ladies were passing your cabin, and one of the company liked the appearance of the neat thatch, and the

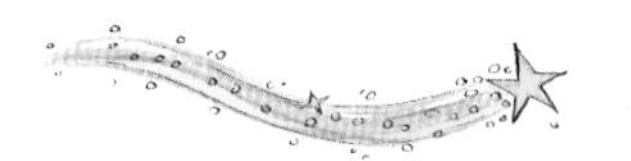

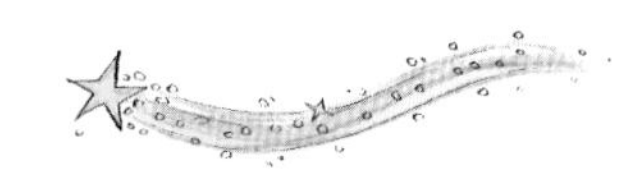

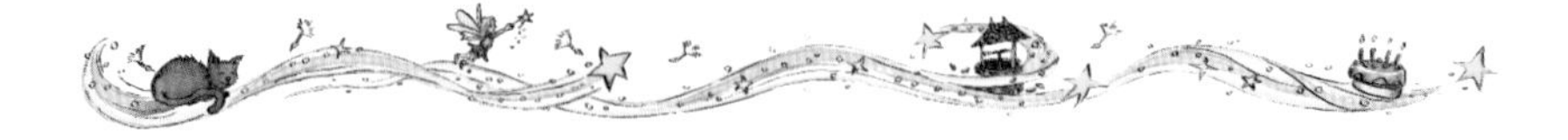

whitewashed walls, and the clean pavement outside the door, so much, that she persuaded us all to go in. We found the cheerful fire shining, the well swept hearth and floor, and the clean pewter and plates on the dresser, and the white table. We were so well pleased, that we sat down on the hearth, and laid our tea tray, and began to drink our tea as comfortably as could be."

"We were vexed enough when we saw your daughter come out of your bedroom, and make towards the fire. Her feet were clean, but one of them would cover two or three of us. On she came, and just as I was raising my cup of tea to my lips, down came the soft flat sole on it, and spilled the tea all over me. I was very much annoyed, and I caught the thing that came next to my hand, and hurled it at her. It was the tea pot, and the point of the spout is in her leg from that night till now."

"Oh, lady! The poor girl didn't know you were there!"

"Well, take this ointment, and rub it where you will see the purple mark, and I hope that your thoughts of me may be pleasant."

With that, Nora returned home, stripped the clothes off her daughter's leg, rubbed some of the stuff on it, and in a few seconds she saw the skin bursting, and a tiny spout of a tea-pot working itself out.

From then on, they took good care never to let their feet stray after bedtime, for fear of hurting any unseen visitors.

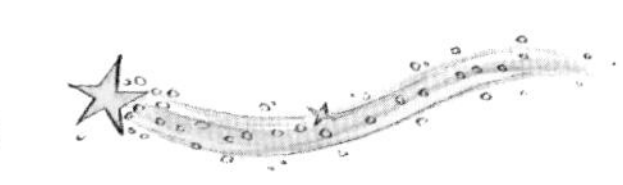

Farmer Mybrow and the Fairies

By William H Barker

Farmer Mybrow was one day looking about for a suitable piece of land to convert into a field. He wished to grow corn and yams. He discovered a fine spot, close to a great forest – which was the home of some fairies. He set to work at once to prepare the field.

Having sharpened his great knife, he began to cut down the bushes. No sooner had he touched one than he heard a voice say, "Who is there,

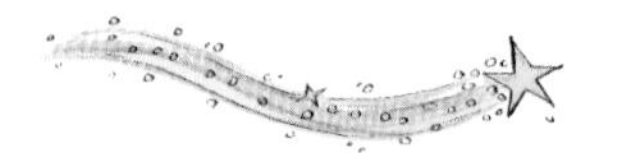

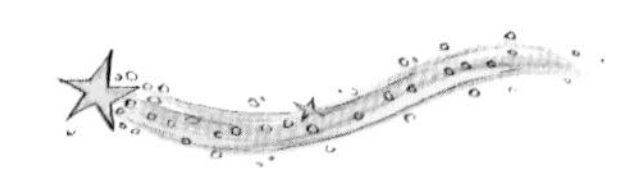

cutting down the bushes?"

Mybrow was too much astonished to answer. The question was repeated. This time the farmer realized that it must be one of the fairies, and so replied, "I am Mybrow, come to prepare a field."

Fortunately for him the fairies were in great good humour. He heard one say, "Let us all help Farmer Mybrow to cut down the bushes." The rest agreed. To Mybrow's great delight, the bushes

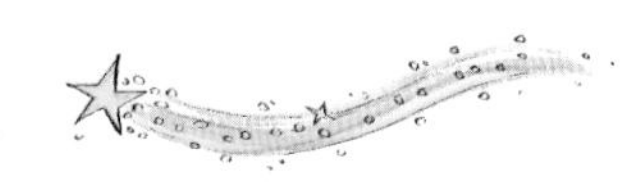

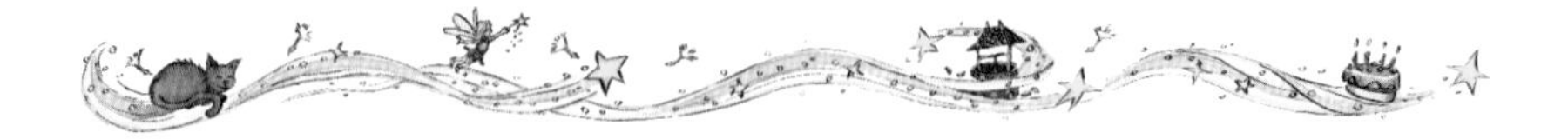

were all rapidly cut down with very little trouble on his part. He returned home, exceedingly well pleased with his day's work, having resolved to keep the field a secret even from his wife.

Early in January, when it was time to burn the dry bush, he set off to his field, one afternoon, with the means of making a fire. Hoping to have the fairies' assistance once more, he intentionally struck the trunk of a tree as he passed. Immediately came the question, "Who is there, striking the stumps?"

He promptly replied, "I am Mybrow, come to burn down the bush." Accordingly, the dried bushes were all burned down, and the field left clear in less time that it takes to tell it.

Next day the same thing happened. Mybrow came to chop up the stumps for firewood and clear the field for digging. In a very short time his

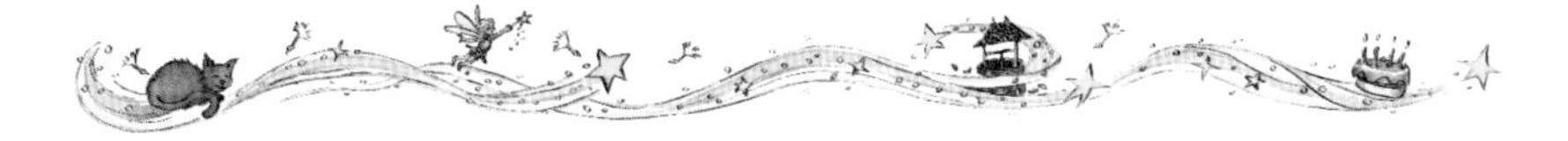

faggots and firewood were piled ready, while the field was bare.

So it went on. The field was divided into two parts – one for maize and one for yams. In all the preparations – digging, sowing, planting – the fairies gave great assistance. Still, the farmer had managed to keep the whereabouts of his field a secret from his wife and neighbours.

The soil having been so carefully prepared, the crops promised exceedingly well. Mybrow visited them from time to time, and congratulated himself on the splendid harvest he would have.

One day, while maize and yams were still in their green and milky state, Mybrow's wife came to him. She wished to know where his field lay, that she might go and fetch some of the firewood from it. At first he refused to tell her. Being very persistent, however, she finally succeeded in

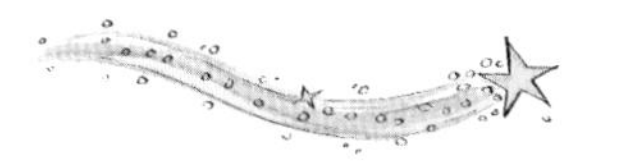

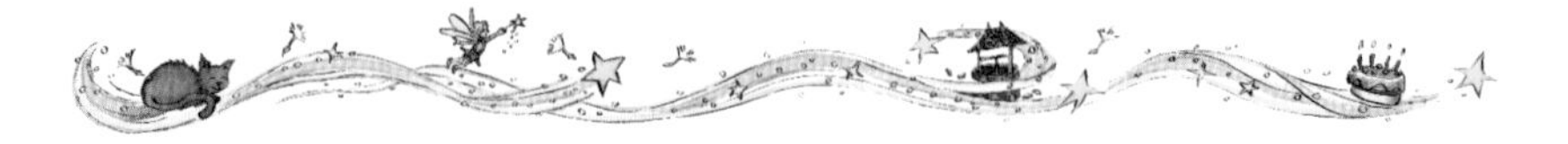

obtaining the information – but on one condition. She must not answer any question that should be asked her. This she readily promised, and set off for the field.

When she arrived there she was utterly amazed at the wealth of the corn and yam. She had never seen such magnificent crops. The maize looked most tempting – being still in the milky state – so she plucked an ear. While doing so she heard a voice say, "Who is there, breaking the corn?"

"Who dares ask me such a question?" she replied angrily – quite forgetting her husband's command. Going to the field of yams she plucked one of them also.

"Who is there, picking the yams?" came the question again.

"I, Mybrow's wife. This is my husband's field and I have a right to pick." Out came the fairies.

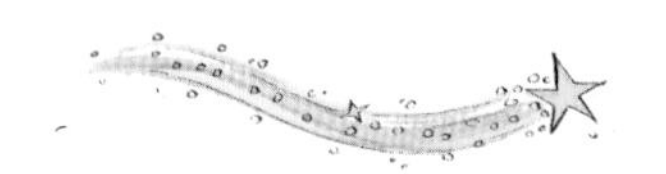

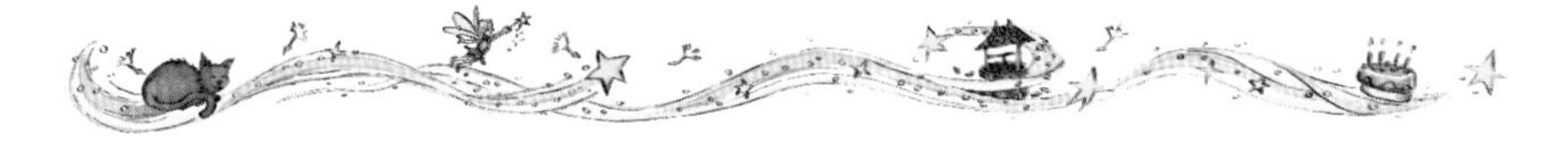

"Let us all help Mybrow's wife to pluck her corn and yams," said they. Before the frightened woman could say a word, the fairies had all set to work with a will, and the corn and yams lay useless on the ground. Being all green and unripe, the harvest was now utterly spoiled. The farmer's wife wept bitterly, but to no purpose. She returned slowly home, not knowing what to say to her husband about such a terrible catastrophe. She decided to keep silent about the matter.

Accordingly, next day the poor man set off gleefully to his field to see how his fine crops were going on. His anger and dismay may be imagined when he saw his field a complete ruin. All his work and foresight had been absolutely ruined through his wife's forgetfulness of her promise.

In the Castle of Giant Cruelty

Retold from an original tale in John Bunyan's
The Pilgrim's Progress

There was once a dark, ugly city where no one seemed to be happy. But none of the grumpy citizens ever thought of leaving because they knew nothing of life outside the city walls. Huge, flat plains of mud surrounded the city as far as the eye could see. No one had ever braved the danger of trying to wade through them, so no one even knew if there was anything beyond the swamps. There were rumours of a distant city where the sun

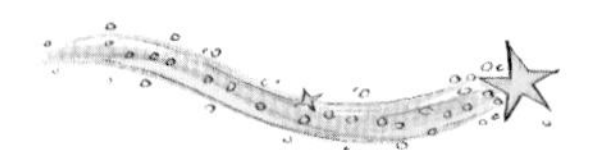

always shone and where the people lived happily together – but no one really believed it existed... that is, except for a man called Christian.

For a long time, Christian had been growing more and more miserable with his life in the grim, depressing city. But it was the strange, glowing light that finally made him decide to leave. It was some weeks ago that Christian had first glimpsed the light, far away in the distance, beyond the mud flats. No one else seemed to be able to see it. They just shuffled around with their hands in their pockets, looking at the pavements as usual. But Christian thought the light was beautiful. "I shall leave this dreadful city and somehow reach the place the light is coming from," he decided. "Or I shall die in the attempt," he added.

Christian didn't take anything with him. He just got up the next morning and instead of making

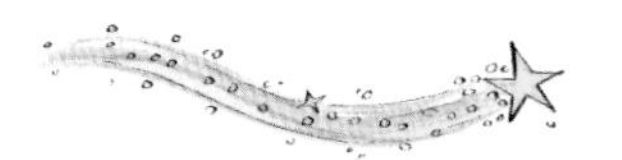

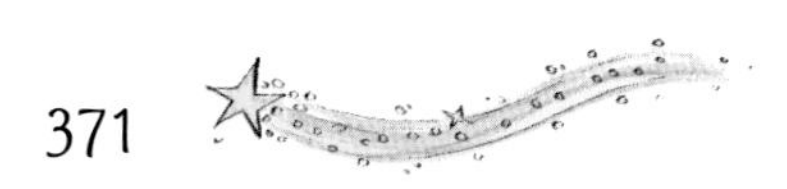

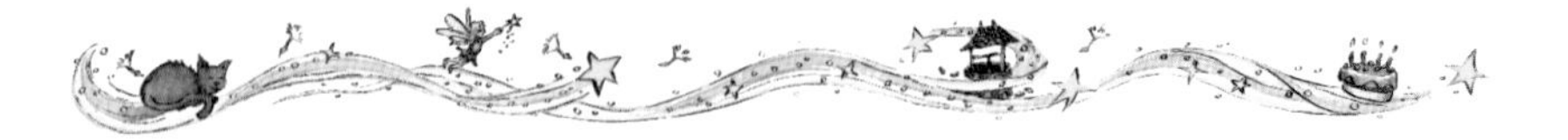

his usual way to work, he walked towards the gates that led out of the city. As people realized that Christian meant to leave town, they began to laugh and jeer at him. "You must be mad!" they mocked. "You'll be floundering in that mud by nightfall and no one will come to rescue you!" But Christian didn't listen to them. He just heaved open the rusty, creaky city gates and strode out into the swamps.

As soon as Christian was outside the city, he felt as if he had left his cares and troubles behind him. Determinedly, he began walking towards the light in the distance. He walked... and walked... and

walked... until he had left the city so far behind that he couldn't see its dark, smoky outline any more. He walked and walked until he dropped with thirst and hunger and exhaustion. Christian didn't have the strength to lift himself back up. He closed his eyes and everything went black.

It was having a huge bucket of water sloshed over his face that finally brought Christian back to his senses. He sat bolt upright, spluttering out the iciness that filled his nose and mouth.

"I am the Giant Cruelty!" boomed the loudest voice that Christian had ever heard. He looked up and began to tremble. He was in a stone room the size of a cave, and standing over him was a man as tall as his house back in the city. The giant had blood-shot eyes and blackened teeth and long, claw-like nails. "What were you doing, trespassing on my land?" Giant Cruelty thundered.

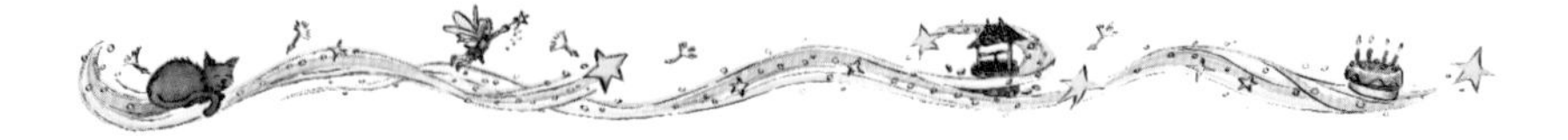

"I'm v-v-very s-s-s-orry," Christian stuttered. "I d-d-didn't realize I was trespassing."

"That is a pitiful excuse!" the giant bellowed. "Now you are no longer a trespasser. You are a prisoner," he boomed, and scooped Christian up in his mighty fist.

Christian's heart thumped as he felt himself being carried down a long flight of steps. He shivered at the echoing of the giant's footsteps and at the damp chill in the air. He wrinkled his nose in disgust as a vile stench filled his nostrils.

Suddenly, the giant's fist opened and Christian was thrown onto the stone floor of a dungeon. A rat scampered up and squeaked in his face, and Christian sprang to his feet with shock.

"Have this bread and water," Giant Cruelty ordered, hurling a

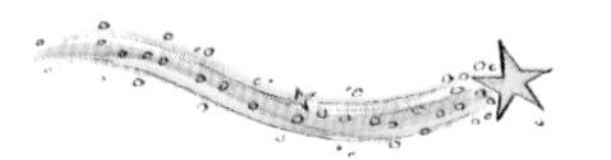

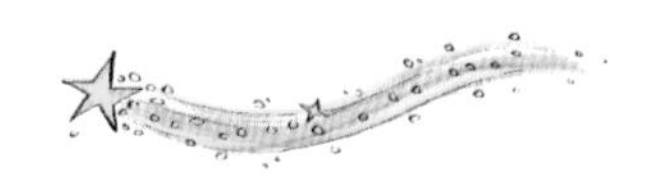

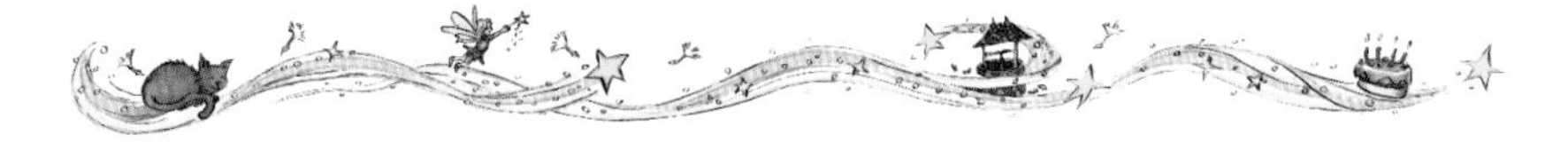

mouldy loaf at Christian and slamming down a bucket of foul-smelling water.

"You have to stay alive so I can come back tomorrow and watch you scream and cry and beg for mercy." Giant Cruelty chuckled. He slammed the door of the dungeon, locked it with a massive iron key, and stomped back up the stairs.

Christian swallowed hard and turned away from the locked door. He wasn't the only prisoner after all. Six faces peered out from the shadows.

"How long have you been here?" Christian gulped.

"So long that we have forgotten our own names," one man sighed.

"The giant only feeds us once a week," a woman whimpered, eyeing Christian's bread and water.

"Here, share with me. If we stay strong and help each other, maybe we can find a way out of here."

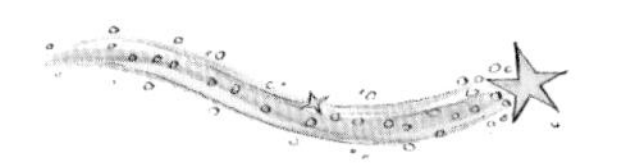

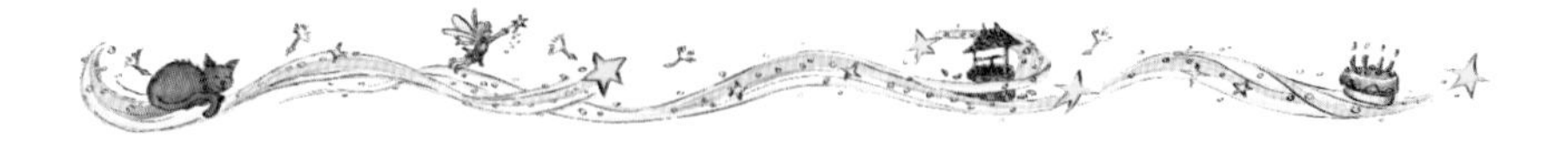

The men and women didn't need inviting twice, and ate the bread hungrily.

At that very moment, a spine-tingling CREAK! filled the air and the dungeon door swung wide open. To Christian's astonishment, a golden key had appeared in the lock. There were words down the shaft which read: the Key of Kindness.

Christian grabbed it and urged, "Come on everybody!" The key fitted every locked door they came to and the giant had disappeared.

Christian and his new friends didn't stop running until they had left the castle far behind them. Christian smiled. Now he could see the faint outline of a golden city – and it was much closer than before. As he set off on his journey once more, he felt a new feeling. It was hope.

Favourite Tales

Chicken Licken

An English folk tale

One fine day Chicken Licken went for a walk in the woods. Now Chicken Licken was not very bright, and he was also rather inclined to act first and think after. So when an acorn fell on his head, he decided immediately that the sky must be falling in. He set off as fast as he could to tell the king. On the way he met Henny Penny and Cocky Locky.

"I am off to tell the king that the sky is falling

in," he clucked importantly.

"We will come too," said Henny Penny and Cocky Locky.

So Chicken Licken, Henny Penny and Cocky Locky set off to find the King. On the way they met Ducky Lucky and Drakey Lakey.

"We are off to tell the king that the sky is falling in," clucked Chicken Licken importantly.

"We will come too," said Ducky Lucky and Drakey Lakey.

So Chicken Licken, Henny Penny, Cocky Locky, Ducky Lucky and Drakey Lakey all set off to find the king. On the way they met Goosey Loosey and Turkey Lurkey.

"We are off to tell the king that the sky is falling in," clucked Chicken Licken importantly.

"We will come too," said Goosey Loosey and Turkey Lurkey.

So Chicken Licken, Henny Penny, Cocky Locky, Ducky Lucky, Drakey Lakey, Goosey Loosey and Turkey Lurkey all set off to find the king. On the way they met Foxy Loxy.

"We are off to tell the king that the sky is falling in," clucked Chicken Licken importantly.

"What a good thing I met you all," said Foxy Loxy with a cunning smile. "I know the way, follow me."

So Chicken Licken, Henny Penny, Cocky Locky, Ducky Lucky, Drakey Lakey, Goosey Loosey and Turkey Lurkey all set off behind Foxy Loxy. He led them all straight to his den where he ate every single one of them for his dinner! So the king never heard that the sky was falling in (it didn't, of course).

The Three Little Pigs

An English folk tale

There once was a mother pig who had three little pigs. They were very poor indeed, and the day came when the mother pig could no longer look after the family. She sent the three little pigs out into the big, wide world to seek their fortunes.

The first little pig met a man carrying a big bundle of straw.

"Oh, please may I have that bundle of straw to build myself a house?" asked the first little pig.

The man was tired of carrying the bundle of straw so he gladly gave it to the first little pig.

The first little pig built a very fine house out of the bundle of straw, and he lived there very happily. Then along came a big bad wolf.

"Little pig, little pig, let me in!" shouted the wolf.

"No, no, not by the hair on my chinny chin chin. I'll not let you in," squeaked the first little pig.

"Then I'll huff and I'll puff, and I'll blow your house down," yelled the wolf. And he did. He huffed and he puffed and he blew the straw house down. The first little pig ran away as fast as his trotters would carry him.

Now the second little pig met a man carrying a bundle of sticks.

"Oh, please may I have that bundle

of sticks to build myself a house?" asked the second little pig. The man was tired of carrying the bundle of sticks so he gladly gave it to the second little pig.

The second little pig built a very fine house out of the sticks, and he lived there very happily. Then along came the big bad wolf.

"Little pig, little pig, let me in!" shouted the wolf.

"No, no, not by the hair on my chinny chin chin. I'll not let you in," squeaked the second little pig.

"Then I'll huff and I'll puff, and I'll blow your house down," yelled the wolf. And he did. He huffed and he puffed and he blew the stick house down. The second little pig ran away as fast as his trotters would carry him.

Now the third little pig met a man carrying a big load of bricks.

"Oh, please may I have that load of bricks to build myself a house?" asked the third little pig. The man was very tired from carrying the big load of bricks so he gave it to the third little pig.

The third little pig built a very fine house out of the bricks, and he lived there very happily. Then along came the big bad wolf.

"Little pig, little pig, let me in!" shouted the wolf.

"No, no, not by the hair on my chinny chin chin. I'll not let you in," squeaked the third little pig.

"Then I'll huff and I'll puff, and I'll blow your house down," yelled the wolf. And he tried. He huffed and he puffed but he could not blow the brick house down.

"Little pig, little pig, I am coming down your chimney to get you," bellowed the wolf.

"Please yourself," called the third little pig who was busy with some preparations of his own.

"Little pig, little pig, I have my front paws down your chimney," threatened the wolf.

"Please yourself," called the third little pig who was still busy with some preparations of his own.

"Little pig, little pig, I have my great bushy tail down your chimney," called the wolf.

"Please yourself," called the third little pig who was now sitting in his rocking chair by the fireside.

"Little pig, little pig, here I come!" and with a great rush and a huge SPLOSH! the big bad wolf

fell right into the big pot of boiling water that the clever little pig had placed on the fire, right under the chimney. The wolf scrabbled and splashed and scrambled out of the big pot and ran as fast as ever he could right out of the front door. And he was never seen again. The third little pig managed to find his two brothers, and they went and fetched their mother. And they are all still living happily together in the little brick house.

The Hare and the Tortoise

An Aesop's fable

The day that Tortoise challenged Hare to a race, all the animals laughed so hard that their tummies ached. But Tortoise was fed-up with Hare whizzing round him all the time, teasing him about how slow he was. 'I'll show that Hare, if it's the last thing I do!' Tortoise promised himself.

Hare thought that Tortoise's little joke was extremely funny. For that's all Hare thought it was – a joke. Hare never expected that Tortoise would

actually go through with his mad idea. So his eyes nearly popped out of his head when he arrived at the starting line to see Tortoise already there, limbering up in a slow, stiff, creaky sort of way.

"Be careful there, old chap!" Hare worried, as he realized his friend was serious. "You don't want to do yourself an injury."

"Don't worry about me," replied Tortoise. "You should be working out how you're

going to beat me. Ha! You won't see me for dust!"

A huge crowd of animals had gathered to watch the race and they all cheered and clapped and jumped up and down at Tortoise's bold remark.

Suddenly, Hare started to feel rather annoyed. "All right then. If that's the way you want it!" he snapped. "I was going to give you a headstart, but obviously you won't be wanting one."

"No need," breezed Tortoise, although his little heart was pumping inside his shell. "First one to the windmill's the winner."

Hare peered into the distance. The windmill was three fields away. He could get there in less than a minute without losing his breath. But surely it would take Tortoise all day to reach it!

"Three! Twit-Two! One!" cried Barn Owl, and Tortoise lifted one leg over the starting line amid thunderous applause.

The stunned Hare watched in amazement as Tortoise began to crawl slowly away. Well, you have to hand it to Tortoise! Hare thought, seeing the funny side of things again. He's certainly got a good sense of humour and a lot of guts!

Hare sat down next to the starting line under a shady tree. It was a beautiful sunny day and

it was very pleasant to sit there in the dappled light, watching Tortoise amble peacefully into the field. Hare's eyes shut and his head drooped before he even realized he was sleepy...

Meanwhile, Tortoise was remembering what his mum had told him as a child: *Slow and steady does it, son. Slow and steady does it.* And Tortoise kept on going and didn't give up.

Hare didn't wake up until the night air was so cold that it was freezing his whiskers. *Where am I?* he thought. And then suddenly he remembered the race. Hare leapt to his feet and squinted into the moonlight, but there was no sign of Tortoise. All at once, he heard a faint sound of cheering coming from a long way off, and he saw tiny dark figures jumping up and down around the windmill. "Surely not!" Hare gasped, and shot off over the fields like an arrow. He arrived at the

windmill just in time to see all the animals hoisting Tortoise – the champion – on their shoulders. And of course, after that, Hare never ever teased his friend about being slow again.

Little Red Riding Hood

An English folk tale

There was once a little girl who lived in the middle of a deep, dark forest with her mother and father, who was a woodcutter. The little girl always wore a red cloak with a hood, and so she was called Little Red Riding Hood.

One day she decided to visit her granny who lived some way from the woodcutter's cottage. She took a basket with a cake her mother had baked and set off. Now the last thing her mother had

said to Little Red Riding Hood was, "Don't leave the path, and don't talk to any strangers." But Little Red Riding Hood was not really listening. So when she saw some bluebells growing under a

tree, she left the path and began to pick a bunch for her granny. Slowly, slowly she wandered further away from the path, deeper into the trees. Suddenly, she was not alone. There in front of her stood a great big wolf. Now Little Red Riding Hood had not met a wolf before so she did not realize that wolves are not the kind of animals to be too friendly with.

"Good day, little girl," said the wolf with a snarly sort of a smile. "What is your name and where are you going?"

"My name is Little Red Riding Hood. I am going to visit my granny, and I am taking her a cake to eat," replied Little Red Riding Hood.

The wolf was delighted. Not only a little girl to eat but a granny AND a cake as well!

"And where does your granny live, little girl?" asked the wolf, trying hard to smile nicely despite

his fierce teeth.

Little Red Riding Hood told the wolf where her granny lived, and went on picking bluebells. The wolf slipped away through the trees and soon found the granny's cottage. He tapped on the door and said, in a disguised voice, "Hello, granny. It is Little Red Riding Hood. I have brought you a cake, will you let me in?"

As soon as the door was open, the wolf bounded in and gobbled the granny all up! He put on her nightcap and shawl and climbed into her bed. Soon he heard Little Red Riding Hood coming and he tried his snarly smile again.

"Hello, granny," said Little Red Riding Hood. "I have brought you a cake and these bluebells,"

and she came up to the bedside.

"Goodness, granny! What great big eyes you have!" she said.

"All the better to see you with," growled the wolf.

Little Red Riding Hood could not help noticing the wolf's teeth.

"Goodness, granny! What great big teeth you have!"

"All the better to eat you with!" snapped the wolf and gobbled up Little Red Riding Hood. He gobbled up the cake in the basket as well and then, very full indeed, he fell fast asleep, snoring loudly.

Now by great good luck, Little Red

Riding Hood's father was passing by the cottage, and when he heard the terrible snores, he put his head round the door to see who was making such a noise. He was horrified to see the wolf so he took his axe and made a great slit down the wolf's tummy. Out jumped Little Red Riding Hood and granny. She stitched up the wolf's tummy and told him to mind his manners in future. Then, as there was no cake left for tea, they all went back home, and Little Red Riding Hood's

mother made pancakes. I am pleased to say Little Red Riding Hood had learnt her lesson, and she never spoke to wolves again.

Goldilocks and the Three Bears

By Andrew Lang

Once upon a time there was a little girl called Goldilocks who lived in a great forest with her mother and her father. Now ever since she was tiny, her mother had told her she must never, ever wander off into the forest for it was full of wild creatures, especially bears. But as Goldilocks grew older she longed to explore the forest.

One washday, when her mother was busy in the kitchen, hidden in clouds of steam, Goldilocks

sneaked off down the path that led deep into the forest. At first she was happy, looking at the wild flowers and listening to the birds singing, but it did not take long for her to become hopelessly lost.

She wandered for hours and hours and, as it

grew darker, she became frightened. She started to cry, but then she saw a light shining through the trees. She rushed forward, sure she had found her way home, only to realize that it was not her own cottage that she was looking at. Even so, she opened the door and looked inside.

On a scrubbed wooden table there were three bowls of steaming hot porridge – a big one, a middle-sized one and a little one. Goldilocks was so tired that she quite forgot all her manners and just sat down at the table. The big bowl was too tall for her to reach. The middle-sized bowl was too hot. But the little one was just right, so she ate all the porridge.

By the warm fire there were three chairs – a big one, a middle-sized one and a little one. Goldilocks couldn't climb up into the big one. The middle-sized one was too hard. The little one was just the right size, but as soon as she sat down, it broke into pieces. Goldilocks scrambled to her feet and then noticed there were steps going upstairs, where she found three beds – a big one, a middle-sized

one and a little one. The big bed was too hard. The middle-sized one was too soft. But the little one was just right and she was soon fast asleep.

The cottage belonged to three bears, and it was not long before they came home. They knew at once that someone had been inside.

Father Bear growled, "Who has been eating my porridge?"

Mother Bear grumbled, "Who has been eating my porridge?"

And Baby Bear gasped, "Who has been eating my porridge, AND has eaten it all?"

The bears looked round the room. They looked at the chairs by the warm fire.

Father Bear growled, "Who has been sitting in my chair?"

Mother Bear grumbled, "Who has been sitting in my chair?"

And Baby Bear gasped, "Who has been sitting in my chair, AND has broken it to bits?"

The bears went upstairs to look at their beds.

Father Bear growled, "Who has been sleeping in my bed?"

Mother Bear grumbled, "Who has been sleeping in my bed?"

And Baby Bear gasped, "Who has been sleeping in my bed, AND is still there?"

Suddenly Goldilocks woke up. All she could see was three very cross-looking bears. She jumped off the bed, ran down the stairs and out of the door. She ran and ran and ran, and by good fortune

found herself outside her own cottage. Her mother and father scolded her, but then gave her lots of hugs and kisses, and a big bowl of soup. Goldilocks had certainly learnt her lesson, and she never ever wandered off again.

The Gingerbread Man

An English folk tale

One fine sunny day, an old woman was making some ginger biscuits. She had a little dough left over and so she made a gingerbread man for her husband. She gave him raisins for eyes and cherries for buttons, and put a smile on his face with a piece of orange peel. Then she popped the biscuits and gingerbread man in the oven. A little while later, she lifted the tray out of the oven when the biscuits were cooked. Suddenly,

the gingerbread man hopped off the tray and ran straight out of the door! The old woman ran after him, and her husband ran after her, but they couldn't catch the gingerbread man. He called out, "Run, run, as fast as you can! You can't catch me, I'm the gingerbread man!"

The old dog in his kennel ran after the old man and the old woman, but he couldn't catch the gingerbread man. The ginger cat, who had been asleep in the sun, ran after the dog, but she couldn't catch the gingerbread man. He called out, "Run, run, as fast as you can! You can't catch me, I'm the gingerbread man!"

The brown cow in the meadow lumbered after the cat, but she couldn't catch the gingerbread man.

The black horse in the stable galloped after the cow but he couldn't catch the gingerbread

man. He called out, "Run, run, as fast as you can! You can't catch me, I'm the gingerbread man!"

The fat pink pig in the sty trotted after the horse, but she couldn't catch the gingerbread man. The rooster flapped and squawked after the pig but he couldn't catch the gingerbread man. He called out, "Run, run, as fast as you can! You can't catch me, I'm the gingerbread man!"

He ran and ran, and the old woman and the old man, the dog and the cat, the cow and the horse, the pig and the rooster all ran after him. He kept running until he came to the river. For the first time since he had hopped out of the oven, the gingerbread man had to stop running.

"Help, help! How can I cross the river?" he cried.

A sly fox suddenly appeared by his side.

"I could carry you across the river," said the sly fox.

The gingerbread man jumped onto the fox's back, and the fox slid into the water.

"My feet are getting wet," complained the gingerbread man.

"Well, jump onto my head," smiled the fox, showing a lot of very sharp teeth. And he kept on swimming.

"My feet are still getting wet," complained the gingerbread man again after a while.

"Well, jump onto my nose," smiled the fox, showing even more very sharp teeth.

The gingerbread man jumped onto the fox's nose, and SNAP! the fox gobbled

him all up. When the fox climbed out of the river on the other side, all that was left of the naughty gingerbread man was a few crumbs. So the old woman and the old man, the dog and the cat, the cow and the horse, the pig and the rooster all went home and shared the ginger biscuits. They were delicious.

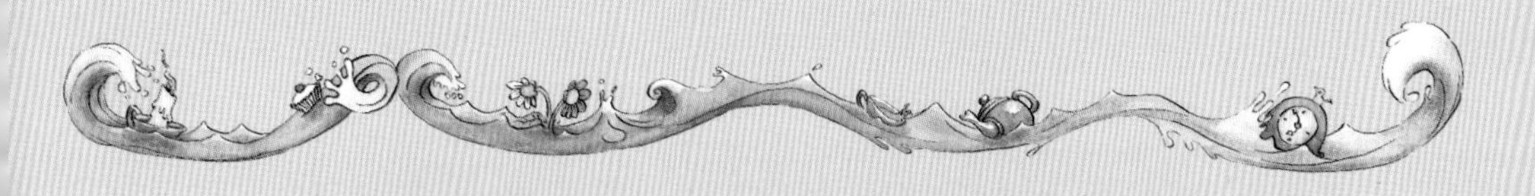

Fun and Nonsense

The Pied Piper of Hamelin

An Irish folk tale

Imagine what it would be like to live in a town overrun by rats. Rats in the streets, shops and gardens! Rats in the town hall, hospital and police station! Rats in your school corridors, classroom and desk! Rats in your kitchen, bath and bed! Well, that's what it was like to live in the town of Hamelin, which lay beside the River Weser.

No one knew where the rats had come from or how they had managed to take over the town in

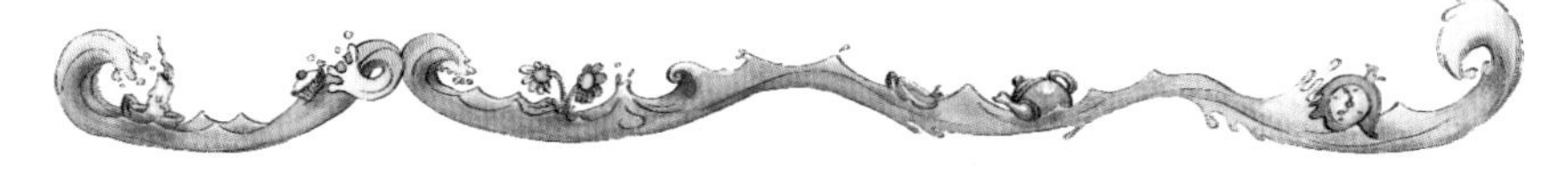

such numbers. The townspeople of Hamelin were desperate to be rid of them. They couldn't eat without rats nibbling off their plates. They couldn't get dressed without uncovering rats nesting in their clothes and boots. They couldn't put their babies down to sleep without finding rats cuddled up in the cradles. They couldn't even chat to each other in comfort, for the noise of all the squeaking and scampering.

So you can see why the mayor put up a poster outside the town hall saying:

There will be a reward of ONE THOUSAND GUILDERS to anyone who can get rid of the rats!

Yes, one thousand guilders! Everyone began to imagine what they would do with such a huge fortune – but of course, they could only dream. No one had the first idea how to begin claiming back their town from the rats.

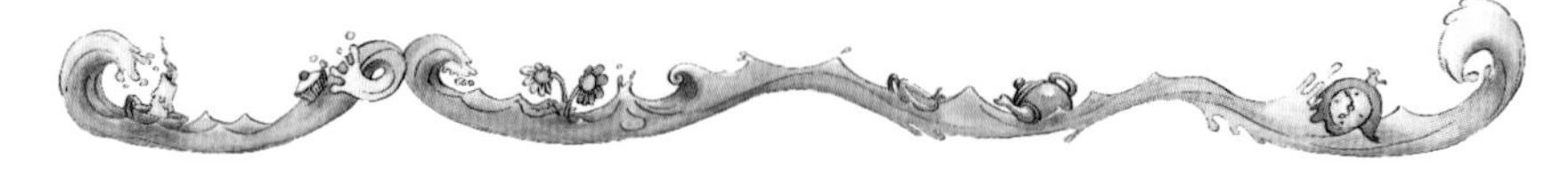

By the time the stranger came knocking on the door of the town hall, the mayor was panic-stricken. He would have listened to anybody who said they could help. So when the stranger announced confidently, "I can get rid of all the rats for you," the mayor didn't worry too much about the stranger's odd, multicoloured costume. The mayor paid no attention to the stranger's extraordinarily long fingers and the unusual pipe that hung on a cord round his neck. The mayor didn't think too much about the sad smile on the stranger's face or the wistful gleam in his eyes. The mayor just beamed with relief.

"Right now," replied the stranger, and he raised his pipe to his lips. Off he went, out of the town hall and into the street, playing a lilting tune that filled

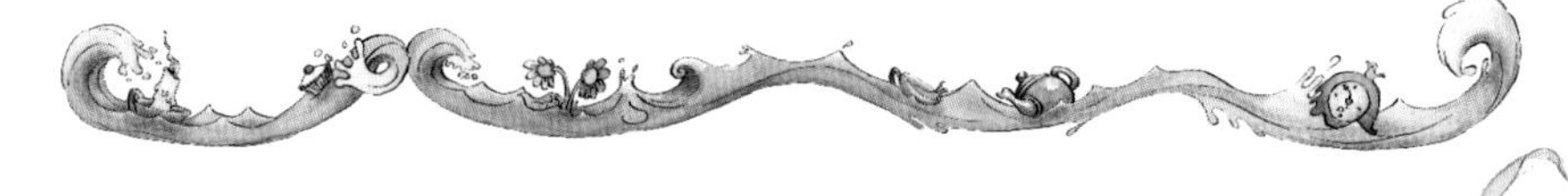

the air. Instantly, the rats stopped scuffling, pricked up their ears, and listened. For the first time in many, many months, there was silence for a moment. Then the scampering and squeaking began again, as the rats followed the Pied Piper.

The townspeople of Weser couldn't believe their eyes. All through the town strolled the Pied Piper, his fingers continually moving on his pipe and the haunting notes rippling through the air. And out of all the houses swarmed the rats; out of every garden and gutter, out of every nook and cranny they came streaming. Down stairwells and through streets, out of passages and alleyways, over rooftops and along roads the rats came hurrying after the strange musician. And the Pied Piper didn't stop playing all the way

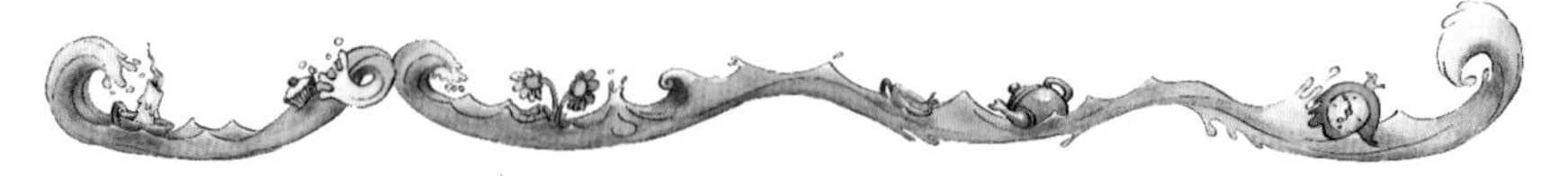

to the wide River Weser. He didn't stop playing as he dipped one brightly coloured foot into the rushing waters and the thousands of rats began to plunge off the bank into the river. He didn't stop playing until the very last rat had drowned.

Then the church bells rang out in celebration, the townspeople hugged each other, the children danced and sang – and the Pied Piper strode quietly back to the town hall to fetch his reward.

"My one thousand guilders, if you please," said the Pied Piper, calmly.

The mayor just smiled what he thought was a charming smile. Now the rats were dead and gone he certainly didn't plan on giving away what was nearly the entire contents of the town council bank account! "Come, come now, my dear fellow," the mayor coaxed. "One thousand guilders is somewhat over-the-top for playing a pretty ditty

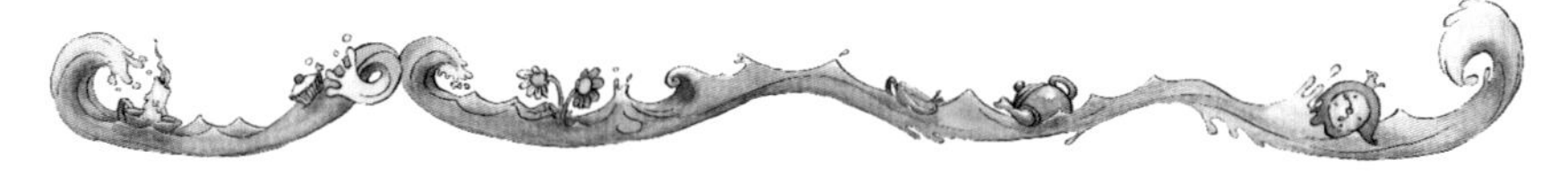

on a tin whistle, surely you'll agree! Why don't we settle on fifty guilders, and I'll throw in a nice bronze medal and even put up a statue of you and me together in the market place, eh?"

The Pied Piper simply turned on his heel and walked out into the street. As he went, he once more lifted his pipe to his lips. But this time, he played a different tune. Enchanting notes rippled all around and down the roads the children came dancing, running and leaping after the Pied Piper.

The men and women of Hamelin were struck still with horror as the children swept past them and were gone through the town. Playing his strange melody, the Pied Piper led the children past the River Weser and skipping happily along a path that led up to a steep, craggy mountain. He piped a burst of airy notes and a little door appeared in the mountain slope. The Pied Piper led the children

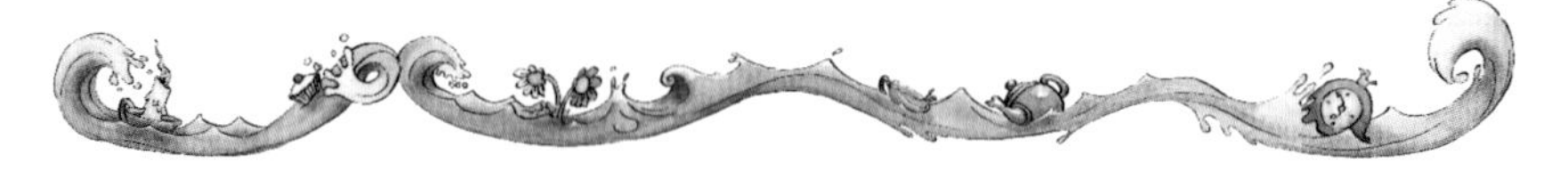

inside. The townspeople could hear the echo of his pipe and the children's laughter grow fainter and fainter as they went deeper and deeper into the earth. Then suddenly, the little door slammed shut and disappeared. The children were gone – all except for one little boy who was lame and so hadn't been able to keep up with the others. He stood on the mountainside and sobbed, calling out for his friends. But the little door had vanished.

No one ever saw the Pied Piper or the children again. But on sunny days, some townsfolk swore they could hear ripples of childish laughter floating down from the mountain. And from that day to this, there has never been a single rat in the town of Hamelin.

The Greedy Dog

An English tale

There was once a very greedy dog who just ate and ate. Whenever he saw anything that looked good enough to eat, he would just open his mouth and gobble it all up. The postman wouldn't come near the house anymore, ever since the greedy dog mistook his ankle for an early breakfast. He would stand at the gate and throw the letters in the general direction of the letterbox. The paperboy just refused to go anywhere near.

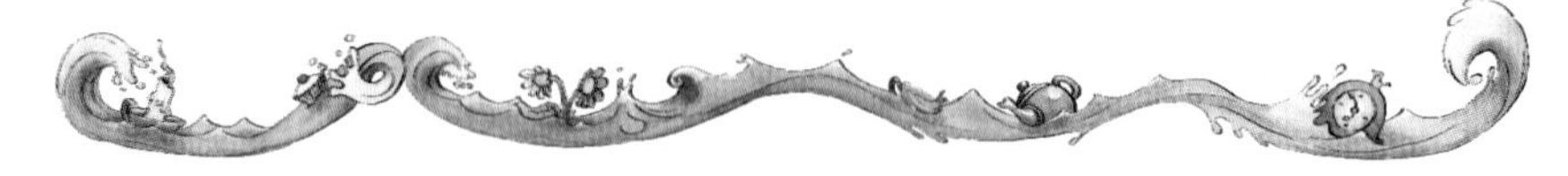

Visitors knew they had to come with a juicy bone or they wouldn't get as far as the front door.

One day, the greedy dog was out wandering round the shops. He loved doing this as there were always lots of good smells for him to investigate, and sometimes old ladies, who didn't know any better, would give him sticky buns to eat.

As he walked past the butcher's shop, the greedy dog started to lick his lips. There in the window was a great big steak. It looked juicy and very good to eat. The greedy dog decided that the steak would make a very nice meal. So he watched and waited outside the shop. Soon one of his favourite old ladies walked down the street and into the butcher's shop. The

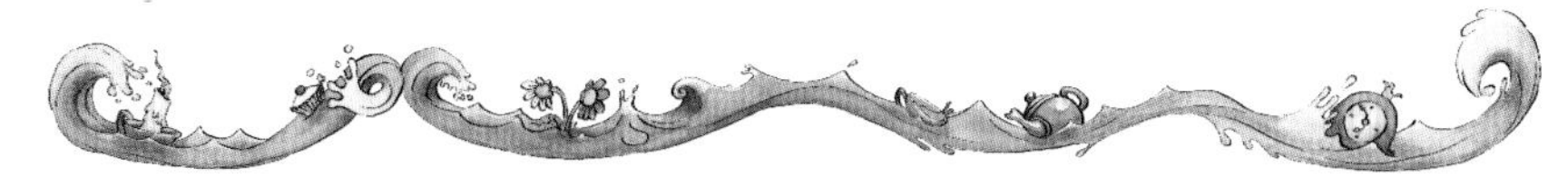

greedy dog sidled in alongside the unsuspecting old lady. She wanted sausages and mince and goodness knows what else, so while the butcher was looking after her, the greedy dog pounced. He grabbed the steak and galloped out of the shop.

Then there was a great hue and cry. The butcher ran out of his shop, the little old lady fainted, and everyone in the street joined in the chase. But the greedy dog knew all the back streets, and he was soon far away and longing to eat his steak. He ran through the back streets until he came to the canal. He was just about to cross the bridge when he caught sight of another dog, right in front of him, and this dog also had a great juicy steak in his mouth! Well now, you and I know that what he was looking at was his own reflection, but the greedy dog did not know that. All he saw

was a second steak that he might have so, with a great fierce bark, he leapt at the other dog.

But instead of gaining another meal, the greedy dog found himself very wet indeed, and he had lost his own steak! It would be good if I could tell you that from that day onwards the greedy dog was better behaved. But I am afraid his manners did not improve, and he is still looking for the other dog …

A Tall Story

An Indian folk tale

Five blind men were once sitting under a shady palm tree by the bank of the River Ganges in India, when they sensed that someone or something had silently crept up and joined them. "Who's there?" asked the first blind man. There was no reply, so he got to his feet and walked forwards with his arms outstretched. After a few steps, his hands hit something flat, rough

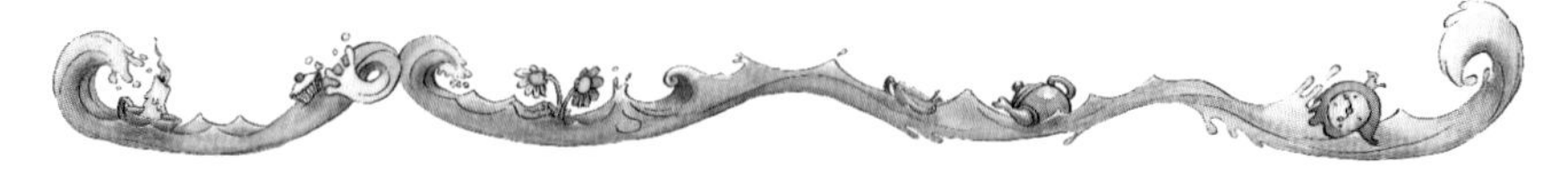

and solid in front of him. "It's a wall!" he cried.

"Don't be stupid!" cried the second blind man, standing up. "How could someone have built a wall right under our noses without us hearing?" He, too, felt about in front of him. "Aha!" he said, delightedly, as he ran his hands down a hard, smooth, stick-like thing. "It's a spear, definitely a spear!"

At that, the third blind man got up to join them. "A wall and a spear!" he sneered. "Obviously, neither of you have any idea what this thing is." His fingers closed around something tatty and wiggly. "It's nothing more than a piece of old rope!" he laughed.

"How can you say that?" argued the fourth blind man, who had jumped up and joined in without anyone noticing.

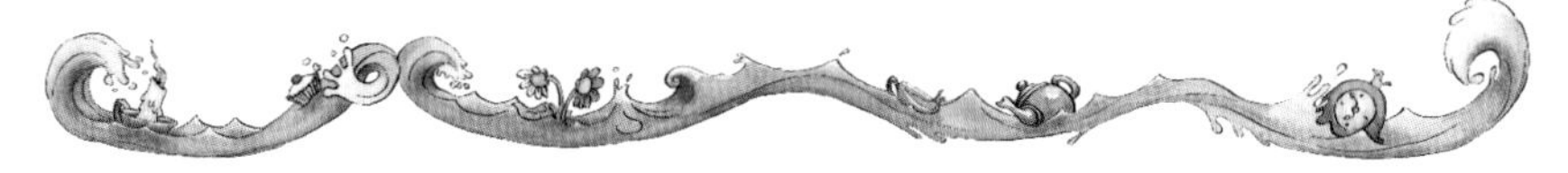

"I'm standing here with my arms wrapped around something so big that my fingers are barely touching together. It's a tree trunk, I'm telling you. A tree trunk!"

"I suppose I'll have to settle this," sniffed the fifth blind man, as he rose. He stuck out his hand confidently and grabbed hold of something long and swaying. "HELP!" he shouted. "It's a snake! It's a snake!"

Suddenly, whoops of laughter filled the air and the five blind men heard a little boy giggle, "You're ALL wrong! You're actually holding parts of an elephant – and you all look REALLY SILLY!"

At that, the five blind men all stopped what they were doing. And from that moment on, they never argued again.

Nasreddin Hodja and the Pot

Anon

Nasreddin Hodja went to his neighbour to borrow a large cooking pot for a few days. When he returned it, the neighbour was surprised to find a smaller pot inside, that he had never seen before.

"What's this, Nasreddin?" he said

"Oh, your pot gave birth while in my house," Nasreddin replied, "and naturally as the larger pot is yours, the smaller pot belongs to you also so I

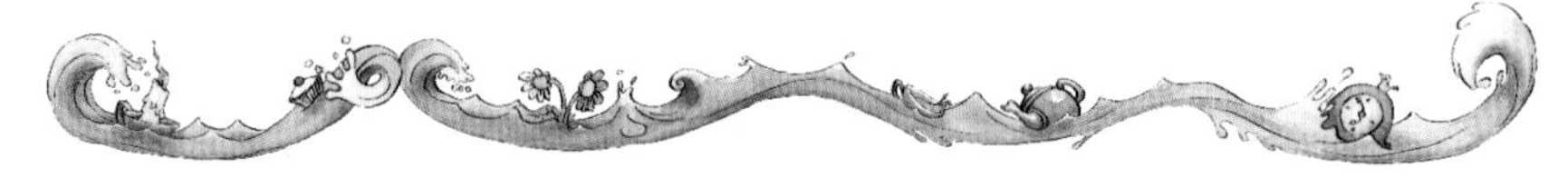

have brought it to you."

'What a fool!' thought the man, but he smiled and accepted the pot, pleased at his good fortune.

Some days later, Nasreddin asked if might borrow the pot again. After a few weeks, the neighbour went to Nasreddin's house to ask for it back.

"Oh, I am sorry to tell you," said Nasreddin, "but your pot has died."

"Don't be so foolish" said the neighbour angrily. "Cooking pots don't die!"

"Are you sure?" said Nasreddin. "You didn't seem surprised when you heard it had given birth."

Nasreddin Hodja and the Smell of Soup

Anon

A beggar was walking along the road of the market. He had begged a small piece of bread for himself, dry and old, and that was all he had to eat that day. Hoping to get something to put on it, he went to a nearby restaurant and begged for a small portion of food, but was ordered out of the inn empty-handed. As he walked out, he stopped to stare at the rich people enjoying the bowls of good savoury soup. He lent over one of the

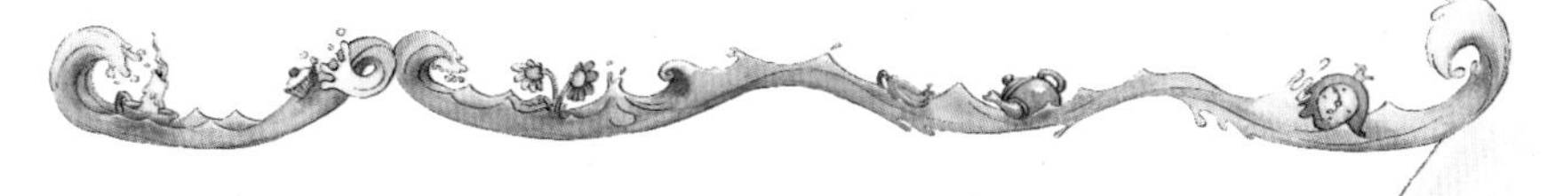

cauldrons and took a deep breath to savour its good smell. At that moment the innkeeper came out and seized his arm.

"Not so fast! You haven't paid!"

"Payment? But I have had nothing," stammered the confused beggar, "I was only enjoying the smell."

"Then you must pay for the smell," insisted the innkeeper. "Do you think I cook my soup for a beggar to steal a smell from? I saw you take it."

The poor beggar had no money to pay, of course, so the innkeeper dragged him off to the Nasreddin Hodja, the judge. Hodja listened most carefully, considering both the innkeeper's angry

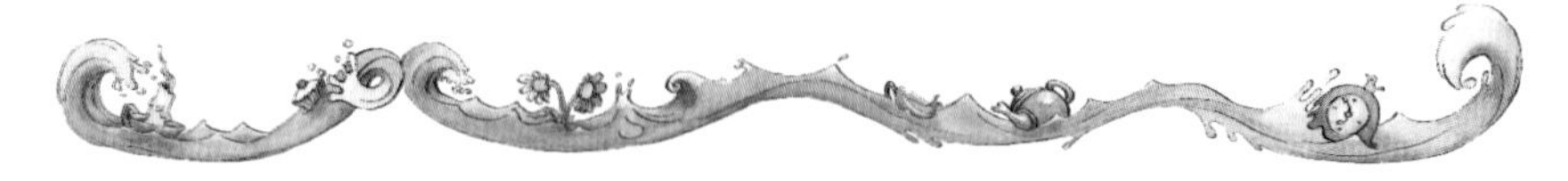

exclamations, and the beggar's protests that he had taken nothing.

"And you say you have no money?" he asked the poor man.

"Not a penny," stammered the terrified beggar.

Then Hodja turned to the innkeeper.

"So you insist on being paid for the smell?"

"Indeed I do," said the innkeeper.

"Then I myself will pay you," said Hodja.

He drew some coins out of his pocket, and beckoned the innkeeper closer. Hodja held the coins in his hands up to the innkeeper's ear and shook his hand gently so the coins rang together.

"You may go," he said.

The innkeeper said angrily, "but my payment..."

"This man took the smell of the soup," said Hodja, "and you have been paid with the sound of the money. Now go on your way."

Lazy Jack

By Flora Annie Steel

Once upon a time there was a boy whose name was Jack, and he lived with his mother on a common. They were very poor, and the old woman made her living by spinning, but Jack was so useless that he was called Lazy Jack. His mother at last told him that if he did not begin to work for his porridge, she would turn him out.

This roused Jack, and he went out and hired himself for the next day to a neighbouring farmer

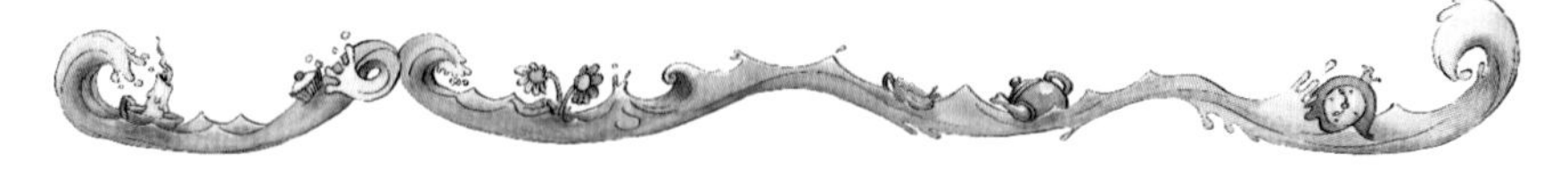

for a penny, but as he was coming home, never having had any money before, he lost it.

"You stupid boy," said his mother, "you should have put it in your pocket."

"I'll do so another time," replied Jack.

Well, the next day, Jack went out again and hired himself to a cowkeeper, who gave him a jar of milk for his day's work. Jack put the jar into his jacket pocket, spilling it all before he got home.

"Dear me!" said the old woman, "you should have carried it on your head."

"I'll do so another time," said Jack.

So the following day, Jack hired himself again to a farmer, who agreed to give him a cream cheese for his services. In the evening Jack took the cheese, and went home with it on his head. By the time he got home the cheese was all spoilt, part of it being lost, and part matted with his hair.

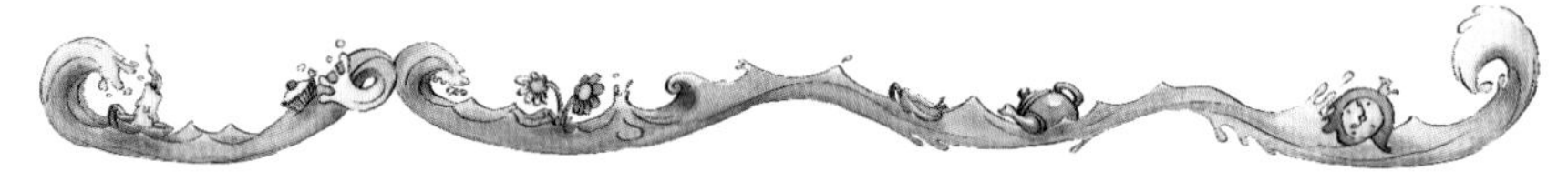

"You stupid lout," said his mother, "you should have carried it very carefully in your hands."

"I'll do so another time," replied Jack.

Now the next day, Lazy Jack again went out, and hired himself to a baker, who would give him nothing for his work but a large tom-cat. Jack took the cat, and began carrying it very carefully in his hands, but in a short time pussy scratched him so much that he was compelled to let it go.

When he got home, his mother said to him, "You silly fellow, you should have tied it with a string, and dragged it along after you."

"I'll do so another time," said Jack.

So on the following day, Jack hired himself to a butcher, who rewarded him by the handsome present of a shoulder of mutton. Jack took the mutton, tied it with a string, and trailed it along after him in the dirt, so that by the time he got

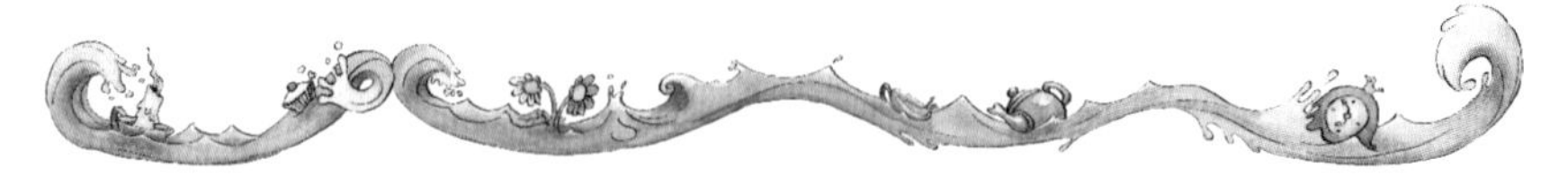

home the meat was completely spoilt. His mother was this time quite out of patience with him.

"You ninney-hammer," said she to her son, "you should have carried it on your shoulder."

"I'll do so another time," replied Jack.

Well, on the Monday, Lazy Jack went once more and hired himself to a cattle-keeper, who gave him a donkey for his trouble. Now though Jack was strong he found it hard to hoist the donkey on his

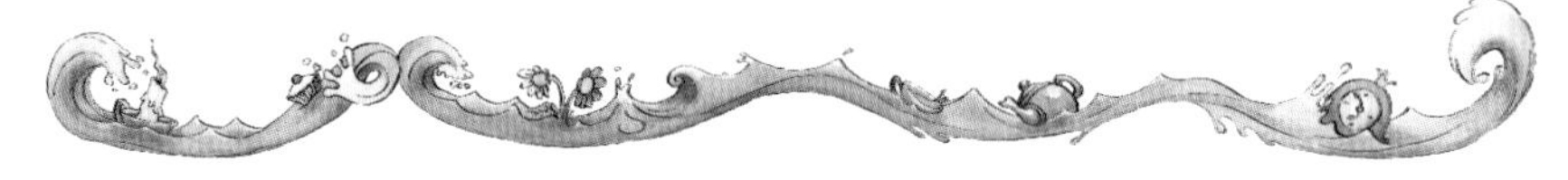

shoulders, but at last he did it, and began walking home.

Now it so happened that he passed a house where a rich man lived with his only daughter, who had never spoken in her life. The doctors said she would never speak till somebody made her laugh. So the father had said that any man who made her laugh would receive her hand in marriage. Now this young lady happened to be looking out of the window when Jack was passing by with the donkey on his shoulders. Well, the sight was so comical that she burst into a fit of laughter, and immediately recovered her speech and hearing. Her father was overjoyed, and fulfilled his promise by marrying her to Lazy Jack, who was thus made a rich gentleman. They lived in a large house, and Jack's mother lived with them in great happiness until she died.

Tikki Tikki Tembo

Anon

Once upon a time in faraway China there lived two brothers, one named Sam, and one named Tikki Tikki Tembo No Sarimbo Hari Kari Bushkie Perry Pem Do Hai Kai Pom Pom Nikki No Meeno Dom Barako.

Now one day the two brothers were playing near the well in their garden when Sam fell into the well, and Tikki Tikki Tembo No Sarimbo Hari Kari Bushkie Perry Pem Do Hai Kai Pom Pom

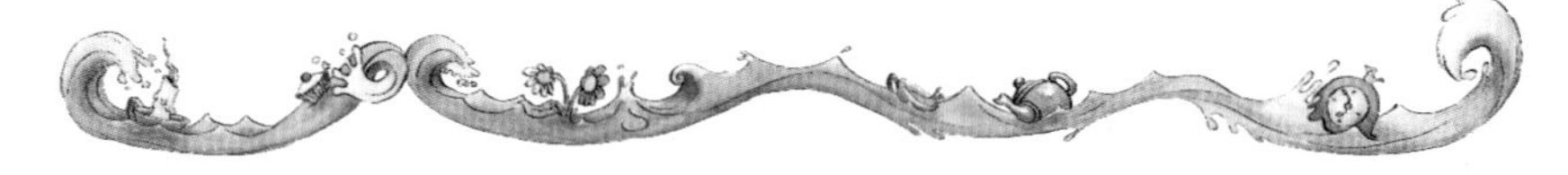

Nikki No Meeno Dom Barako ran to his mother, shouting, "Quick, Sam has fallen into the well."

"What?" cried the mother, "Sam has fallen into the well? Run and tell father!"

Together they ran to the father and cried, "Quick, Sam has fallen into the well."

"Sam has fallen into the well?" cried the father. "Run and tell the gardener!"

Then they all ran to the gardener and shouted, "Quick, Sam has fallen into the well."

"Sam has fallen into the well?" cried the gardener, and then he quickly fetched a ladder and pulled the poor boy from the well, who was wet, cold and frightened.

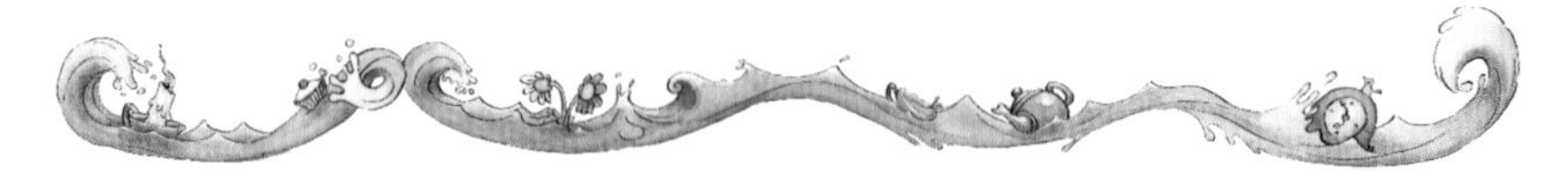

Some time afterward the two brothers were again playing near the well. This time Tikki Tikki Tembo No Sarimbo Hari Kari Bushkie Perry Pem Do Hai Kai Pom Pom Nikki No Meeno Dom Barako fell into the well, and Sam ran to his mother, shouting, "Quick, Tikki Tikki Tembo No Sarimbo Hari Kari Bushkie Perry Pem Do Hai Kai Pom Pom Nikki No Meeno Dom Barako has fallen into the well."

"What?" cried the mother, "Tikki Tikki Tembo No Sarimbo Hari Kari Bushkie Perry Pem Do Hai Kai Pom Pom Nikki No Meeno Dom Barako has fallen into the well? Run and tell father!"

Together they ran to the father and cried, "Quick, Tikki Tikki Tembo No Sarimbo Hari Kari Bushkie Perry Pem Do Hai Kai Pom Pom Nikki No Meeno Dom Barako has fallen into the well."

"Tikki Tikki Tembo No Sarimbo Hari Kari

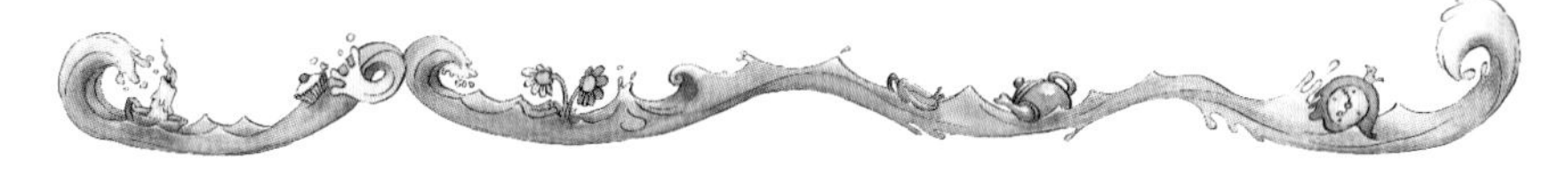

Bushkie Perry Pem Do Hai Kai Pom Pom Nikki No Meeno Dom Barako has fallen into the well?" cried the father. "Run and tell the gardener!"

So they all ran to the gardener and shouted, "Quick, Tikki Tikki Tembo No Sarimbo Hari Kari Bushkie Perry Pem Do Hai Kai Pom Pom Nikki No Meeno Dom Barako has fallen into the well."

"Tikki Tikki Tembo No Sarimbo Hari Kari Bushkie Perry Pem Do Hai Kai Pom Pom Nikki No Meeno Dom Barako has fallen into the well?" cried the gardener, and then he quickly fetched a ladder and pulled Tikki Tikki Tembo No Sarimbo Hari Kari Bushkie Perry Pem Do Hai Kai Pom Pom Nikki No Meeno Dom Barako from the well, but the poor boy had been in the water so long that he had drowned.

And from that time forth, the Chinese have given their children short names.

The Husband who was to Mind the House

By Peter Christen Asbjørnsen

Once upon a time there was a man who was so bad tempered and cross that he never thought his wife did anything right in the house. One evening, in hay-making time, he came home, scolding and shouting.

"Dear love, don't be so angry, that's a good man," said his wife, "tomorrow let's change jobs. I'll go out with the mowers and mow, and you can mind the house at home."

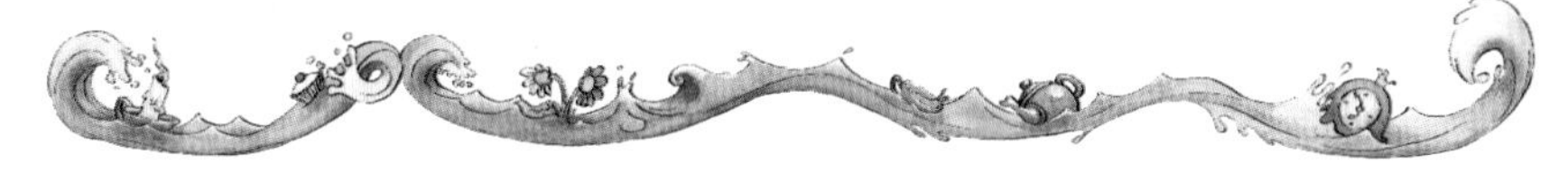

Yes, the husband thought that would do very well. He was quite willing, he said.

So early the next morning, his wife took a scythe over her neck, and went out into the hay field with the mowers and began to mow, but the man was to mind the house, and do the work at home.

First of all he wanted to churn the butter, but when he had churned awhile, he got thirsty, and went down to the cellar to tap a barrel of ale. He had just knocked in the bung, and was putting in the tap, when he heard the pig come into the kitchen above. As fast as he could, he ran up the cellar steps, with the tap in his hand, to keep the pig from upsetting the churn, but when he got

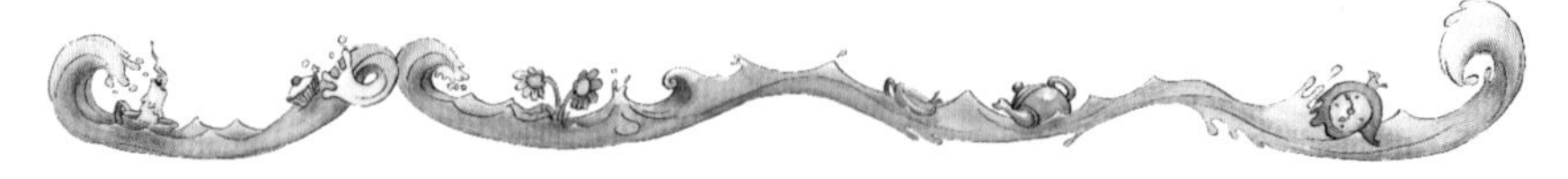

there, the pig had already knocked the churn over, and was rolling in the cream on the floor.

He got so angry that he quite forgot the ale barrel, and ran at the pig as hard as he could. He caught it and gave it such a powerful kick that he killed it on the spot. Then he remembered he had the tap in his hand, but when he got down to the cellar, all the ale had run out of the barrel.

Then he went into the milk shed and found enough cream left to fill the churn again, and so he began to churn, for they had to have butter at dinner. When he had churned a bit, he remembered that their milk cow was still shut up in the barn, and hadn't had a bit to eat or a drop

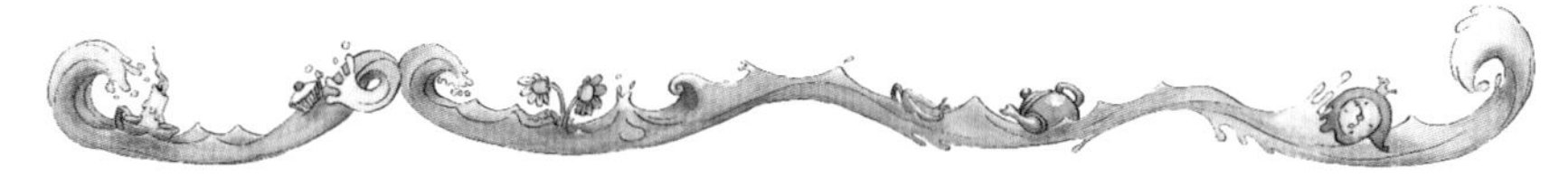

to drink all morning, although the sun was high. It occurred to him that it was too far to take her down to the meadow, so he'd just get her up on the roof, for it was a sod roof, and a fine crop of grass was growing there.

But he couldn't leave the churn, for his baby was crawling about on the floor. 'If I leave it,' he thought, 'the child will tip it over.' So he took the churn on his back and went out, but then he thought he'd better draw water for the cow before he put her on the roof. So he picked up a bucket to draw water out of the well, but, as he stooped over the edge of the well, all the cream ran out of the churn over his shoulder and down into the well.

Now it was near dinner time, and he hadn't even got the butter yet, so he thought he'd best boil the porridge, and filled the pot with water and hung it over the fire. When he had done that, it occurred

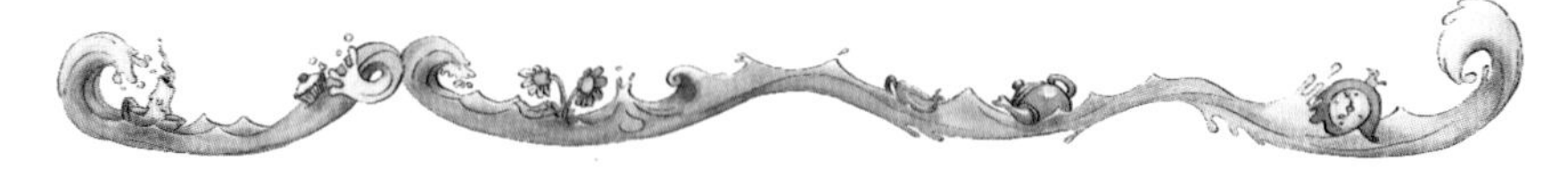

to him that the cow might fall off the roof. So he tied one end of a rope to the cow's neck. He slipped the other end down the chimney and tied it around his own leg. Then he had to hurry, for the water was now boiling in the pot, and he had still to grind the oatmeal. As he began to grind away, the cow fell off the roof, dragging the man up the chimney. There he stuck fast, and the cow hung halfway down the wall.

Now the wife waited for her husband to call her home to dinner, but he never came. At last she thought she'd waited long enough, and went home. But when she got home and saw the cow hanging there, she ran up and cut the rope with her scythe. When she did this, her husband fell down from within the chimney. When the old woman came inside, she found him upside down with his head in the porridge pot.

Teeny-tiny

An English folk tale

Once upon a time there lived a teeny-tiny old woman. She lived in a teeny-tiny house in a teeny-tiny street with a teeny-tiny cat. One day the teeny-tiny woman decided to go out for a teeny-tiny walk. She put on her teeny-tiny boots and her teeny-tiny bonnet, and off she set.

When she had walked a teeny-tiny way down the teeny-tiny street, she went through a teeny-tiny gate into a teeny-tiny graveyard, which was a

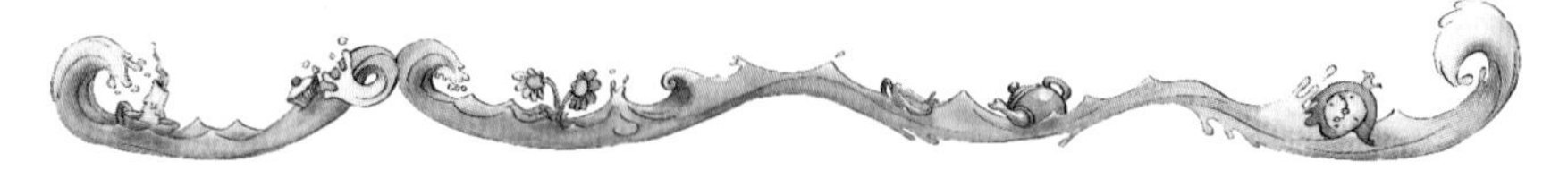

teeny-tiny shortcut to the teeny-tiny meadow. Well, she had only taken a few teeny-tiny steps when she saw a teeny-tiny bone lying on top of a teeny-tiny grave. She thought that would do very well to make some teeny-tiny soup for supper so she put the teeny-tiny bone in her teeny-tiny pocket and went home at once to her teeny-tiny house.

Now the teeny-tiny woman was tired when she reached her teeny-tiny house so she did not make the teeny-tiny soup immediately, but put the teeny-tiny bone into her teeny-tiny cupboard. Then she sat in her teeny-tiny chair and put her teeny-tiny feet up and had a teeny-tiny sleep. But she had only been asleep a teeny-tiny time when she woke up at the sound of a teeny-tiny voice coming

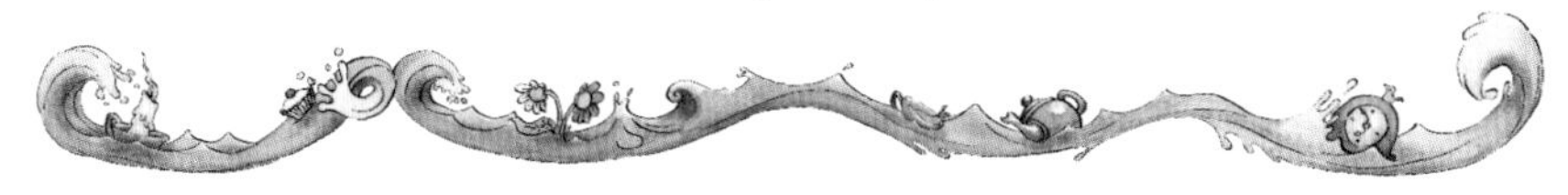

from her teeny-tiny cupboard. The teeny-tiny voice said, "Where is my teeny-tiny bone?"

Well, the teeny-tiny woman was a teeny-tiny bit frightened so she wrapped her teeny-tiny shawl round her teeny-tiny head and went to sleep again. She had only been asleep a teeny-tiny time

when the teeny-tiny voice came from the teeny-tiny cupboard again, a teeny-tiny bit louder this time. "Where is my teeny-tiny bone?"

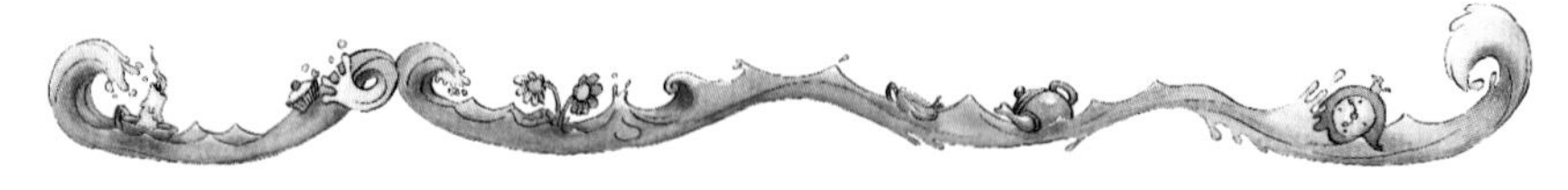

The teeny-tiny woman was a teeny-tiny bit more frightened than last time so she hid under the teeny-tiny cushions, but she could not go back to sleep, not even a teeny-tiny bit. Then the teeny-tiny voice came again and this time it was even a teeny-tiny bit louder. "Where is my teeny-tiny bone?"

This time the teeny-tiny woman sat up in her teeny-tiny chair and said in her loudest teeny-tiny voice, "TAKE IT!"

There was a teeny-tiny silence, and then a teeny-tiny ghost ran out of the teeny-tiny house, down the teeny-tiny street, through the teeny-tiny gate into the teeny-tiny graveyard – with the teeny-tiny bone clutched very tightly in its teeny-tiny hand! And the teeny-tiny woman never took even a teeny-tiny walk there ever again!

Magic and Mystery

The Fairy Cow

By Jeremiah Curtin

In the parish of Drummor lived a farmer called Tom Connors. He had some land, four cows, a wife and five children.

Connors had one cow that was better than the other three, and she went by the name of Cooby. On one corner of Connors' farm there was a fairy fort, and the cow Cooby used to go into the fort, but Connors always drove her out, and told his wife and boys to keep her away from the fort.

One morning when Connors went to drive his cows home to be milked he found Cooby in the field with her legs broken. He killed the cow that minute for the family to eat.

One morning after Tom had gone to the bog to cut turf, his wife went out to milk their remaining cows, and what should she see but a cow walking into the fort that looked just like Cooby. Soon the cow came out, and with her a girl.

"Oh, then," said Mrs Connors, "I'd swear that is Cooby, if we hadn't eaten her."

The girl milked the cow, and then cow and girl disappeared. The following day Tom's

wife went to milk again, and again she saw the cow go into the fort, and the girl come out to milk it.

'God knows 'tis the very cow. I'll tell Tom tonight, and he may do what he likes,' she thought.

When Connors came home in the evening, his wife said, "You remember Cooby?"

"Why shouldn't I remember Cooby, after eating most of her?"

"Indeed then, Tom, I saw Cooby today, inside the fort with a girl milking her."

"Well, I'll go in the morning, and if it's our Cooby I'll bring her home with me," said Tom, "Even if all the devils in the fort are before me."

Early in the morning Tom started across his land, and never stopped till he came to the fort, and there, he saw the cow walking in through the gap to the fort, and he knew her that minute.

"'Tis my cow Cooby," said Connors, "and I'll

have her. I'd like to see the man who would keep her from me."

That minute the girl came out with her pail and stool and walked towards Cooby.

"Stop where you are – don't milk that cow!" cried Connors.

"Let the cow go," said Tom, "this is my cow. Go to your master and tell him to come out to me."

The girl went inside the fort and disappeared, but soon a fine-looking young man came and spoke to Connors. "What are you doing here, my man," asked he, "and why did you stop my servant from milking the cow?"

"She is my cow," said Tom, "and by that same token I'll keep her."

"But I've had this cow a long time. And didn't you eat your own cow?"

"I don't care what cow I ate," said Tom. "I'll have

this cow, for she is my Cooby."

They argued and argued. Tom declared that he'd take the cow home. "And if you try to prevent me," said he to the man, "I'll tear the fort to pieces."

"Indeed, then, you'll not tear the fort."

Tom got so vexed that he made as though to fight the man. The man ran and Tom after him into the fort. When Tom was inside, he forgot all about fighting. He saw many people dancing and enjoying themselves, and he thought, 'Why shouldn't I do that myself?' With that he went up to a fine-looking girl, and, taking her out to dance, told the piper to strike up a hornpipe.

The young man came up and said, "Well, you are a brave man and courageous, and for the future we'll be good friends. You can take the cow."

"I will not take her, you may keep her, for you

are all very good people."

"Well," said the young man, "the cow is yours, and it's why I took her because there were many children in the fort without nurses, but the children are reared now, and you may take the cow. I put an old stray horse in place of her and made him look like your own beast, and it's an old horse you've been eating all the year. From this day forwards you'll grow rich and have luck. We'll not trouble you, but help you."

Tom took the cow and drove her home. From that day forwards Tom Connors' cows had two calves apiece and his mare had two foals and his sheep two lambs every year. Every acre of his land gave him as much crop in one year as another man got in seven years. At last Connors was a very rich man – and why not, when the fairies were with him?

Paddy Corcoran's Wife

By William Carleton

Paddy Corcoran's wife was for several years afflicted with a kind of complaint that nobody could properly understand. She was sick, and she was not sick, she was well, and she was not well, she was as ladies wish to be who love their lords, and she was not as such ladies wish to be. In fact nobody could tell what the matter with her was. The poor woman was delicate beyond belief, and had no appetite at all.

She lay bedridden, trying doctors of all sorts and sizes, and all without a farthing's benefit, until, at the long run, poor Paddy was nearly brought to despair.

Then one harvest day, as she lay moaning about her hard condition, on her bed by the kitchen fire, a little woman dressed in a neat red cloak came in, and sitting down by the hearth, said, "Well, Kitty Corcoran, you've had a long lie of it there on the broad of yer back for seven years, and you're just as far from being cured as ever."

"Ay" said the other, "in truth that's what I was this minute thinking of."

"It's yer own fault, then," says the little woman.

"Ah, how is that?" asked Kitty, "sure I wouldn't be here if I could help it? Do you think it's a pleasure to me to be sick and bedridden?"

"No," said the other, "I do not – but I'll tell you

the truth – for the last seven years you have been annoying us. I'm here to let you know the reason why you've been sick so long as you are. For all the time you've been ill, your children have thrown out yer dirty water after dusk and before sunrise, at the very time we're passing yer door, which we pass twice a day. Now, if you avoid this and throw it out in a different place, at a different time, the sickness will leave you and you'll be as well as ever you were." She then bade her goodbye, and disappeared.

Kitty immediately did as she was asked, and the next day she found herself in good health once more.

The Three Wishes

An English folk tale

There was once a poor fisherman who lived by the sea in a tumbledown old cottage. He lived with his wife, who was always grumbling no matter how hard the fisherman worked.

One evening he threw the nets out for one last try before it grew dark. He had caught nothing all day. As he began pulling the nets in, the fisherman's hopes rose – the nets were heavy. But when he hauled them in, there was only one tiny

fish lying at the bottom. Then the fish spoke. The fisherman rubbed his eyes in astonishment.

"Please throw me back," said the fish. "I am so small I would not make much of a meal for you."

But the fisherman was tired and hungry.

"Even though you are small I cannot throw you back. My wife would not be pleased if I came home empty-handed." he said with a deep sigh.

"I will grant you the first three wishes made in your cottage if you let me go," said the fish, "but I should warn you that wishes do not always give you what you really want."

Well, the fisherman did not hear the fish's warning. All he heard was the bit about three wishes, and he thought that finally his grumbling wife could have whatever she wanted. So he carefully untangled the tiny fish from the nets and placed it back in the sea. With a flick of its tail the fish disappeared deep, deep under water.

The fisherman ran home and told her all about the tiny fish. But instead of being pleased, she just shouted at him as usual.

"Trust you to believe such a thing! Whoever heard of a talking fish. You must be daft," and she slammed down a plate of dry bread and a rind of cheese in front of the poor fisherman.

"I wish this was a plate of fine sausages, I am so hungry," said the fisherman wistfully.

No sooner were the words out of his mouth than there was a wonderful smell and there in front of

him was a plate of sizzling sausages! He was delighted and reached for his knife when his wife yelled at him,

"Why couldn't you have wished for something better? We could have had chests of gold and fine clothes to wear!" and this from the woman who had refused to believe his story only a few moments before. "You stupid fool! I wish the sausages were at the end of your nose!"

There was a ghastly silence as the wife looked at her poor husband. Hanging from the end of his nose was a great string of sausages. The fisherman remembered what the fish had said – the first three wishes made in the cottage.

The fisherman and his wife pulled at the sausages, but they were stuck . There was nothing for it, they would have to use the last wish.

"I wish the sausages would disappear," said the fisherman sadly, and they did in a flash. So there they sat, the poor fisherman and his grumbling wife. No delicious supper of sizzling sausages and, much worse, no magic wishes. The fisherman never caught the tiny fish again, and his wife never stopped grumbling. Wishes do not always give you what you really want!

The Mermaid of Zennor

A Cornish legend

The bell was ringing, calling the villagers of Zennor to Sunday service. It was a simple little granite towered church, built to withstand the wild winds that could roll in from the sea. Matthew stood in the choir stalls and looked at the new bench he had been carving. It was nearly finished and wanted only one more panel to be carved.

As the voices of the congregation rang out in the hymns, a sweet, pure voice was heard. A voice that

no one had heard before. When the villagers turned to leave at the end of the service, there at the back of the little church stood the most beautiful woman any of them had ever seen. Her dress was made of silk, at one moment green, the next blue, like the sea. Round her neck she wore a gleaming necklace of pearls, and her golden hair fell down her back almost to the floor.

As Matthew walked out, the woman placed her hand on his sleeve.

"Your carving is beautiful, Matthew."

Matthew blushed and turned his rough cap round and round in his great red hands.

"Why, thank you ma'am," he managed to stutter before he fled out of the church. Where the beautiful lady went no one quite saw.

The next day Matthew was hard at work, carving the decoration of leaves that went round

the edge of the bench when he heard the soft rustle of silk. There stood the woman again.

"What will you put in the last panel, Matthew?" she whispered. Matthew sensed a strong smell of the sea in the tiny church as he bent to get up off his knees but when he looked up again, there was no sign of the woman.

The next Sunday the lady was in church again. She looked deep into Matthew's eyes as she sang the hymns, and when he walked slowly out, she was waiting for him.

"Will you carve my image in the last panel, Matthew?" she asked and her voice was gentle. Matthew's deep blue eyes gazed far over her head, out towards the sea, but he did not reply. Only the schoolmaster and his wife noticed that the seat where the woman had sat was wet with sea water.

Time passed, and every Sunday the woman

came to church. Matthew seemed like a man in a dream, his eyes always looking out to sea. The final panel was still not finished on the bench. November came, and with it the mist curled up from the sea. Night after night a light was to be seen late in the church. The gentle sound of wood chipping drifted out with the mist, but no one ventured into the church.

It was the parson who discovered the finished bench when he went in to open up the church one morning. The church floor was wet with sea water. The stub of a candle stood among a great pile of wood shavings on the floor. The final panel of the bench was the best Matthew had

ever carved. It was a mermaid, long hair falling down her back, the scales of her great fish tail in deep relief. She looked almost alive.

Matthew had not slept in his bed that night, nor was he ever seen again in Zennor. The mysterious woman never came to church again. The schoolmaster and his wife never talked of the wet seat. Only the fishermen would shake their heads as they sat talking on the winter's evenings. They would talk of the mermaid they had seen off the coast, and of the young man with the deep blue eyes who was always swimming by her side.

Pandora's Box

A Greek myth

When the world was first created, it was a happy place of light and laughter; there was no such thing as sadness or pain. The sun shone every day and the gods came down from heaven to walk and talk with the humans.

One afternoon, a man called Epimetheus and his wife, Pandora, were outside tending their flower garden when they saw the god Mercury approaching. He was bowed down by a dark

wooden chest that he was carrying on his shoulders. Pandora rushed to get the god a drink, while Epimetheus helped him lower the chest to the ground. It was tied shut with golden cords and was carved with strange markings.

"My friends, would you do me a great favour?" sighed Mercury. "It is so hot and the box is so heavy! May I leave it here for a while?"

"Of course you can," smiled Epimetheus.

The man and the god heaved the chest indoors.

"Are you sure that no one will find it?" asked Mercury anxiously. "NO ONE under ANY circumstances must open the box."

"Don't worry," laughed Epimetheus and Pandora, and they waved goodbye to the god.

All of a sudden, Pandora stopped still and frowned. "Listen, Epimetheus!" she hissed. "I am sure I heard someone whispering our names!"

Epimetheus and Pandora listened hard. At first, they heard nothing but the twittering of the birds. Then, they heard the distant sound of their names being called from outside.

"It's our friends!" cried Epimetheus, happily.

But Pandora looked puzzled and shook her head. "No, Epimetheus, those aren't the voices I heard," she said, firmly.

"They must have been!" Epimetheus laughed. "Come on now, let's go and see everyone."

"I'd rather stay here for a while," Pandora insisted.

As soon as Epimetheus was gone, Pandora hurried over to the strange box and waited. After only a few seconds, she heard it again – distant voices calling "Pandora!" The voices were so low and whispery that Pandora wasn't sure whether she really was hearing them or was just imagining

it. She bent down closer and put her ear to the lid. No, she was sure.The box was calling to her!

"Let us out, Pandora! We are trapped in here in the darkness! Please help us to escape!"

Pandora jumped back with a start. Mercury had expressly forbade anyone to open the box... and yet the voices sounded so sad and pitiful.

"Pandora!" they came again. "Help us!"

Pandora could stand it no longer. Hurriedly, she knelt down and worked at the tight golden knots. All the time, the whispering and pleading voices filled her ears. At last the knots were undone and the gleaming cords fell away. She took a deep breath and opened the lid.

At once, Pandora realized she had done a terrible thing. The box had been crammed with all the evils in the world – thousands of tiny moth-like

creatures that stung people with their wings and caused hurt and misery wherever they went. Now, thanks to Pandora, the evils were free! They flew up out of the chest in a great swarm and fluttered all over Pandora's skin. For the very first time, Pandora felt pain and regret. She began to wail with despair, and all too late, she slammed the lid back down onto the box.

Outside, Epimetheus heard his wife's cries and came running as fast as he could. The creatures fluttered to sting and bite him, before speeding off through the window into the world beyond. For the first time ever, Epimetheus began to shout at his wife in anger. Pandora yelled back, and the couple realized in horror that they were arguing.

"Let me out!" interrupted a high voice. Pandora and Epimetheus grabbed onto each other in a panic. The voice was coming from inside the box.

"Don't be afraid of me! Let me out and I can help you!" came the voice.

"What do you think?" Pandora whispered to Epimetheus, wide-eyed.

"Surely you can't do any more mischief than you already have done," he grumbled. So Pandora shut her eyes and opened Mercury's chest for a second time.

Out of the deep, dark box fluttered a single shining white spirit like a butterfly. It was Hope. Pandora and Epimetheus sobbed with relief as she fluttered against their skin and soothed their stinging wounds. Then she was gone, darting out of the window and into the world after the evils. And luckily, Hope has stayed with us ever since.

Rapunzel

By the Brothers Grimm

Once upon a time there lived a man and his wife who for years and years had wanted a child. One day the wife was looking sadly out of the window. Winter was coming but in the garden next door, which was surrounded by a huge great wall, she could just see rows and rows of delicious vegetables. In particular, she could see a huge bunch of rapunzel, a special kind of lettuce. Her mouth watered, it looked so fresh and green.

"Husband, I shall not rest until I have some of that rapunzel growing next door," she whispered.

The husband clambered over the wall and quickly picked a small bunch, which he took back to his wife. She made it into a salad, and ate it all up. But the next day, all she could think of was how delicious it had been so she asked him to pick her some more.

He clambered over the wall, and was picking a small bunch of the rapunzel when a voice behind him hissed, "So you are the one who has been stealing my rapunzel!"

When he spun round, there stood a witch and she looked very angry indeed. The husband was terrified, but he tried to explain that his wife had been desperate for some fresh leaves for her salad.

"You may take all the leaves you require then, but you must give me your first child when she is

born," smiled the witch, and it was not a nice smile. The husband was greatly relieved, however, for he knew that there was little chance of his wife ever having a daughter so he fled back over the wall, clutching the bunch of rapunzel. He did not tell his wife of his meeting with the witch for he thought it would only frighten her, and he soon forgot all about his adventure.

But it all came back to him when nine months later his wife gave birth to a beautiful baby girl. No sooner had she laid the baby in her cradle, than the witch appeared to claim the child. The wife wept, the husband pleaded but nothing could persuade the witch to forget the husband's awful promise, and so she took the tiny baby away.

The witch called the baby Rapunzel. She grew into a beautiful girl with long, long hair as fine as spun gold. When she was sixteen, the witch took Rapunzel and locked her in a tall tower so no one would see how beautiful she was. The witch threw away the key to the tower, and so whenever she wanted to visit Rapunzel she would call out, "Rapunzel, Rapunzel, let down your hair." Rapunzel would then throw her golden plait of hair out of the window at the top of the tower so the witch could slowly scramble up.

Now one day, a handsome young prince was riding through the woods. He heard the witch call out to Rapunzel and he watched her climb up the tower. After the witch had gone, the prince came to the bottom of the tower and he called up,

"Rapunzel, Rapunzel, let down your hair," and he climbed quickly up the shining golden plait. You can imagine Rapunzel's astonishment when she saw the handsome prince standing in front of her but she was soon laughing at his stories. When he left, he promised to come again the next day, and he did. And the next, and the next, and soon they had fallen in love with each other.

One day as the witch clambered up Rapunzel exclaimed, "You are slow! The prince doesn't take nearly as long to climb up the tower," but no sooner were the words out of her mouth than she realized her terrible mistake. The witch seized the long, long golden plait and cut it off. She drove Rapunzel far, far away from the tower, and then sat down to await the prince. When the witch heard him calling, she threw the golden plait out of the window. Imagine the prince's dismay when he sprang into the room only to discover the horrible witch instead of his beautiful Rapunzel! When the witch told him he would never see his Rapunzel again, in his grief he flung himself out of the tower. He fell into some brambles, which scratched his eyes so he could no longer see.

And thus he wandered the land, always asking if anyone had seen his Rapunzel. After seven long years, he came to the place where she had hidden herself away. As he stumbled down the road, Rapunzel recognized him and with a great cry of joy she ran up to him and took him gently by the hand to her little cottage in the woods. As she washed his face, two of her tears fell on the prince's eyes and his sight came back. And so they went back to his palace and lived happily ever after. The witch, you will be pleased to hear, had not been able to get down from the tower, so she did NOT live happily ever after!

The Fairy Blackstick

From *The Rose and the Ring*
by William Makepeace Thackeray

Between the kingdoms of Paflagonia and Crim Tartary, there lived a mysterious person, who was known as the Fairy Blackstick, after the ebony wand that she carried.

When she was young, and had been first taught the art of conjuring by her father, she was always practising her skill, whizzing about from one kingdom to another upon her black stick. She had turned numberless wicked people into beasts,

birds, millstones, clocks, pumps, boot jacks, umbrellas, or other absurd shapes, and, in a word, was one of the most active of the whole College of Fairies.

But after two or three thousand years of this sport, I suppose Blackstick grew tired of it. Or perhaps she thought, 'What good am I doing by sending this princess to sleep for a hundred years? By fixing a black pudding on to that fool's nose? By causing diamonds and pearls to drop from one little girl's mouth, and vipers and toads from another's? I might as well shut my incantations up, and allow things to take their natural course.' So she locked up her books in her cupboard and only used her wand as a walking cane.

When the Princess Angelica was born, her parents did not ask the Fairy Blackstick to the christening party and gave orders to their porter to

refuse her if she called. This porter's name was Gruffanuff, and he had been selected by their Royal Highnesses because he was a tall fierce man, with a rudeness that frightened people away.

When the Fairy Blackstick called upon the prince and princess, Gruffanuff made the most vulgar sign as he started to slam the door in the fairy's face! "Get away, Blackstick!" said he. "I tell you, Master and Missis ain't at home to you."

But the fairy, with her wand, prevented the door being shut, and Gruffanuff came out again in a fury, asking the fairy 'whether she thought he was going to stay at that there door all day?'

"You are going to stay at that door all day and night, for many a long year," the fairy said.

Gruffanuff, coming out of the door, burst out laughing, and cried, "Ha, ha! This is a good un! Let me down –O–o!" and then he was dumb!

For, as the fairy waved her wand over him, he felt himself rising off the ground, and fluttering up against the door, and then he was pinned to the door. He felt cold, as if he were turning into metal.

He was turned into metal! He was neither more nor less than a knocker! And there he was, nailed to the door in the blazing summer day, till he burned almost red-hot, and there he was, nailed to the door all the bitter winter nights, till his brass nose was dropping with icicles. And the postman came and rapped at him, and the boy with a letter came and hit him up against the door.

And that evening, when the king and queen came home from a walk, the king said, "Hello, my dear! You have had a new knocker put on the door. Why, it's rather like our porter in the face! What has become of that lazy man?" And the

housemaid came and scrubbed his nose with sandpaper, and once, some larking young men tried to wrench him off, and put him to the most excruciating agony with a screwdriver. And then the queen had a fancy to have the colour of the door altered, and the painters dabbed him over the mouth and eyes, and nearly choked him, as they painted him pea-green.

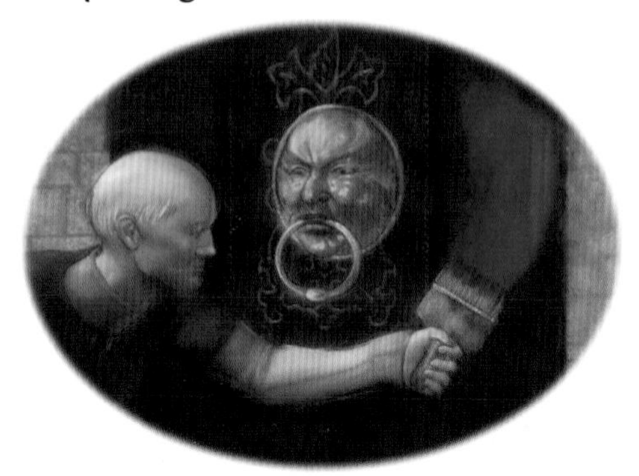

As for his wife, she did not miss him, and when the prince and princess chose to become king and queen, they left their old house, and nobody thought of the porter any more.

The Smith and the Fairies

By Kate Douglas Wiggin

It was a superstition in Celtic lands that fairies stole babies and left fairy babies (changelings) in their place.

Years ago there lived a smith called MacEachern who had a boy of about thirteen years of age, cheerful, strong, and healthy. All of a sudden he fell ill. No one could tell what was the matter with him, and the boy could not tell how he felt. His father and friends were afraid that he would die.

After the boy had been lying in this condition for a long time, getting neither better nor worse, an old man walked into the smith's workshop and the smith told him about his son.

The old man listened, and after sitting a long time, he said "It is not your son you have got. The boy has been carried away and they have left a fairy baby in his place."

"Alas! And what then am I to do?" said the smith. "How am I ever to see my own son again?"

"I will tell you how," answered the old man. "But, first, to make sure that it is not your own son you have got, take as many empty eggshells as you can, go into his room and spread them out. Then draw water with them, carrying them two and two in your hands as if they were heavy, and arrange them around the fire."

The smith had not been long at work before

there arose from the bed a shout of laughter, and the sick boy exclaimed, "I am eight hundred years of age, and I have never seen the like of that before." The smith told the old man.

"Well, now," said the old man to him, "I told you that it was not your son you had. Your son is in the round, green hill of the fairies. You must light a very large, bright fire before the bed on which this stranger is lying and throw him into it. If it is your son you have got, he will call out to you to save him, but if not, the thing will fly through the roof."

The smith again followed the old man's advice. The sick boy gave an awful yell, and sprang through the roof, where a hole had been left to let the smoke out.

The old man told the smith that on a certain night the green, round hill, where the fairies kept the boy, would be open. On that night the smith,

taking a sword, went to the hill. He heard singing and dancing, and much merriment going on. On entering the hill, he stuck the sword in the doorway, to stop the hill from closing upon him.

On entering, the fairies asked him, with a good deal of displeasure, what he wanted. He answered, "I want my son, whom I see down there, and I will not go without him." The angry fairies threw the smith and his son out of the hill and in an instant all was dark.

For a year and a day the boy hardly spoke a word. At last one day, sitting by his father and watching him finishing a sword, he suddenly exclaimed, "That is not the way to do it," and taking the tools from his father's hands he set to work himself in his place, and soon made a sword, the like of which was never seen before.

From that day the young man became the

inventor of a fine sword, making the father and son famous far and wide.

Billy Beg, Tom Beg and the Fairies

By Sophia Morrison

Not far from Dalby, Billy Beg and Tom Beg, two humpback cobblers, lived together on a lonely croft. Billy Beg was cleverer than Tom Beg. One day Billy Beg gave Tom a staff and said, "Tom Beg, go to the mountain and fetch home the white sheep."

Tom Beg took the staff and went to the mountain, but he could not find the white sheep. At last, when he was far from home, and dusk was

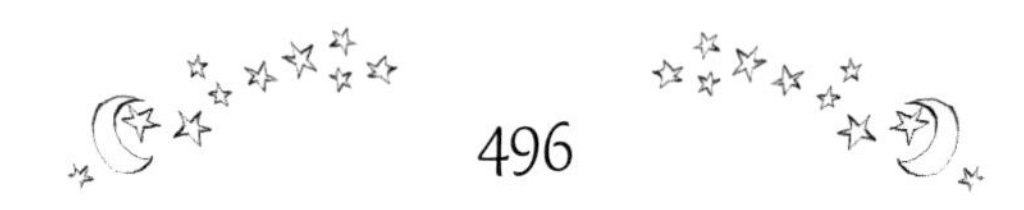

coming on, he began to think that he had best go back. The night was fine, and stars and a small crescent moon were in the sky. Tom was hastening home, and had almost reached Glen Rushen, when a grey mist gathered, and he lost his way. But it was not long before the mist cleared, and Tom Beg found himself in a green glen such as he had never seen before. He was wondering where he could be, when he heard a faraway sound coming nearer to him.

"Aw," said he to himself, "there's more than me in the mountains tonight."

The sound grew louder. First, it was like the humming of bees, then like the rushing of a waterfall, and last it was like the marching of a crowd. It was the fairies. All of a sudden the glen was full of fine horses and of little people riding on them, with the lights on their red caps shining like

the stars above and making the night as bright as day. There was the blowing of horns, the waving of flags, the playing of music, and the barking of many little dogs. Tom Beg thought that he had never seen anything so splendid as all he saw

there. In the midst of the dancing and singing, Tom saw coming towards him the grandest little man he had ever set eyes upon, dressed in gold and silver silk, shining like a raven's wing.

"It is a bad time you have chosen to come this way," said the little man, who was the king.

"But it is not here that I'm wishing to be," said Tom.

"Are you one of us tonight?" asked the king.

"I am," said Tom.

"Then," said the king, "it will be your duty to take the password. You must stand at the foot of the glen, and as each group goes by, you must take the password – it is: 'Monday, Tuesday, Wednesday, Thursday, Friday, Saturday'."

"I will," said Tom.

At daybreak the fiddlers took up their fiddles, the fairy army set itself in order, the fiddlers played

before them out of the glen, and sweet that music was. Each group gave the password to Tom as it went by, "Monday, Tuesday, Wednesday, Thursday, Friday, Saturday."

Last of all came the king, and he, too, gave it, "Monday, Tuesday, Wednesday, Thursday, Friday, Saturday."

Then he called to one of his men, "Take the hump from this fellow's back," and before the words were out of his mouth the hump was whisked off Tom's back and thrown away.

How happy Tom was, who could stand up straight! He went down the mountain and came home early in the morning with light heart and eager step. Billy Beg wondered greatly when he saw Tom Beg so straight and strong, and when Tom Beg had rested, he told his story about how he had met the fairies.

The next night Billy Beg set off along the mountain road and came at last to the green glen. About midnight he heard the trampling of horses, the lashing of whips, the barking of dogs, and the fairies and their king, their dogs and their horses, all at drill in the glen as Tom Beg had said.

When they saw him they stopped, and one came forward and crossly asked his business.

"I am one of yourselves for the night, and should be glad to do you service," said Billy Beg.

So he was set to take the password, 'Monday, Tuesday, Wednesday, Thursday, Friday, Saturday.' And at daybreak, group after group came by, giving Billy Beg the password, "Monday, Tuesday, Wednesday, Thursday, Friday, Saturday."

Last of all came the king with his men. and gave the password also, "Monday, Tuesday,

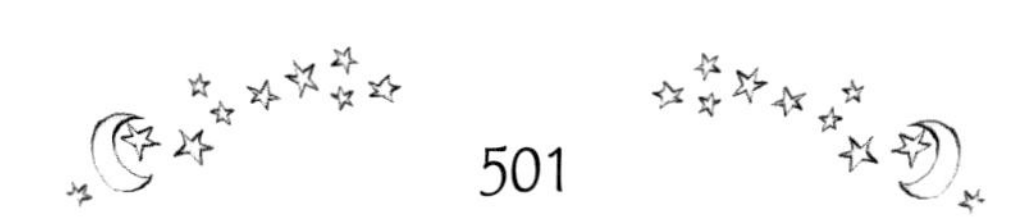

Wednesday, Thursday, Friday, Saturday."

"And Sunday," said Billy Beg, thinking himself clever. Then there was a great outcry.

"Get the hump that was taken off that fellow's back last night and put it on this man's back," said the king, with flashing eyes, pointing to the hump that lay under the hedge.

Before the words were well out of his mouth, the hump was clapped onto Billy Beg's back.

"Now," said the king, "be off, and if ever I find you here again, I will clap another hump onto your front!"

And they all marched away, leaving poor Billy Beg standing there, with a hump growing on each shoulder. And he came home the next day dragging one foot after another, with a cross face and two humps on his back.

The Magic Porridge Pot

A Swedish folk tale

This is the story of an old porridge pot. One day, just before Christmas, a poor old farmer and his wife decided that they needed to sell their last cow as they had no money left, and no food in the cupboard.

As the farmer walked sadly to market with the cow, he met a very strange little man on the road. He had a long white beard right down to his toes, which were bare, and he wore a huge black hat,

under which the farmer could only just see the bright gleam of his eyes. Over his arm he carried a battered old porridge pot.

"That's a nice looking cow," said the little man.

"Is she for sale?"

"Yes," said the farmer.

"I shall buy your cow," declared the little man, putting the porridge pot down with a thump. "I shall give you this porridge pot in exchange for your cow!"

Well, the farmer looked at the battered old porridge pot, and he looked at his fine cow. And he was just about to say, "Certainly not!" when a voice whispered, "Take me! Take me!"

The farmer shook himself. Dear me, it was bad

enough to be poor without beginning to hear strange voices. He opened his mouth again to say, "Certainly not!" when he heard the voice again."Take me! Take me!"

Well, he saw at once that it must be a magic pot, and he knew you didn't hang about with magic pots, so he said very quickly to the little man,"Certainly!" and handed over the cow. He bent down to pick up the pot, and when he looked up, the little man had vanished into thin air.

The farmer knew he was going to have a difficult time explaining to his wife just how he had come to part with their precious cow for a battered old porridge pot.

She was very angry indeed and had started to say a lot of very cross things when a voice came from the pot,

"Take me inside and clean me and polish me,

and you shall see what you shall see!"

Well, the farmer's wife was astonished but she did as she was bid. She washed the pot inside and out, and then she polished it until it shone as bright as a new pin. No sooner had she finished than the pot hopped off the table, and straight out of the door. The farmer and his wife sat down by the fire, not saying a word to each other. They had no money, no cow, no food and now it seemed they didn't even have their magic pot.

Down the road from the poor farmer, there lived a rich man. He was a selfish man who spent all his time eating huge meals and counting his money. He had lots of servants, including a cook who was in the kitchen making a Christmas pudding. The pudding was stuffed with plums, currants, sultanas, almonds and goodness knows what else. It was so big that the cook realized she didn't have

a pot to boil it in. It was at this point that the porridge pot trotted in the door.

"Goodness me!" she exclaimed. "The fairies must have sent this pot just in time to take my pudding," and she dropped the pudding in the pot. No sooner had the pudding fallen to the bottom with a very satisfying thud, than the pot skipped out of the door again. The cook gave a great shriek, but by the time the butler and the

footman and the parlour maid and the boy who turned the spit had all dashed into the kitchen, the pot was quite out of sight.

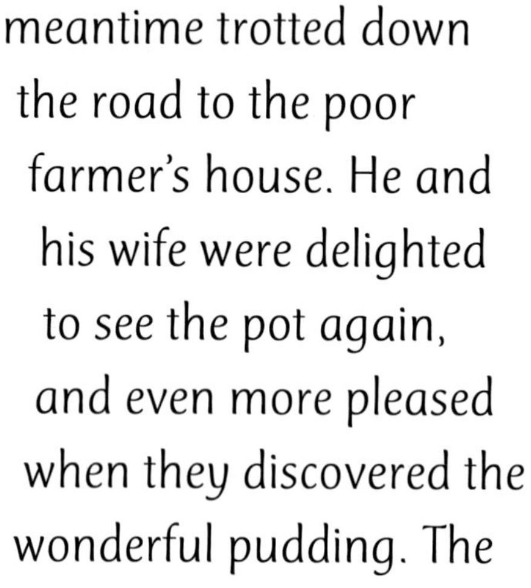

The porridge pot in the meantime trotted down the road to the poor farmer's house. He and his wife were delighted to see the pot again, and even more pleased when they discovered the wonderful pudding. The wife boiled it up and it lasted them for three days. So they had a good Christmas after all, while the old porridge pot sat quietly by the fire.

Spring came, and still the porridge pot sat quietly by the fire. Then one day the pot suddenly trotted over to the farmer's wife and said,

"Clean me, and polish me, and you shall see what you shall see."

So the farmer's wife polished the pot till it shone as bright as a new pin.

No sooner had she finished than the pot hopped off the table, and straight out of the door.

You will remember that the rich man was very fond of counting his money. There he sat in the great hall, with piles of golden guineas and silver sixpences on the table, and great bulging bags of coins on the floor at his feet. He was wondering where he could hide the money when in trotted the pot. Now the cook had been far too frightened of the rich man's temper to tell him about the pot stealing the Christmas pudding, so when he saw the pot he was delighted.

"Goodness me!" he exclaimed, "The fairies must have sent this pot just in time to take my money,"

and he dropped several bags of money in the pot. No sooner had the bags fallen to the bottom with a very satisfying clink, than the pot skipped out of the door again. The rich man shouted and hollered, but by the time the coachman and the head groom and the stable lad had run into the great hall, the pot was quite out of sight.

It trotted down the road to the poor farmer's house. He and his wife were delighted to see the pot again, and even more pleased when they discovered the bags of gold and silver. There was enough money to last them for the rest of their days, even after they had bought a new cow.

As for the battered old porridge pot, it sat quietly by the fire for many a long year. Then, one day, it suddenly trotted straight out of the door. It went off up the road until it was out of sight, and the farmer and his wife never saw it again.

Index of Stories

Amal and the Genie 35

Androcles and the Lion 342

Billy Beg, Tom Beg and the Fairies 496

Cap o' Rushes 192

Cat and the Mouse, The 114

Chicken Licken 378

Clever Apprentice, The 24

Dick Whittington and his Cat 313

Elves and the Shoemaker, The 353

Fairies and the Envious Neighbour, The 27

Fairy Blackstick, The 486

Fairy Cow, The 454

Fairy Cure, The 359

Fairy Fluffikins, The 85

Farmer Mybrow and the Fairies 364

French Puck, A 109

Frog Prince, The 253

Giant Who Counted Carrots, The 66

Gingerbread Man, The 409

Girl who Owned a Bear, The 41

Golden Touch, The 228

Goldilocks and the Three Bears 402

Greedy Dog, The 423

Hansel and Gretel 203

Hare and the Tortoise, The 388

Haughty Princess, The 259

Hillman and the Housewife, The 54

Honourable Minu 307

Hop-Toads and Pearls 328

How the Camel got his Hump 145

How the Rhinoceros got his Skin 73

Husband of the Rat's Daughter, The 151

Husband who was to Mind the House, The 444

Iktomi and the Ducks 103

Iktomi and the Muskrat 30

In the Castle of Giant Cruelty 370

Jack and the Beanstalk 58

Lazy Jack 435

Liam and the Fairy Cattle 335

Lion and the Mouse, The 345

Little Matchgirl, The 216

Little Red Riding Hood 394

Magic Porridge Pot, The 503

Mermaid of Zennor, The 468

My Own Self 211

Nasreddin Hodja and the Pot 430

Nasreddin Hodja and the Smell of Soup 432

Ogre's Bride, The 96

Old Woman and her Pig, The 163

Paddy Corcoran's Wife 460

Pandora's Box 473

Peter and the Wolf 174

Pied Piper of Hamelin, The 416

Pot of Gold, The 90

Precious Stove, The 290

Princess and the Pea, The 241

Rapunzel 479

Red Shoes, The 185

Rosy's Journey 319

Sagacious Monkey and the Boar, The 139

Selfish Giant, The 178

Seven Little Kids, The 133

Seven Ravens, The 222

Singh Rajah and the Cunning Little Jackals 49

Smith and the Fairies, The 491

Sorcerer's Apprentice, The 198

Straw, Coal and Bean 310

Sword in the Stone, The 234

Tall Story, A 427

Tattercoats 274

Teeny-tiny 449

Three Aunts, The 282

Three Billy Goats Gruff, The 127

Three Little Pigs, The 382

Three Sillies, The 296

Three Wishes, The 463

Thunder God Gets Married, The 12

Tikki Tikki Tembo 440

Twelve Dancing Princesses, The 247

Twelve Windows, The 266

Two Frogs, The 303

Ugly Duckling, The 121

Under the Sun 79

Whippety Stourie 348

Why the Manx Cat has no Tail 168

Why the Swallow's Tail is Forked 158

Wonderful Tar Baby, The 19